Serving Up
HOPE

Cover Design: Megan Parker-Squiers of EmCat Designs
Editing by: PWA & IDIM Editorial
Shander, H.M., 1975—Serving Up Hope

My hope is that
You as a reader
Know how much I adore
And appreciate you.

Chapter One

"What a flipping waste of time," I muttered while I twisted in front of my computer screen, filling out an online dating profile. "There has to be another way."

Desperation oozed from my fingers and onto the screen where I bared way too much of my private life.

My only hope was no one I knew searched me out and discovered what I was about to voluntarily post. Online dating was supposed to make things easier and yet I was wracked with more nervousness than I would be harmless flirting with the produce manager at the market down the street. Sheesh, and the kicker was, I wasn't looking for a husband or even a long-term boyfriend, just a one-time accomplice to a wedding. And not just any wedding – my former fiancé's wedding. The one who failed to show up for *our* wedding.

As I contemplated the trajectory my life was on, I ran my fingers through my lightly lavender scented hair, detangling the squeaky clean, yet still damp strands.

My male friends, as in all two of them, were busy or thought it ridiculous that I even needed a date for a wedding.

Especially *this* wedding.

"You don't need a date," my trusted friend and neighbour said. "However, go, be yourself and you'll show them all that you are better off without that mess in your life."

My shift manager actually thought the opposite. "Wouldn't taking a date actually hinder your chances of finding a man and having a wonderful fling?" But he was also all for going and enjoying myself to the fullest.

I cussed under my breath, daring the image of my ex to flick away rather than grow larger and stronger in my head. What nerve he had to send me an invitation. What was his reasoning behind it? Or had it all been her idea? Get some kind of last laugh at my expense?

I picked up the invitation, tracing my finger around the cream-embossed edges, wondering again if it represented some kind of sick joke. With a quiet resolve, I placed it back down and returned my attention to Mingle More's dating website.

This could be the perfect opportunity to show Scumbag how leaving me at the altar four years ago on our wedding day didn't leave any lasting scars on my heart. How marrying the person who I thought was my friend didn't hurt even more. It was asinine I'd even received an invitation to attend. I secretly thought it was a joke—just to see if I'd actually show up.

I'll show them.

I reread my profile, deleting the information about my employment. A fake boyfriend didn't need that information, right? All I needed was someone my age or older and good-looking, although I typed in *older, preppy-looking guy*. The guy could be a total player and a complete jerk just as long as for one night he looked like he was hopelessly in love with me.

A feeling of shallowness clouded my heart as I added a part about needing a recent photograph to accompany any correspondence, because Mr. Dreamy needed to be perfect; in looks and employment. The employment thing was key. Scumbag was not the best employee and had transitioned through numerous jobs, or at least he had when he was with me.

I clicked back and added in: *steady employment.*

Bonus points if similar in nature to a Disney Prince. I laughed out loud at that comment and took a sip of Chardonnay.

The ad was simple enough.

Single lady looking for a single male to accompany to former fiancé's wedding.
Must be willing to spend the entire day with me – three weeks from Saturday; from an hour before the ceremony (so we can meet and become acquainted) until after the cake is cut.
All food and refreshments will be covered; limited alcohol.
May provide own transportation or share with me. Applicant must have steady employment, look great in a suit as dress code is semi-formal/business and be between the ages of 25 – 40.
Please note – I am not looking for a one-night stand or anything beyond this event. I simply need a charming date. Serious inquiries only.

There it was. I leaned back in my comfy office chair, twisting slightly, my naked feet gripping the base. I admired my dating want ad, and followed the reading with a deep groan, placing my head into the palms of my hands.

How pathetic had my life become? I owned and operated a busy restaurant, with detailed plans to open another soon, but finding a date for a wedding? Mission impossible.

Tucking my slight embarrassment into the base of my

stomach, I reviewed my carefully selected words. For the fifth flipping time.

Hmm… should I have said more? Nope. It's exactly what I was looking for. It bore a striking similarity to the want ads I placed for work, which, once I thought about it, I needed to remember to place again. Two of my staff had moved into shift manager positions, which left the door open for more entry-level jobs on the floor. At least two full-time servers were needed, and if that wasn't going to work, then four part-time ones. I jotted it down on a mile-long to do list. A low sigh rolled out of me, and I took another sip of wine, licking the dribble with my tongue. An owner's work was never done.

In the corner of my computer, the time flashed two-twelve. The late hour didn't bother me since I was a night-owl by nature, and mainly because I didn't get home from Westside until after eleven. By the time I checked my lacklustre social media pages and ran a few reports, the clock had struck one. Add to the night my foray into the online dating world, and time disappeared. However, it was late, and I had other projects tomorrow to attend to needing more of my energy.

I was almost ready to hit the submit button when I stopped. My ad was blunt and to the point, but aside from the free food and beverages, what was in it for him? What would motivate someone to spend the day with a complete stranger, especially when there would be no sex? I pinched the bridge of my nose as my thoughts climbed into a headache inducing process.

There wasn't much I had to offer as enticement for someone to give up a Saturday and hang out with me. As a workaholic, I easily logged sixty plus hours at Westside in person, not including the hours spent away from there establishing the new location I'd hoped to open in a few short

4

months. I wasn't an avid movie goer, or up-to-date on the latest reality tv show, so chatting about the latest Star Wars movie or Marvel comic book recreation wouldn't work. At least that eliminated the nerdy types from applying.

Physically, I wasn't even much of a catch. My hair was shorter, but easy to take care of especially since I swam four days a week. My apartment complex had a great 25m length pool, perfect for laps, and since I was the only one who ever seemed to be there, I swam for an hour each time. My ultimate goal was to compete in a triathlon, but I'd still need to learn how to ride a bike. I hadn't since I was a child of single digits. However, I refused to put that on my dating profile.

What if I added I was a total loner and lived alone? On second though, it opened the door for all sorts of hooligans to reply and put me into an awkward position. Nope, it's better I kept it off my profile.

The chardonnay touched my lips, and I swallowed down the last of the red wine, contemplating further on what interesting bullshit to add. What about *enjoys long walks under the maple trees?* Nah, I wasn't even sure where the nearest maple tree was. For crying out loud, this was hard, even though I needed something personal. I wasn't the sharpest tack in the drawer, but I wasn't a pushover either.

Thinking of something personal, but not too out there, I typed the words from a song sung by Neil Diamond.

If the words "When no one else would come, Shilo you always came" mean anything to you, please respond with recent photo.

That was better. A smile bubbled out. It would also narrow down a lot of applicants. For good measure, to funnel the short list even more, I added *If Captain Picard played the best Hamlet, I'd love to talk further with you.*

Still, it didn't dangle any carrots in front of would be applicants. Maybe it would be better to show up to this thing with the greatest lie I've ever told? Something along the lines of my boyfriend needed to fly over to Boston for an emergency conference for a company he was taking over and that's why I came alone. It was believable, right?

"Hah." I laughed.

If anyone accepted that as truth well... I had some ocean front property in Saskatchewan I wanted to sell them.

The wine glass beside the laptop sat empty, so my time in front of the ad was over. With a final swallow of my pride, I hit the submit button. Nothing ventured, nothing gained.

Immediately a bright red error message appeared on the screen.

"Dammit," I said, pulling my chair in closer and rubbing my temples.

Tomorrow would be better, I was sure. It was too late to be doing this, and the error was karma's way of preventing a huge mistake, according to the words the angel on my shoulder whispered. But I brushed her aside and read the error. Apparently, I needed to upload a photo. Guess appearances went both ways.

Begrudgingly I opened my phone and flipped through. There weren't many selfies at all, perhaps three. I hated the whole idea of them, hated being a part of them, and as soon as one of my friends pulled their phone out and took aim, I was out of there. Despite their reassurances to the contrary, I believed I wasn't photogenic. Like at all. I suffered from R.B.F. – Resting Bitch Face – and most, if not all the pictures I'm sporting a pissed off look, except I wasn't. It just appeared that way. My constant pout would certainly prevent guys from applying. Plus, I just wasn't model thin and pretty. I was a healthy size eight with no health issues, but it wasn't enough for a lot of guys. Obviously, or I'd have a date for the fracking wedding.

"Fuck it."

I held up my empty wine glass with one hand while I smiled into my camera. Meh, it was decent, if not a little bit goofy. Whatever. I uploaded it onto my computer.

A couple clicks later, I added it to my profile.

"Good luck."

My mouse hovered over the submit button and before I could change my mind, it clicked and sent my profile off to either be accepted or rejected. Let the chips fall where they may. Nothing could stop it now. My future lay in the hands of the internet now.

Oh crap – what had I done!

Chapter Two

"Good morning, Meghan," the pool man said as he stacked a fresh set of towels by the change room door.

Don't get excited by the idea of the pool man – he's old enough to be my grandfather, if I were Italian; a gentle soul with a weathered exterior who hunched and shuffled with each step.

"Good morning, sir," I said, exiting the cool water.

It was the perfect temperature to push a little harder to keep warm and as it was, I managed to beat my score of 93 laps in 59 minutes. I'd only been swimming for four months, but my strokes were longer and more powerful, and my speed was increasing. It shouldn't be long before I hit a 100 in 60… as long as I remembered to eat an hour before, like I did this morning.

The scratchy towel he'd passed me dried my face, exfoliating my damp skin as I ran it over my cheeks and neck. I gave my head a solid drying off, drowning out the elevator music management thought was best for a pool facility. Wrapping the towel around my waist, I tipped my head from side to side to drain the water from my ears.

"How's the missus?"

"She good. Grandkids come to keep her young today."

"That's nice."

He held out another towel for me, a soft expression of wanting to talk crossed his face.

"I'm good, Paolo, thanks." On both the towel and the further conversation.

The old man kept chatting, "She loves them kids. To me they too loud, but not her. Scream all day." He laughed an old man laugh, deep and wide. "Her ear aide is broke not like mine." A crooked finger tapped against his ear.

"It keeps her young, right?" I placed my hand on the handle for the woman's change room.

He grinned. Paolo once told me he'd been married for over fifty years. I couldn't even imagine loving someone for so long. These days, one night seemed hard enough, let alone times that by 365 by 50. Craziness, if you asked me.

"You have good day, miss." He gave me a soft nod. "Don't be forgetting they be changing the pool codes over the next day or two, in case it don't work."

"Right."

I'd forgotten the tenant's board had agreed to a new security company, who were also changing all the exterior locks in the next 48 hours. Another item to add to my mental list of things to do.

With a quick nod, and a flick of my wrist, I hopped into the change room and deposited the heavy towel into the basket. My dark shorts slipped up over my legs, and I fiddled for my key hidden within.

Thankfully my apartment was in the building beside the pool, and it was a short jaunt from there to the back entrance. It was a short walk on the industrial strength carpet past four doors over to the elevator. Up I went to the seventh floor and back down the length of hall to my place at the end. If I leaned far over my balcony and twisted my body, which I'd never do, but if I did, I'd be able to see the pool house.

My key slid into the lock of my home for the past three years. When my life fell apart after I got the ultimate dumping at the altar, I moved in with a friend, mostly to rebuild my life. But she packed up and headed to warmer climates in the southern US to become a Ravenclaw. Last I heard she was getting closer as she worked in one of the Harry Potter themed shops in Disney World. I guess we all needed to start somewhere.

My apartment was home, and very modern having only been built within the last five years. I made enough money to live within my means and decorated accordingly. My mom called it rustic chic, but I leaned more towards classic. Clean lines, white walls with huge bold paintings, the kind of paintings you'd get from Ikea, not from a gallery. Actually, a lot of my furniture was from Ikea—affordable and they delivered—so thanks to a little retail therapy, I never needed to venture into their maze of a store. Win-win for everyone, but mostly me.

I dropped my key in the bowl by the door, and clicked the lock shut. The nice thing about living alone was everything was exactly where I left it. I had no one but myself to blame if anything was out of place. My phone sat on the table, the screen lit with text messages and calendar notifications.

Nothing important, just a reminder of Joy's baby shower this afternoon. I graciously agreed to close the restaurant between the hours of 2 PM – 4 PM so the staff could ogle and cuddle with her baby. Just as I'd been ready to give her a full-time management position, she dropped her pregnancy bomb on me and I found myself scrambling to fill it since my other, dependable manager was leaving to join her boyfriend's company. Thankfully, Robin - another employee I'd debated promoting - was able to fill the vacant role in tandem with Joy, and he became my newest shift manager. But I can't complain as there haven't been too many issues – both Joy and Robin took to their new positions like ducks in water. It certainly made my job a tad less stressful.

I thumbed open my phone and opened the dating app, thinking, or hoping for maybe a couple of views of my profile. I did not expect there to be seven inbox messages, but I was sure most of them were a joke.

Before I settled down to read any of them, I cleaned myself up and made myself some lunch. Fingers clicking rapidly, I opened the site and logged in, readying for the interesting mail I expected.

The first message read "Hey, Megs," and I instantly deleted it. Hearing that horrid nickname reminded me of Scumbag, his apparent term of endearment, which always made my blood curdle.

On to the next.

It sounded hopeful, and the guy referenced to being a Next Generation fan, so there was a plus. 'Cory' was over forty and had two young children. He was lonely and claimed his therapist encouraged him to get out of his comfort zone and hang out with adults every once in a while. The thought of trying to impress an ex at a wedding sounded like fun way to spend the day and, he added, his ex-wife had always said he looked good in a suit.

Does someone have lingering issues?

His picture was adorable; dark hair, dark eyes, tanned face nestled up beside a Golden Retriever. I flagged his message for follow-up.

The next message was a joke, it had to be. Either that or

the guy didn't even read my posting as he mentioned he was in town and we could Netflix and chill. He even posted his number for me to text. No, thank you, and with a quick click on the mouse, another message disappeared from my screen.

The fourth message was intriguing. 'Hudson' said Neil Diamond's Shilo was overrated and much preferred the later released Heartlight album but agreed Patrick Stewart was magnificent in Hamlet.

I raised an eyebrow in suspicion. No way did he actually catch both of my vague drop ins, there had to have been some research. I continued to read his comments and mentally tallied up a couple of brownie points in his favour.

Nothing personal was shared, nor was there any information pertaining to his employment which I found rather disappointing, but he did include a photo. Decked out in a brown leather jacket, he had the look of someone with a ton of confidence. It practically leaked out the edges of the photo. Definitely good looking, but more in a self-assured way than Cory's handsome one. I stared harder at the photo noting the jagged scar along his chin running up towards his left eye. There was a story there for sure. However, scar aside, I flagged his email.

Confidence sells, and I've always told that to my staff, especially my front-end staff. Act confident and be confident and your tips will reflect that. And most of the time, it was true. But there were always a few assholes to prove the theory wrong.

Email five and six were instantly deleted, especially when #5 contained pornography. Nope, never asked for a dick pick, no desire to see it on a strange man either. It's simply not an attractive part of the male anatomy. Give me soulful eyes and a winning smile and a guy who treats a lady right, and I'll be yours any day. Sad part was I wasn't seeing any of that lately.

Seven was just as interesting as the other two I'd flagged but 'Seth' included personal details. He was divorced two years ago and recently moved to the city as a new marketing director, so he didn't know anyone. Saturday nights were free nights and he typically hung out alone playing online video games with people he presumed were teenagers. Picard ruled, he said, with Starship Mine being his favourite all time episode.

I was impressed and kept reading.

> *I think it's rather noble of you to want to attend your former fiancés wedding and agree one should not venture into such an event unaided. However, I would like to request of you that we meet for a coffee firsthand, on the premise of making sure we click and can then lay out the terms of the agreement. One would not want to be caught off hand and have our cover blown because we arrived unprepared.*

Nodding at his words, it made a lot of sense--meeting an hour prior to the ceremony wouldn't be enough time to properly come across as being in a strong relationship. Should I meet the three flagged potentials beforehand and make my decision based on a quick coffee date, rather than blind trust. It would make it more like an interview, which made me laugh out loud, although I was great with those.

There was something fun about sitting across from someone and asking random questions just to see how they reacted. When I hired Robin a few years back, at the end of his rather spectacular interview, I asked him if he preferred red or blue. Without missing a beat, he declared blue because it was soothing. He was hired on the spot, and I've never regretted adding him to payroll. I enjoyed people who can think on their feet and don't get frazzled.

I scrolled down, finished reading, and stared at Seth's picture. If I was to choose based on looks alone, he would be the clear-cut winner. Gorgeous dark hair, brown irises with an amber ring encircling them and a mischievous expression on his face. Fun photo for the win. I imagined suits fit perfectly on his body, perhaps even tailored a bit to make his best assets stand out. His age never came up, but based on the photo, I'd peg him as mid-thirties, just a hair older than me.

I emailed the three potential candidates, asking Hudson and Cory if they were okay with meeting for a quick coffee before the wedding day. But the other – Seth's – his I replied to, inquiring if Saturday morning would work for a biscuit and java.

I pandered into work through the main entrance and quickly surveyed the dining room. A lone table of three, tucked near the south wall, sat with empty glasses before them. They must be nearly finished as no cutlery and napkins remained. Great. Someone was doing her job well.

"Greetings, Boss Lady," Robin said as he carried a handful of baby shower balloons through the kitchen and out onto the floor, keeping them to the staff table area for now.

From anyone else, Boss Lady would be a horrible nickname, but I tolerated it from Robin. He was punctual, polite and a hard worker, so I let the name slid. Besides, it was always said in the nicest tone without a hint of defiance.

I walked over and dropped off my tray of homemade cupcakes decorated in pink swirls and a bag full of newborn supplies the department store led me to believe were much needed necessities plus a few cute baby girl clothes added on top. Soon, my staff would arrive, and the festivities would begin. Celeste, one of my front-end servers, was in charge of games and had assured me it would be a lot of fun.

I wasn't a baby shower type of person, more of the here's-a-bag-full-of-goodies for you. Holding babies wasn't my thing, nor doting on their every little whimper. I wasn't the neighbourhood sitter as I lacked the patience for kids. My mother said someday I would change. I still don't believe her.

Day shifters not on schedule arrived and joined their evening counterparts and rolled into the restaurant, some bringing their spouses or significant others. The afternoon party was getting ready to begin, and I was sure Celeste had some fun party activities planned.

Since the staff and guests were mingling amongst themselves and keeping a fair distance away from me, I headed to my office quickly to scan the reports and see how the day went. Things went well. Steady. Totals were within the expected range. A couple of things to add to the next supply order. All in all, I was pleased. Provided the evening went as it usually did, closing the place down for a couple of hours wouldn't have an impact on revenue.

Robin was doing a great job in his new managerial role, having been one of my best front-end staff. And actually, when the invitation for the wedding came addressed to me here at Westside, he was one of two people I thought to ask. Too bad he said no though as he was a nice enough guy. A little lanky for my liking, and perhaps a bit of a player if the word around the server station was true when I'd approach on the sly and they didn't immediately disperse into the wind. It was always unnerving when they suddenly stopped talking and instantly found something they'd forgotten to do.

15

Oh well. I'd see how the potential dates go and reassess. I had been more than curious as to why I'd received the invitation, but I couldn't turn it down. I needed to save face in front of these people who had almost became family. Taking a date would just solidify to the world I was better off without him and being stood up on my wedding day didn't ruin me. Because it didn't. I didn't mind being a workaholic.

There were about twenty people in attendance when I walked back on to the floor, passing around cups of coffee and helping themselves to non-Westside food. My establishment wasn't the type to serve pizza, but as long as they disposed of the boxes in the dumpster before four o'clock, I'd let it slide this one time.

Joy, or Josephine as it stated on her paycheques, had arrived with James, the father of her baby. I hadn't seen her since her last day of work seven weeks ago when she was all pregnant belly. It was remarkable how different she looked in her sundress, and not the standard issue apparel. Motherhood suited her, even with the tired expression she wore on her face.

"Hi, Joy," I said, calling her by her nickname.

All front-end staff were given one, for protection and to keep their work lives separate from their private lives. I started it when I took ownership of Westside a few years back and whenever we were within the walls of my second home, nicknames were used.

Joy gave me a gentle hug, which I begrudgingly accepted. I wasn't a hugger.

"You look great."

Her hand smoothed down the front of her dress. "Thanks. Breastfeeding helps."

I laughed, and it probably sounded as awkward as I felt. "Say no more. Where's the baby?"

16

"James took her. She did a doodle on the way in."

"Oh," I said.

Joy was so colourful in her speech, she never swore, instead choosing to use other, more obscure words and because of that, it took me a minute to figure out she meant pooped.

"There she is." Joy's face lit up as she spotted her newborn daughter.

"All clean," James said, passing his baby girl to her.

"Meghan, this is Destiny."

"Destiny, eh?" What a unique name. I looked at the little bundle of pink blankets tucked into Joy's arm. As far as babies go, Destiny was a cutie. "She's gorgeous. How old is she?"

"Thanks, she's thirty-six days." Joy beamed and leaned her head against James's shoulder. "Taking care of a baby is a lot harder than I thought. Good thing he's around."

A loving look blossomed over her as she gazed up at James.

"You're a natural," he said, his focus on his baby girl as he pushed his finger towards the little baby's hand.

"Would you like to hold her?" Joy asked me.

My eyes fell to the baby and jumped back up to my employee. "Nah, I'm good. A newborn should stay with it's mother." I gave her my best friendly pat on the shoulder. "Have some cupcakes and coffee before Celeste brings out the games."

She held her little one closer like I was some sort of a monster for not wanting to hold a newborn. They were too breakable and not something I wanted to be responsible for. She and James pulled back from their conversation with me and mingled amongst the other staff members who fought like vultures for the chance to baby snuggle.

I hung near the back of the group, happier there

anyways, as guests raved about the wonderful choice in baby name and asked probing questions into the birth. When I heard her gushing about how she gave birth in James's car, I figured my talents were best used in the back office. I had no problem in closing the restaurant down for a couple of hours during the slow period, but I didn't feel I needed to be out celebrating and listening to breastfeeding horror stories and the raging competition between the moms in the crowd over who had it worst.

Everyone—myself included—had a story, except no one knew mine because I was never going to share it.

Chapter Three

ucked into the corner of the local coffee shop buzzing with activity, I opened my laptop and connected to their wi-fi. I'd arrived early enough before meeting Seth so I could:

a) check him out before he saw me

b) run some reports so if things went south, I'd have an easy out and most importantly

c) if he didn't show, then I'd have something to work on and it won't look like I've been stood up.

I expected the third possibility.

My iced caramel latte with non-fat milk swirled around in its plastic container, the coolness keeping my hands from burning up. I wasn't sure why I was so nervous, I'd been on a few blind dates before. And this wasn't even a blind date, I'd seen his picture—if it was truly him and if his name was really Seth.

The nervousness reminded me of how things turned out between my former fiancé, Giovanni and I, how he completely caught me off guard when he failed to step out from the holding area when Wagner's Bridal Chorus played on the pipe organ.

The best man was also surprised as he walked ahead of me with my maid of honour; his sweeping glances around the church told me he was just as surprised as I was. I started walking, waiting to see Scumbag's face and the more I walked, the more the butterflies swarmed. It was embarrassing to not see the groom. At all. For four long days after I waited for him to call or text or something.

Ever since that day, I've hated surprises. I needed full control of everything. It calmed me. Sitting in the café, twenty minutes early to meet this mystery man was as much control as I was going to get. That's why I chose the place and time. And I'd even ordered my drink, although I didn't plan on tasting much of it until he arrived. Didn't want to look too early.

And arrive, he did. The living breathing picture I stared at in my inbox sauntered in through the glass door looking as though he'd stepped off the cover of a magazine. Dark hair pushed back, shades on, skin that appeared more bronze thanks to the blue tee and a pair of khaki shorts highlighting his toned and taunt legs. As far as appearances went, he was off the chart. A cool confidence radiated off him as he slipped the shades off his face, and folded them, slipping the arm into the crook of his v-neck.

His head bobbed each way, eyes searching out.

Like a bat out of hell, I dropped my gaze quickly to my computer screen pretending to not have noticed him. As I checked out the time, he was ten minutes early. Impressive. Was he wanting to be early for the same reasons I did? I looked up and stared at his gorgeous body.

"Are you Meghan?"

I rose. "Depending on who's asking?"

He extended his hand. "Seth Morrison."

I gave it a quick pump. "Then yes, I'm Meghan."

20

God, his hands were soft.

A quizzical narrow to his eyes. "No last name?"

"We'll go with that. Meghan No-last-name."

Safety first. I would've used an alias for the dating site and had considered it, however seeing as though I'd run into Scumbag's family and they knew my name... Well, I squashed the hairbrained idea. But for now, I'd be last name-less.

"Well, Meghan No-last-name, may I grab you a drink?"

I pointed to my plastic-encased iced latte.

"Never mind. You beat me to it. I'll be right back."

I lowered myself back into my seat and took a sip to put out the fire that had suddenly roared up, and I aimlessly scanned through a report. Seth re-joined me, a mug of plain old black coffee in his hands.

He was stunning gorgeous, and I found it difficult to keep myself from staring.

Treat this like an interview.

I needed to keep reminding myself, as that's all this was. I was interviewing him for a one-time date. As long as I kept it in the back of my mind, his corded muscular arms would be useless.

"So..." I began, looking back at my screen. With a quick click, I had brought up a list of questions to ask. The first one being, "Tell me a bit about yourself." How cliché.

A small grin cut through his chiselled face. "I'm thirty-one. Divorced two years ago." He held up two fingers to confirm it for me. "I just moved here from Thunder Bay a couple of months ago, and I'm the marketing director for a huge investment company." He lifted the mug to his lips.

"That's excellent." Thirty-one wasn't too bad, three years younger than me. Totally workable. The second question stared back at me, having already been answered. I skimmed the

21

questions until I got to the fifth. "And what made you decide to submit your ad to Mingle More?"

He set the mug down, lacing his fingers together. They were long with the right amount of curl, like they could play the piano perfectly. "Same reasons as you I suppose."

I kept my face as stoic as possible. "And have you had any success finding anyone?"

He peered over the top of my screen, a gentle laugh breezing out of him. "Is that on there?"

"Yes," I said, closing the lid a hair. He didn't need to know it wasn't the truth, at this point I was flying by the seat of my pants. And... the report was still trying to finish running.

"Interesting." He straightened himself out as a pensive thought controlled his features. "No, I haven't yet found the right person."

"And how long has your ad been running?"

"Are you really going to treat this like an interview?"

I took a long sip of the ice-cold drink. It did nothing to cool me down. "I'd planned on it."

"Why?"

I looked long and hard into his dark brown eyes ringed with amber. It was easy to find myself getting lost in them. "Because, Seth, that's all this is. I'm too busy for interpersonal relationships, and I need an impressive date for a wedding."

"What is it you do that you are too busy for fun?"

"I own and manage a restaurant and am preparing to open another one in the new year."

There was still so much to do, I wasn't sure if I'd truly be ready in five months. Staff management was the least of concerns for the new location. There was still codes and permits and–

"Two? Well, that's impressive on its own merits."

22

"Thank you," I said, checking on the report. It had finally finished downloading. I closed the lid to my laptop, questions be damned. "So business keeps me very busy."

"Yes, I imagine it would. So, tell me, this wedding... You'd mentioned in *your* ad it was your former fiancé who's wedding you're crashing."

"I never said crashing." I scowled while I tried to remember if that's what was said. I was ninety-nine percent sure I hadn't.

"Fooled you."

And one point deducted for inserting humour into the wrong space.

"I received an invitation, so there's no crashing involved." My tone filled with indignation.

"Did you run out on him, or he on you?"

I scoffed at his first suggestion of me bailing.

"Ah, so he did the dumping, and you're going to save face." His eyes widened in what I hoped was surprise. It still stung to hear it. No one likes being dumped, especially not in front of 200 guests of friends and family.

"I need to show him I've moved on."

"And a one-time date will show that?"

I dug deep into myself and pulled out my best business voice. "Yes. If I have the right chemistry with a certain someone, I believe it will be easy to fool him. He wasn't the sharpest knife in the drawer."

"Yet you were ready to marry him?"

"Love is blind." And deaf. And dumb. Like really dumb. The warning signs were there.

"Are you still in love with him?"

The question hung between us, thickening the air, and pressing in on my chest. The mere thought of still being in love with Scumbag rendered me speechless. I was deeply in love with him once, but I hadn't given it much thought in the past year or so. Figured maybe I was growing out of it.

"How longs it been?"

"Four years," I said after my heart started beating again.

"Wow." He leaned back against the back of the wooden chair. "It is evident for an event such as this, given the brief set of circumstances I have heard, a date is an absolute must."

I nodded, pleased, wishing my friends had agreed so easily. "Thank you."

My friends thought it was better if I showed up single, to prove I was stronger than Scumbag thought possible. I completely disagreed. He had to know I'd moved on, with someone else. Even if it was total bullshit.

"Looking forward to the big day, being that this is an interview and all, how do you see it working out?"

"Great question," I said as I straightened myself out and rested my forearms on the table, clasping my hands together. This I had all worked out. "I see us meeting an hour before the ceremony to familiarize ourselves with any last-minute details in the parking lot of this coffee shop and you joining me as I drive there. We sit and watch, laugh and enjoy each other as he exchanges vows with her. Between that and the reception, we can network…" I gave him a small wink.

He was new and perhaps this would be an added perk of having to be my date for a day.

"And mingle. We'll eat dinner, regale our table mates with some funny anecdotes about how we met, having hashed out those details in the pre-ceremony meet and greet. We can talk about your job, my job, and the upcoming civic election."

"Interesting, and detailed." He ran his ring fingernail up and down his thumb pad a few times.

It was mesmerizing in its oddity.

"I like to be prepared."

"Clearly." He nodded at my laptop. "And physical contact?"

A flush of adrenaline tingled through my body, and I inhaled nice and slow to tamper it down. "What about it?"

He placed his hands atop mine. "If we're to be believable as a couple, we should have modest touching."

I rather enjoyed the electricity pulsing intensely through my hands but pulled them back regardless. "Contact is allowed, but it would be dignified, borderline professional. Hand holding, gentle touches on the shoulder, that kind of thing. There will be no sexual contact."

"Odd but noted." His eyes closed slightly as if in deep thought. "I assume kissing is off the list?"

"Completely and totally." Was this guy for real?

"That does make it difficult to prove to your former betrothed you are in a committed, fulfilling relationship."

"It will have to. It's all I'm able to give." I pressed my shoulders down and lifted my chin.

He crossed his muscular arms over what I could only imagine was a sculpted chest. "Interesting."

I grew weary of the handsome man sharing my table and constantly repeating the word *interesting*. I shifted in my seat and crossed my legs. Mingle More wasn't specifically for hookups like its competitor, all I needed from it was a date, plain and simple, and I was pretty sure I had made the point clear. I was baffled why it was a hard concept to grasp.

"Is there anything further you need to know about the details?"

"Nope." The 'p' made a popping sound.

I suspected the interview had taken an unpleasant turn

somewhere, and I was confused as to when and where it happened. When I planned the meeting, everything was supposed to go easy, and he was supposed to look forward to signing the contract. Apparently, I misread the situation. How unlike me. Dating was impossible.

"You've grown quiet behind those greenish eyes of yours. What are you thinking?"

"I'm just contemplating."

"I gathered." He leaned closer and pushed his empty mug to the side. "On what?"

Honesty was always the best policy, but I didn't want to say anything hurtful or offensive, however I didn't know him very well and wasn't sure how to proceed. "A great many things."

"Anything you care to share?"

"Not really."

He was a handsome man, and would be arm candy for just about anybody, except me it seemed. I wasn't into contact with other people and avoided hugs and the friendly arm pats like the plague. I hadn't worked through the physical details, but it would need to be done if I was going to prove to Scumbag I had moved on, and he hadn't destroyed me.

Seth laughed, a nice jolly sound. "So, am I passing the interview?"

Until a minute ago I would've wholeheartedly agreed, but I wasn't so sure. "You're doing fine. You've answered everything I asked, and you've agreed to my rigid terms."

"Exceptionally rigid." He gave his well-maintained beard a rub as he leaned against the backrest. "Can I ask you a few things?"

This man was good. Most of my interviews, the interviewee merely nodded along and agreed to pretty much everything I stated. Only the truly invested would have questions, and usually, those go-getters got the job. Maybe there was hope.

A smile spread on my face. "Sure, just know I may not answer if I feel it's too personal."

"Fair enough." He gave his lips a lick and a pensive look crossed his face as if he hadn't expected me to say yes.

"Are there others you'll be meeting with?"

I nodded. "Yes, at this point, two others."

"And when will you make a decision?"

Not quite the questions I was expecting, but then again, I was treating this like an interview. These are questions I'd expect them to ask. "The wedding is September long weekend, a mere three weeks away, so I'll probably get an answer to you at least a week before hand. Is that fair?"

"Totally."

"One more, if I may." He waited until I nodded. "Would you have swiped left or right for me?"

I narrowed my eyes. "I don't know what that means."

"Really?"

"Really."

A perplexed expression crossed his face. "Interesting."

I fought to keep the eye roll to a minimum while I studied him. Good lord he was handsome, and a tad charming, and if that was all I needed, I'd already have my date picked out. But shopping for a date wasn't like selecting what dress to wear, was it?

I wasn't looking for anything aside from some charming eye candy to prove to Scumbag I'd moved on. Apparently, it meant I'd become a shallow pig and was willing to pick a date based only on superficial qualities. Sigh what had my life become?

Chapter Four

a knock sounded on my door, and I threw a glance at the clock. It was after eight, not a time for many guests to come for a visit—except one. I put my laptop on the coffee table and padded over to the door.

"Hey, Gabe," I said, unhooking the chain.

"Hey. Saw your car in the parkade and figured you were home."

Gabe and I had only become friends in the last couple of years, after passing each other in the common area of the building for months beforehand. After the first couple of friendly hellos, things progressed to a friendship level.

I laughed. "My calling card."

Chances are if the car was there, I was home. I didn't often venture out, even though there were a lot of places I could visit on foot. I preferred being in my sanctuary.

"Not working tonight?"

"Not at work, no, but I am working."

The dark-haired gentleman winked a greyish-blue eye at me. "Like always. Am I interrupting anything?"

"Not at all. Come on in, I could use the break."

Gabe was older than me by a few years, but if you were to judge him by the grey flecks near his temples… well, he'd seem much older. But some guys were just unlucky in the grey hair department and mother nature cursed them early with it. Gabe wasn't model perfect, but he was comfortable in his own skin and that confidence radiated from him. Plus, there was an air of wisdom about him how he'd been through a lot, so I figured any grey hairs on his head he'd likely earned.

"Oh, I got this for you." He passed me a small, yet heavy box.

I peeked under the flap. A candle; its fragrance filling up the space around me with orange and spice.

"I remember how you commented you liked the one in my apartment, and I was at the market and there it was. It was the last one."

"Thanks, Gabe." It found its new home on the coffee table and since I was there, I grabbed my wine glass from the living room and refilled it, pouring one for Gabe. As I returned to my seat, I passed it to him. "Figured you wouldn't say no."

"Not a chance." He swirled the red liquid in the glass and took a sip. "Merlot? Thought I had you upgraded to a more sensible wine than this." A gentle smirk curled up the corner of his lip.

"I ran out."

The brands Gabe suggested I purchase from Wine and Beyond were a little bit beyond my reasonable price range for drinking alone. If I were to have company on the other hand...

He nodded towards my trusty laptop. "What are you working on?"

"Looking over figures for the new store, but I'm having trouble making some of the numbers work."

"Yeah, it makes for fun times."

29

"You know it." And he really did.

I'd consulted with Gabe a number of times as he owned his own business, an insurance company, and he was great with numbers.

"Anything you want me to take a look at? Maybe it's a quick miscalculation."

"I really couldn't ask that of you, Gabe, you've been more than helpful already." Besides, I'd already checked and rechecked the numbers. I thought it came down to a cash flow possibility but now I wasn't confident.

"Are you sure?" He drew out the last word, in such a way it would be impossible to tell him no. There was a sweetness to the way he asked.

I turned my laptop in his direction, the excel spreadsheet fanned open in all her glory, nasty numbers, and all. What could it hurt? Keeping to myself, I leaned against the back of the couch and pulled my legs underneath me.

Gabe tapped on the screen. "What's this?"

Shit. That was supposed to stay hidden. "That's for the staff, allotted money set aside in hopes of trying to find ways to make them like me."

At least with Gabe I could be honest, there was something comforting about him.

"They don't like you now?" His tone sounded bewildered.

"If you could see the way the staff look at me and hear the things they say when they think I can't hear them, well, you'd agree with my assessment."

At least once a week, I caught the roll of an eye, or the whispered shhs as I walked towards a group of staff. They were not paid to stand around and gossip, they were paid, and paid well, to do their job and keep the restaurant nice and tidy.

"I suspect you're imagining things."

"I'm not." Too often, their comments floated over to me with enough dislike I needed to excuse myself to the back office and close the door. Not that I would give them the satisfaction of knowing their words had power. It was better, in a way, to let them think I was Mean Meghan.

His short finger moved the mouse on the track pad so the cursor hovered over the total. "That figure seems pretty high."

I shrugged. "It's coming out of the bottom line and it's not excessive."

"And how do you plan to dole out this *bonus* money?"

"Some cash bonuses at the end of the year, some in sporting tickets, some in arts and entertainment. I'm trying to think if buying a couple season seats to share with the staff would be good or not. A season of football tickets for two seats is very affordable."

"You know it's only eleven games, right?"

"Sure. But the staff total is only that. Each staff would get a pair of tickets."

"What if they don't like football?"

"That's their problem. They could give them away or sell them."

Like the air let out of a balloon, I deflated. Sure, football tickets weren't for everyone, but if they were getting them free, wouldn't it be good? Maybe I should include transportation and food costs? Nah, that's being excessive.

"They all still get a cash bonus at Christmas and something on their birthdays. This was just a little extra something to let them know they are appreciated. Besides, I pay them more than the minimum wage."

"I'm just being difficult. I know you treat your staff

31

well. Your turnover is very low given the industry."

It was. In the service industry, most companies have a constant hiring going on. I haven't had to hire anyone for a while, nearly two months ago, and months before that. "I just want them to like me."

He cleared his throat. "I've got news for you, they will never like you. You are their boss. However, I do believe they respect you, and you can't buy that."

"And I respect *them*. I appreciate everything they do for me. Without them, I'd never be able to keep Westside floating."

Gabe leaned back against the couch. "Precisely. So, whatever you're doing now, it's working, right?"

I nodded slowly, agreeing.

"Say it."

A small smile leaked from my lips. "You're right."

"That's better." His own sly smile rivalled mine, and his finger moved the cursor to another mark. "Is this your salary?"

"Yes."

"You're paying yourself from the store's earnings, correct?"

"Yes."

"And that's all you're paying yourself?"

It wasn't much. In fact, my next in line made way more than what I took home, and even my newest shift managers were on par with my salary. But I also took a small percentage of the revenue. Not a lot but enough to give me a healthy vacation in the sunshine in the dead of winter each year, plus extra. If I ever used it.

"I reroll most of the earnings back into the company. Wage increases and additional staff have to get paid from somewhere."

He backed away. "I'm not discounting that, or telling you to stop doing what you're doing, but honestly you can afford to increase your personal pay. You certainly put in enough hours."

"Meh, I'm happy, and I hope the bonuses for the staff will keep them happy. A happy staff member is a long-term team member."

"That's certainly true." He scrolled through a few other totals and checked out the formulas. "Ah, here's your problem." The cursor rolled over and highlighted one group of numbers. "The math doesn't add up here." With the nearby pen in hand, he scratched out the figures on a sheet of paper. "See?" He pushed the correct math in my direction.

How had I missed that? I'd checked and rechecked those numbers dozens of times. My eyes flickered to the screen and compared the two. Yep, I had messed up. It wasn't a critical mistake, but one when corrected would trickle through the spreadsheet and right the wrongs it had created. I fixed the error and watched with joy as the number I expected showed up.

"Thank you so much."

"My pleasure. Usually it's a number issue."

"I'm so glad it was. I worried I was going to have a bigger problem on my plate." I hit save and closed out of the program. Relieved, I took a healthy swallow of Gabe's idea of a sub-par wine and watched as he did the same.

"Feels pretty good, eh, to have the error corrected?"

"It really does." Another swallow of red slipped down my throat with less effort than before.

Gabe stretched out his jean-covered legs beside the coffee table and placed his arm on the back of the couch. "How did the date interviews go?"

I laughed, the wine nearly coming out my nose. With

Gabe there was no subtlety. I liked that about him. "So far, there's just been the one guy, Seth. But he seemed a decent enough fellow."

"Old? Young?"

"Thirty-one."

"Decent." He enjoyed a taste of the wine and swirled it around in his goblet. I was sure he was categorizing the toxicity of my poor choice. He studied it way too much to be able to look past where it sat on the wine food chain.

"Are you going to pick him?"

"I think it would only be fair to the other candidates if I met with them."

He nodded. "I agree. Two others, right?"

"Correct."

"I think I've told you before how unnecessary this is, right? You don't need to go with anyone to prove anything. He's not worth it, in my opinion, the ex-fiancé I mean."

I shrugged. "I disagree."

Gabe had been my first choice when the invitation arrived, and he politely turned me down because he had a girlfriend, Jordan, and didn't think it would fly with her. Which made sense. However, he would've been nearly perfect. A business owner, charmingly handsome, and someone I felt comfortable with. The only problem was there was no romantic interest. I was just the neighbour down the hall.

"I still don't understand why you're going through this foolishness." Gabe set the half-full wine glass on the table. "I sure hope you find what you're looking for."

"A cheap date with interesting stories? Someone who doesn't expect anything from me, and can accept a onetime date? Someone who'll look good on my arm and be memorable, but not so much that Scumbag won't take too much interest?"

He winced. "That's where you're wrong. Whoever you bring, he'll search out. If Jordan and I were to get married, and for whatever crazy reason I invited my former witch of a wife, you can bet your bottom dollar I'd be checking out who she brought, although she's not allowed with a hundred feet of me."

Gabe never talked about life with his ex-wife. Whatever had happened between them didn't end well. He'd once mentioned, and only once as I think it slipped, that he filed a restraining order against her and her new husband. But I couldn't figure out why, despite the myriad of options floating in my head. And I was curious to know more.

"Why? Why would you care so much about who your ex brought? That relationship ended."

Gabe shrugged and set the mostly empty glass on the table. "Maybe it's a guy thing. Maybe it's a sense of morbid curiosity, but deep down I guess I'd want to know she still held on to me. It's kind of an ego boost in a sick way."

"You'd want your ex-wife to still pine after you?" I certainly didn't want Scumbag to lust after me.

"Not really. Mir– She was a total bitch and the guy she married…" He shook his head and ran his fingers through his hair. "Anyways, a part of me would want to see her stumble. Even if just for a fraction of a second. To know maybe, just maybe, she remembered how good we used to be together." He got a far away look in his eyes.

"So, you'd want to know who she brought, and yet want to know she stumbled after you? That it wasn't easy moving on?" It didn't make a lick of sense.

"Something like that." His distant look faded away and the smirk deepening the lines in his face returned. "But getting over her was difficult."

His hands rested on his lap and a sadness crept across

his face. Clearly, the ex had really done a number on him. It broke my heart a little knowing how much the rarely talked about ex hurt him so.

Time to deflect a little. "And that's exactly why I need to take a date. To show him I didn't stumble. How I'm better off without him. Like you without... her."

"No, you crashed."

I contorted my face and scowled at him.

"And rightfully so. What he did was unthinkable. But I think you're going about this the wrong way. Taking a guy you've known for a few hours won't prove anything, how desperate you were. And you don't want to come across like that, do you?"

But I was desperate. Gabe had turned me down. My shift manager did the same. My scowl faded as realisation set in.

"What am I supposed to do?"

"Honestly?"

I twisted and turned my body to face him dead on. "Please, hit me with the truth."

"I don't know what the right answer is, but I think taking an unknown is a bad idea. Toss the invitation and forget about it."

I grabbed a nearby pillow and swung it at him, laughing as it connected with his chest. "Thanks a lot."

He giggled. "I'm no Dear Abby."

"No, you're not." I rested my head on the top of the couch. "I'm hopelessly screwed, aren't I?"

"Well, you're certainly not hopeless, and the screwed part? I wouldn't know." He braced his hands in front of his body as if I were going to toss something else at him.

I gave him a playful push on the shoulder rather than

throw another pillow.

"Seriously though, I hope your meet and greets with these guys yield you whatever it is you're looking for. I don't want to see you crash and burn. You haven't mentioned with details how your relationship ended aside from him not showing up at the church, but I sense you're not healed as you're still holding on to it."

He was easy to talk with and never pressed for more information than I was willing to give. Despite the rather abrupt turn his life had taken, he was fairly upbeat and usually had some solid advice for me. Mind you, it was all work related as I think we both took the prize for having been attached to Class A jerks. It was only recently I'd shared with him about Scumbag, and he danced around his ex.

"Maybe that's why I need to go to his wedding. To get some closure." I often wondered if he'd gotten closure and had healed. Sometimes it seemed like the wound was still fresh.

He shrugged. "Maybe. I doubt it, but maybe. You're different than I am. When are you meeting with the other two guys?"

"I'm meeting Hudson tomorrow before I go to work, and Cory the day after."

"Hudson? Sounds pretentious."

I cocked an eyebrow. "Actually, I'm rather intrigued. In the pic he sent, there's a scar on his cheek that likely has a story behind it."

"Probably got beaten up for not handing over his lunch money." He scoffed and rose from the couch. "I should get going. I have an early meeting with a company in London I need to prep a little more for." He walked himself to the door. "Keep me posted on Mr. Pretentious and the other guy."

"Thanks for your help. Have a good night."

If Gabe had agreed to be my date, even as friends, I could close the door to this whole online dating shenanigans joke. Taking Gabe would be so much easier than a perfect stranger. Maybe I could sweet-talk Jordan into letting him go, especially after I explained the whole situation. She seemed like a nice enough person the couple of times we'd briefly talked in the hallway.

What was so wrong in my life that this was the level I now resorted to?

~Chapter Five

After a lengthy battle with myself and weighing the positives and negatives about treating these dates like interviews, I led with logic and brought my laptop...tucked into my bag. It banged against the door in my rush to find street parking. Dang, I wanted to be early and here I was borderline on time. By time I found this place, I was sure the minute hand would've ticked well past the top of the hour.

I was way out of my comfort zone agreeing to meet Hudson at the Royal Mayflower Hotel, assuming it was a darkened hotel bar we'd be meeting at. Racing breathlessly into the grand foyer with high ceilings dripping with opulence and bright chandeliers, I felt totally out of place in my simple sundress and wrap. If the entrance was any gauge to the rest of the place, even a full tuxedo and ball gown wouldn't be fancy enough wear.

Treading softly in my flats over the marble-esque floor tiles, I searched the area. He'd said the bar was off to the left of the entrance. A giant table with a bouquet of fresh flowers sat in the middle of the foyer, effectively blocking my view. I walked around it, on the left, and spotted a gilded open door.

The bar was brightly lit, and as I stepped inside, it transported me to another time and place. Sunlight streamed in the stain-glass windows and dark wooden chairs sat around tables of varying size. A long, polished bar stretched out beside me, a lone patron drinking from a tall thin glass sat on one of the bar stools closest to the back wall. Overall, the bar itself was fancy looking, which fit the hotel it was nestled into.

"Can I help you?" A young lady in a slim-fitting black top and skirt stood before me.

"I'm meeting someone." I glanced around. "A guy."

There weren't many people in there, so it shouldn't be difficult to locate him.

"Is he good-looking?" She giggled like a schoolgirl.

"I suppose." I raised an eyebrow at her behaviour. Based on how she was dressed, I would've expected her to act a little more mature.

She pointed to the corner to her left. "He's over there." A dreamy look blanketed her face. "I'll take you."

"I see him, thanks."

The volume of the Irish music playing on the overhead speakers increased as I walked closer, and thankfully faded as I approached his table. Suddenly, I understood why the hostess was giddy – Hudson was drop dead gorgeous, even from twenty feet away. How was a guy like that single still?

"Hudson?" I asked as I got to the table. He hadn't even noticed me approach.

He dropped the leather-bound menu on the round table. "Meghan, I presume?" He stood and extended his hand, his suit pants hanging perfectly off his body. The lavender dress shirt unbuttoned at the top complemented his pale skin tone.

"Pleased to meet you," I forced out, breaking my gaze

when he squeezed my hand a little too tightly. I tucked my dress under me and sat down, my laptop bag resting against my shin.

Hudson sat down after me and crossed his legs, his pointy right shoe poking out from under the table.

"This is quite the place." I glanced around again.

"It's a hidden gem within the city. Plus, it's only a few blocks from my office."

I draped my purse on the back of my chair. "What is it you do? You never mentioned anything in your ad."

"Nor did you." His arm stretched out over to the chair beside him.

And a point to Hudson. "I don't work any place exciting."

"Me either."

Downtown was littered with high rise offices I imagined contained investment employees, bankers, lawyers, or marketing directors like Seth; something super sexy. All the high-end businesses had offices there, at least I thought so.

"Really? I don't buy it. You're dressed pretty sharply."

The compliment softened him. He dropped his leg and tucked it back under the table. "I'm a lawyer for the LAPP."

I nodded my head like I knew what the LAPP was. "That would keep you busy."

It was a stretch, but I'd heard lawyers were famous for working ridiculously long hours, something I could relate to, although the pay scales were light years apart.

"Seventy hours a week."

Most weeks I felt I'd worked the same number of hours. It never ended.

The schoolgirl with a giddy laugh approached our table. "May I get you something from the bar?"

Hudson answered right away. "A pint of draught. The

darker the better." He tipped his head in my direction. "And you?"

"Sangria?" I asked.

She never took her eyes off him. "I'll be right back with those."

"What about you?" He eyed me up and down, taking the casual glance to a level I wasn't comfortable with. "I take it you're not a lawyer?"

"A business owner. I'm opening up a restaurant in the new year."

"I see. I'd offer you some legal advice, but I'm not that type of lawyer."

"To offer the advice?" It wasn't meant to come out snarky, but it did. Oh well.

He chuckled. "No, but that's cute. I work with the government on pension plans, so restaurant management is not my area of expertise."

I nodded, swallowing down a morsel of guilt. At least he took it well. "I understand; however, I do have a great lawyer who helps me with that."

In moving my leg, the laptop bag slid, and I reached down to right it. Should I retrieve it and ask some questions, or just go with the flow?

"Excellent." He unlocked his gaze from me, his focus falling to the menu on the table. "Do you know what you'd like to eat?"

The menu was heavy in my hands as I opened it up. Limited selection for main courses, but a long list of bar appropriate plates. I didn't want anything messy or dripping with sauce. Scanning the items, I settled on a clubhouse sandwich and closed my menu.

"So, you're looking for a date, and just one night,

correct?" Hudson pushed his menu towards the centre of the table and stared at me like I was a client on the stand; intently and unblinking.

"Correct." I swallowed.

"When's this wedding?"

"September long weekend."

The server approached and set down our drinks, starting with his. My staff knew better than to lead with the male, even if he was eye candy. Mind you, his eyes didn't stray far from her either. So far, I'd say this date was a total flop, but yet, I believed it was still salvageable. He didn't seem as pretentious as Gabe thought, given his name, but I could see Gabe being genuinely annoyed with Hudson.

We ordered our food, Hudson first, and she disappeared.

"Back to the meeting." He gestured. "What would be required of me?"

"To be my date." I thought I had been clear.

"That's cute." He leaned back in his chair, crossing his legs again. "How?"

"What do you mean?" I pulled my laptop out and fired it up.

Hudson tipped his head to the side in a curious expression. "How long should it appear like we've been together? Obviously, you don't want it to be happenstance that we met outside the venue."

"A couple of months maybe?" I hadn't really thought about a timeline aside from the fact I didn't want it to appear like what he'd just suggested.

"Okay, I can work with that. Dancing is allowed?"

"Of course." Dancing was a preferred way to interact and be seen without *being seen,* if you followed my thinking.

"And drinking?"

"It's an open bar, but I respectfully ask you keep the intoxication level to a buzzed feeling and not a fall-over drunk level."

He appeared mildly disappointed, but answered, "I can live with that."

Thank goodness. Nothing worse than those partygoers who drink to excess just because it's free, and then get loud, rude and obnoxious.

"Good. Now, I suppose I should check some items off my list before we get into too many specifics. Do you mind?" I pointed to the laptop where a snapshot of the list projected onto the screen. Standard questions first that I'd neglected to ask. "Married?"

"No."

"Divorced?"

"Not yet." He said it in such a way I hesitated before continuing on. What kind of answer was that? Were they separated, but seeing other people? His answer didn't make any sense.

"Are you currently in a relationship?"

"Not at the moment, but should I meet someone prior to this wedding, would that be okay?" He inched himself closer as he asked.

Another thing I hadn't considered. What if between now and the wedding he did find someone? Should he be allowed to cancel on me, or should he honour his commitment, as it was only for one night?

"I suppose," I said, weighing the correct way to answer. "It wouldn't be a problem if you started dating anyone as I only need your companionship for a few hours, and nothing beyond the cake cutting. However, if I agreed to take you as my date, it would be nice to have you honour that commitment, even if you had met another."

His hand wrapped around the mug of dark ale. "Fair enough. And if I meet someone at the wedding?"

There's a scene I wanted to avoid. Nothing like being left at the altar to ruin one's self esteem, but to take a date to a wedding and have him leave with someone else? The fact he even brought it up worried me it would likely happen. That kind of bad luck followed me like a shadow.

"I'd respectfully ask you not pick up anyone at the wedding. This night is about closure for me, not for my date to dump me in favour of someone better looking."

A Cheshire grin filled his face.

"Moving on…" My eyes scanned the list of questions, trying to pick which I really wanted answers to. Any would've worked. Instead, my mouth was as dry as cotton and my heart pounded loud enough to drown out any thoughts. I swallowed. "How old are you?"

"Thirty-five. Too old for you?"

"Hardly, why?"

"You look like you are in your late twenties."

I took a sip of sangria, hoping the coolness would give me something to focus on. Instead, it felt like it was souring on my lips. "I'm flattered but I'm closer to your age."

"Really." Slowly, he lifted the mug to his full lips and as he swallowed, his Adam's apple bobbed. A fascinating movement that had me reaching for my own neck, if only for a brief rub.

Damn, he was good looking, but that was about all. Surely there had to be more beneath his surface.

"You're a fan of Patrick Stewart, right?"

"I know enough to know you were referring to him in

45

Star Trek, but I'm not a sci-fi fan in the least. However, I do love a great Shakespearean play, and Patrick Stewart did a great job in Hamlet."

Ugh, Shakespeare. A high school class I barely made it through. Never did understand it and all the Coles notes in the world didn't help my C+ average.

Another glance to the list of questions. Ah, there's one. "Do you play any sports?" My favourite was curling.

"Hockey, but I haven't since university."

At least they are both on ice surfaces. It's a start.

"That's how I got this scar." He tapped his left cheek. "High stick."

"Ouch, that had to hurt."

The scar was a thin, jagged line. The plastic surgeon, or whoever stitched him back up, did a great job. Unless you really stared, or scaled a picture to make it bigger, it wasn't too noticeable.

"Probably, they gave me great drugs."

"For a stick to the face?" Numbing agents maybe, but enough to knock him out? I doubted it.

"For the cracked ribs after I laid a beat down on the player who hit me."

Yikes. The strikes added up quickly, and an instinctual feeling in the gut, the kind warning you of making a big mistake, it roared up big time.

The waitress set our food down. "Your plate is hot," she told Hudson. "Be careful. I'd hate for you to get hurt."

He smirked, as if the shameless flirting was something that happened every day. Who am I kidding, it probably did.

"I'll be careful."

"Can I get you anything for now?"

I thought she was asking us both, but when I said,

"Ketchup, please," she ignored me and walked away. Yeah, she wouldn't last long in my restaurant. I pushed the laptop off to the side, keeping the screen facing me, and pulled my plate closer.

Hudson took a generous bite of his burger, and with a mouth full of food asked, "How long were you and your fiancé together?"

"Four years."

"That's a long time." He wiped his food with the cloth napkin and tucked it under the rim of his plate.

It went by very quickly. We were on and off for a couple of years through college, only getting together for good a few years later. Perhaps the on and off relationship should've given me a heads up how we were destined for a permanent off, not that I would've honestly believed it. Ah, love was truly blind.

"So, you really need to impress him, or are you going to simply get closure on the whole thing?"

"A bit of both, to be honest."

"Good. So, we need to look like we've been a couple for a couple of months, limited drinking, but we need to enjoy ourselves and dancing is okay. So far am I correct?"

I nodded as I popped a fry into my mouth.

"And sex at the end of the night is off the table?"

Thankfully my snort stayed firmly in my head. No doubt this guy was a total player. "Totally."

"Too bad," he said, just loud enough for me to hear. "That's where I perform best."

A chunk of fry lodged itself in my throat, and I coughed to get it to back up and took a large swallow of my drink to get it down. Eww. Part of me wanted to be flattered that Hudson thought I was attractive enough to want to be intimate with, but the larger, and smarter part, was disgusted by his comment.

47

"I'm curious to know what's in it for me? What can you bring to the table to sweeten the deal, making it impossibly hard for me to say no to? There has to be something in it for me. You'll be going around this party introducing me as your boyfriend to people you know fairly well, and since I won't be getting any booty as a paycheque, what's in it for me?"

"I know it's not much, but there'll be plenty of free food and drinks. You don't need to bring a gift or anything, and I can do the driving, so there's no wear and tear on your vehicle."

"That's cute if you're being funny. Seriously though… what do I get out of it?"

I sat there dumbfounded, holes being poked in what I thought was a well-planned thing. Instead, the lawyer kept finding the gaps of logic. He must be good in court and have the witnesses come unhinged. What did I have to offer my date? I guess going out blindly, so to speak, with someone new isn't what it used to be.

My clubhouse sandwich remained largely uneaten as I lost my appetite, although I picked at a few fries. Hudson seemed to have no issues devouring his burger and ordering another draught while the air between us thickened with awkwardness. All my thoughts kept revolving back to what it was I could offer. On the flip side of the coin, would I accept a date with a random stranger to attend a wedding just because? No. The idea was sheer lunacy.

"You know," Hudson said, his words being the first thing to come out of his mouth since he finished eating. "We could exchange services."

My blood boiled at the mere mention of services.

"I come as a guest to your former fiancé's wedding September long, and you come as a guest to the Regatta at my beach house this weekend." He wiggled his brows as the grin

48

spread across his face.

Relief filled every cell in my body as I knew I was working and there was no way I could, or would want to, get out of being at Westside. There wasn't anything wrong with the idea, and I have a girlfriend who likely would've jumped at the chance to jump Hudson, it just wasn't my thing.

He eyed me up and down, his gaze slowly roving up my body. "It would give us time to work into our roles."

Time to let the guy down easy and politely.

"As lovely as an offer as that is, I feel I should let you know I have already interviewed one person for the role of doting boyfriend, and I'm interviewing another tomorrow, so I'll need time to consider your counteroffer."

"Hope I'm at the top of your list," he said, downing the rest of his dark beer.

"Most definitely."

I didn't mention what list he would be on of course. However, Hudson was not getting a call back. At first, I was concerned why a guy as good looking as him would be without a date or a steady girlfriend, and then his actions spoke loud enough for it to make perfect sense.

As the Proclaimers said *She ain't pretty, she just looks that way.*

Chapter Six

"Oh my god, that was a terrible date. Not the worst in a history of bad dates, but still." I spilled all the gory details to Gabe after I holed myself up into my tiny little office after the supper rush. I needed to vent about Hudson, and since Gabe was the only one who knew what I was attempting, it felt like the most logical thing to share it with him.

His loud, booming laugh echoed through the speakers, and I rushed to click down the volume level. No one in the back of the restaurant needed to hear about the epic lunch disaster. I double checked the door was still closed.

"Well, I'm sorry it happened. He sounds like a winner."

"He's a winner, all right. All I'm getting through this dating website is a group of desperate men who can't get a woman the traditional way because they're jerks. This Hudson is a prime example."

"You know," Gabe said with a voice of reason too hard to ignore, "you could try to be a little more open-minded about the whole thing. Dating websites are the new way to meet someone."

"Or an easy way to get pornography."

Two more lovely pictures of the male anatomy had graced my inbox.

"Well, there's that too."

"What about the first guy? You said he seemed okay. They can't all be complete jerks."

"That's true, I suppose not all of them are." Seth was the winner for now. "I just thought I made it clear in my ad I wasn't looking for a hookup."

Gabe cleared his throat. "Can't fault a guy for trying. It's like that Gretzky quote—"

"You miss one-hundred percent of the shots you don't take."

I knew the quote well as I applied it to my business. If you don't try, you'll never find out. Never in a million years did I think it applied to a dating site where I specifically mentioned I wasn't into hookups. Oh well. There didn't have to be a date two.

"I think I'm just frustrated with the whole thing. Being invited has rattled me to the bones. Why does he want me there? Is it to poke fun at me and remind the others how he and I weren't successful, but look, he's making it with my former friend? What gives? I can't figure out his motivation for inviting me."

"I think, and I could be way wrong here, is figuring out why you are so motivated to attend? Why not just not go? You've moved on, and you're better off without him, clearly, so why the need to go? It can't be just to save face. I know there's more there than that. Unless you're still in love with the guy?"

There was a lengthy pause, longer than needed. Perhaps I should've raced to answer but the comment stung, because I wasn't. That ship had sailed long ago.

Gabe resumed speaking like I'd unclicked a pause

button. "Personally, I think you're desperately grasping for straws."

I sighed and scribbled some numbers on a nearby notepad, glancing up at the staff calendar. A long list of who had what time booked off for holidays stared back at me. Thankfully summer was almost over and my constant juggle with the schedule was also near its end. I preferred regularity and knowing, both mentally and emotionally, who would be working on my shifts. Some were easier to deal with than others.

The wedding date still had an opening for the evening manager as no one had yet volunteered. It would make life easier for me if someone stepped up, but my pickings were slim. Guess I was going to have to bite the bullet and slot someone in. So much for getting people to like me. Whoever I picked was bound to hate me more.

"Are you still there?"

My eyes fell from the calendar back to my phone. "What? I'm sorry. I got distracted. What were you saying?"

"It's all good."

"I'm sorry." I hated hearing an upset tone in his voice. Here I'd been the one to call him and I couldn't even stay focused. What a lousy friend I was.

"Do you have plans tomorrow?"

I flipped through my mental calendar. "Not until the evening."

"Can we meet for lunch?"

"Sure. Why don't you come over?" My hand smacked the desk. "Damnit, I can't. I'm meeting Cory for lunch. Blind date number three."

"Right."

"Maybe I should cancel. This whole thing isn't working out the way I'd hoped. I think I'm too old-fashioned and hoped my inbox would have at least something romantic in nature, instead of it being filled with things I'd rather not see."

Which also included a follow up from Seth, but I wasn't sure how to deal with him just yet. My warm, stinging hand clasped to my forehead which felt surprisingly nice. I pressed the weight of my head into it.

"You need to do what's best for you. But I'm going on record as saying you don't need to attend the wedding. Then your problem is solved."

"Yeah, but I'm still single and stuck in life."

A long-winded sigh blew out of me. Even though my professional life was soaring, my meager personal life suffered. Big time.

A gentle rap sounded from behind me. "Excuse me, Meghan?" The female voice called out.

"Just a sec," I said to the phone and the door, and slid my chair out of the way to inch open the barrier between pouring my heart out and the reality I faced. "Yes, Celeste?"

"I'm sorry to bother you, but there's someone in the dining room asking to talk to a manager."

I nodded and rose. "Table?"

"L9." Celeste disappeared around the corner.

"On my way." I picked up my phone. "Sorry, Gabe, I need to go."

"Go kick some ass." I could almost imagine him air punching and the thought made me smile. "Knock on my door when you get home tonight, and we'll continue this. I think you need to talk."

A moment ago, I was about to let my guard down. Pushing my shoulders back and smoothing out my skirt, my personal walls rose back up to their full strength. "It'll be late."

"I can handle it."

53

"See you later." When he said goodbye, I turned off my phone and steeled myself for what waited me in the dining room.

Whenever I wore heels, the staff was always alerted to my presence. The click-clack no doubt warning them. However, in flats with the rubber sole, I was like the predator sneaking up on the prey, and tonight was no different. I walked through the kitchen first to make sure there was an order sitting for L9 in limbo, and seeing that they were caught up, came around the back side of the wait station.

"—And I told him, in no uncertain terms, that he needed to ditch the bitch."

"You're so in love with him."

"I am not. I just want to have a fun time with him. I think it'll be—"

The two servers, Daisy and Celeste, stopped talking the second I stepped around the corner. No drinks were being loaded onto trays, nothing was being cleaned. I don't mind foolish gossiping when they are working but they were standing around like they were on a break.

"Ladies," I said, giving each of them a stern once-over.

They remained frozen in the spot.

My gaze zeroed in on lack of fresh coffee, to which Daisy jumped to and started rinsing out the pot. The ripped foil package of grounds released its scent all around us. It was instantly soothing.

"Celeste, is L9 your table?"

"Yes, ma'am."

I waited, head leaning closer to her, for an explanation. It wasn't coming without digging. "And?"

"I don't know. They've finished eating and asked for you specifically."

"Okay. Thanks." I was barely around the corner when I heard a sigh escape from one of them.

One of the ladies whispered, "That was close."

Not sure what I almost caught, but I may need to keep a closer eye on them. Shoulders back I walked over to the table in the far corner. Nothing appeared out of place on the floor, and everything looked clean and tidy.

"Hello, I'm Meghan, how can I help you tonight?" I wore on my sweetest smile and calmest voice.

"And you are the manager?"

I took in the couple sitting before me. She was about my age, nicely dressed but not over the top. One hand on her drink, which needed a refill, and the other casually in her lap. She wasn't giving off any unpleasant vibes. The gentleman was dressed in a similar style and he too appeared relaxed.

"Yes, sir."

"We'd like to help you out. I'm Matthew Forsythe, from the Journal."

My insides pulsed suddenly with excitement. I knew his name; he'd rated many top restaurants and here he was sitting unannounced in mine. "You are their top food critic."

A shy grin filled his face. "My reputation precedes me."

Stay calm. Don't get excited.

It was like talking myself off the ledge to remain professional. "And how was everything tonight?"

"Absolutely amazing. I've never had a steak bowl, and the flavours are a perfect mix of tang and savour."

My heart skipped a beat with the glowing way the words rolled off his tongue. Mr. Forsythe was known more his reviews of top-end establishments, not the casual dining experience I offered, so it was thrilling to hear him say such wonderful things.

"A friend raved about this place and on a whim, Patty and I thought to check it out. And I must tell you, the food is top notch, and the service is delightful."

The smile on my face was nothing compared to the one attempting to burst free of me, and it was hard to restrain. But if I went all gushy and over the top, it could taint his opinion of my professionalism. "I'm so very pleased to hear that."

"I'd like to run a review on it in Sunday's section."

"Absolutely. Is there anything I can provide you with?" I had stock photos on file, if need be.

"I took all my photos as they came out. This way, my readers can see the real deal. May I ask you a few questions about the business, or should I contact the owner?"

"I am the owner, so feel free to ask me."

For the next five minutes, he asked about where the idea came from for the steak bowls, how long Westside had been around, and plans for expansion. I filled him in and accepted his business card.

"So, I expect a call from you, Ms. Carter, when the new place opens up."

"You can count on it." I shook his hand, and the lady's who sat silently in waiting. "Is there anything else I can do for you?"

"No, I don't want to take up any more of your time."

"Thank you for coming by and taking a chance on us. I look forward to your review."

With a quick tip of my head, I excused myself from the table and walked with a purposefully normal speed until I reached the back. I punched the air and then pinned his business card to the wall above the calendar.

Surprise drop ins like him, and the secret shoppers were always welcome. It just proved running a tight ship had positive effects. The food was great, the service wonderful, and even the brick-encased interior added the charm, he'd said.

Finally, something to hoot and holler over.

# # #

It was after eleven when I walked down the hall. The evening had been remarkably quiet after Mr. Forsythe left, but I got all the paperwork done, staff clocked out, and the place locked up before ten-thirty. Had to be some kind of record. Still dressed in my work attire consisting of a white blouse, black dress pants and heels, I leaned against Gabe's door and rapped the back of my knuckles on it. I didn't do it too hard, because if he was sleeping, I was going to let him.

There was no response, and I headed down the hallway to my apartment. My key was in the lock when I heard his voice whisper in my direction.

"Giving up so easily?" He wore a pair of shorts and a faded grey shirt, and rubbed the sleep from his eyes. The hairs on one side of his head were standing up, as if that was the side he'd been sleeping on.

"Go back to sleep."

"You're home early."

I glanced at my watch. "A little."

He ran his fingers through the salt and pepper strands, smoothing everything back down and pulling himself together. "I'd set my alarm to wake me up in time to freshen up." He glanced back into his apartment and held up a finger. "Just a sec."

I pulled the key out of the lock and walked back in his direction. A faint buzzing sound came from his kitchen.

"You set an alarm?" It was funny to me, but I think it

was mental exhaustion giggling inside of me.

"Of course. I crashed not long after we hung up."

"That was at eight."

"I know." A shade of embarrassment crossed his face.

"Don't worry, it's okay. I know you were up early."

He nodded, a slow still waking up kind of nod. "This lead guy in London likes to have his meetings before the staff come in, which makes it five am here. And since I need to be at the office for before five, I was up at four."

"You really should get some sleep."

"Nah, I think you need me more than I need the sleep." He pointed inside his apartment. "I've even got wine."

It was never too late for a glass of red. "Oh, this is for you. I know it's your favourite."

It was our Coriki Steak bowl, the same one the food critic enjoyed. I closed the door.

"Thanks. This will make for a tasty lunch tomorrow."

Gabe's apartment was on the corner of the building, and much nicer than mine. His was a two-bedroom verses my single, and where I decorated it with a chic look and kept my colouring to the basic white walls and put together furniture, his was very different.

Behind the grey sofa flanking the wall, he'd put up a distressed wood looking type of mural, giving the apartment a totally warm and cozy look. Who knew it could change the feel of the place? Bookshelves were in abundance, some tall, some short, and plants of varying sizes sat on top of them, giving a contrast of colour to the brick. The best part wasn't the titles of the books, although he had some interesting new age style reads, but the pictures he had scattered around.

None were of the typical landscapes or art deco type, instead all were images of people. Every. Single. One. Family portraits, hanging out with the guys at an Oiler's game, a couple of him in front of famous landmarks, two cute little girls he said were nieces, and a cute pic of him and Jordan posing at the legislative fountain.

I looked around. Wait a sec? Where was that picture? It had been on top of the side table, under the lamp, but it was absent.

Gabe walked toward me brandishing a goblet of red. "It's Australian."

I shook my head as a small smile escaped me. "That doesn't mean anything to me."

"It could if you took the wine lessons seriously."

"Having a glass of wine with you a few nights a week hardly constitutes a lesson."

"What about those trips to Wine and Beyond?" He was starting to look more awake. The reds in his eyes faded to a barely noticeable pink.

I took the wine and sat on the still-warm-from-sleeping couch. It was always so inviting, and I loved running my hand over the fabric, a suede-like material which I knew wasn't suede as Gabe wasn't the type. It was higher end than that.

He sat on the opposite side, smoothing out the throw pillow he placed between us. "So, tell me, you were saying earlier about not wanting to go to the wedding?"

"No," I said, my eyes drifting to the vacant spot where Jordan's picture used to be. "You first. What's going on?"

He turned to see what I was staring at it. "Oh, you noticed."

"Of course, I did. What's going on? You two have a fight?"

"No." He set his wine glass down and gave his tired face a rub. "We broke up."

"Oh." I thought things were getting serious between them. "I'm so sorry."

"She asked me to move in with her, and I turned her down. It was too quick."

"Too quick?"

"We'd only been together three months."

Yeah, then that is quick.

He leaned his head on the top of the couch and crossed his arms over his chest. "We were having a good time and enjoying life, I just didn't think it meant to shift into super serious zone. I loved her but we weren't in the same place."

In all the time I'd known Gabe, he had always been the kind of guy who wore his heart on his sleeve. You never needed to guess what he was thinking or how he was feeling. It was very refreshing.

"I figured we'd still be together, but she totally smashed that. Grabbed the few personal effects she had here and cleared out." He sighed. "It's now officially over."

"I'm sorry." I took a sip of wine.

It was tasty and had a nice fragrance about it. Plus, it was smooth enough to gently slip down my throat with ease. Maybe there was something to these Australian wines.

"Ah, what can I do?" He turned his head over to the vacant space under the light. "It is what it is. Women are so fickle; it's all or nothing, and I couldn't give her my all. She wanted the fairy tale but I'm not her prince."

I knew he was referring specifically to Jordan and not all women in general. I certainly didn't want it all. Mind you, I suppose I didn't really know what it was I wanted, but a no-strings attached date to a wedding would be a start.

"So now what are you going to do?"

"Don't know." He flipped his gaze to me. "Do you think

it was too fast?"

That was a loaded question. It took me forever to decide upon something and matters of the heart were no exception. But I was an oddity. I knew and accepted it. Not sure what the right answer was, I shrugged.

"Obviously, she enjoyed spending time with you and wanted you to be the first person she saw when she woke up and the last when she went go to bed."

"Gee, when you phrase it like that it makes me sound like an incredible dickhead and that's not what I wanted with her." He closed his eyes. "I loved her, but I wasn't ready for a high level of commitment. It's only been recently I've opened myself up to the possibility of ... more."

"She really did a number on you, didn't she?"

When he bolted upright, he understood who specifically I referred to. The ex-wife. Whatever she did, she wrecked him.

I swallowed half the glass of wine before I came up for air. "You're tired. I should let you go."

"No, please stay." He pushed himself up and crossed his legs, attempting to brush away the Sandman who stood ready to pounce. "Now that I've told you my little problem, tell me yours. Let's get to the root of the problem."

"Wondering if I should bother meeting with Cory?" He had sent me another email confirming we were still a go and provided the address. In good conscience I couldn't cancel, but I had a nagging feeling I was just wasting both of our times.

"No, the other one. About feeling stuck."

Oh, that one.

"It flew out of me before I could stop it. It wasn't truth, it was just something I said in the heat of the moment."

"There was truth in it." He let out a yawn and raced to cover it. "Sorry."

It was sweet he wanted to discuss my off-handed remark, but it was clear the man was tired. "Gabe, go to bed. You've had a busy, emotional day. Get some rest." I finished off the rest of my wine, no sense letting it go to waste.

"I'm sorry. I really want to talk."

"Another time."

And about anything else.

I dropped my glass off in his kitchen sink and headed for the door, Gabe right behind me.

"Dinner tomorrow?" He pressed his weary body against the door frame. A hint of cologne falling off him.

"I'm working. But Friday night?" It would make for a better Friday evening to dine with Gabe than to sit alone and stare at my computer.

"Sure."

I stepped out into the hall. "G'nite."

"I'm sorry I wasn't more awake."

My hand flew through the air. "I'll talk to you after meeting with guy number three."

He pointed his finger at me, a lazy man's version of finger guns. "I'm counting on it."

Based on how fast he closed the door, I suspected he was passed out sleeping before I had my key back in my lock.

~Chapter Seven

$\mathcal{M}$y swim session sucked. I couldn't stay focused on maintaining my form, despite the effort I put into my strokes and kicks. I was like an errant missile on some sort of collision course. It was infuriating, and I scrubbed my skin with the exfoliating towel a little too briskly and left my cheeks a roughed-up rouge colour. It was neither healthy looking nor looking as though I'd had too much sun.

My date with Cory was in an hour and there wasn't time to soothe my skin with a chamomile face mask, I'd have to show up looking rough around the edges so to speak. Before I walked out the door wearing capris and a nice, flowery blouse, I gave his profile another quick peek.

He was a father to two, had a golden lab or retriever – I never understood the difference – and was over forty. Plus, he double-checked *again* if we were still good to go. A little unnerving how he needed constant reassurance I wasn't going to stand him up.

About to close the lid on the laptop and pack it in my bag, my eyes darted to the battery readout – enough for ten minutes worth of screen time. Shit. That wasn't going to be enough. Even a decent coffee date took the better part of an hour, and even if I didn't look at the screen the whole time, it still needed some juice to be awake. What was I going to do without my computer?

Dang it, I was going to be late if I didn't get moving. The clock ticked loudly as I hopped in my car, sans laptop, and drove to the Italian bistro he wanted to meet at. Not that I minded. I knew the place and was comfortable there.

Pulling into a stall, I watched as a couple walked in, and a couple of suits exited. A guy in nice dress pants and a button up walked in, holding the door for a lady with a baby in a car seat. Even from his profile, with his chiseled chin and long nose, I recognized the face from Mingle More – my date had arrived.

Taking a deep breath, I exited the car and strode into the restaurant.

"You must be Meghan?" He was taller than he appeared outside a moment ago but had an instantly soothing voice.

"Yes, you're Cory?"

We shook hands and he turned to the hostess. "For two please."

"Right this way," she said.

"After you," Cory said, pointing in front of him.

I followed the hostess and like a fine gentleman, Cory pulled out my chair. Thankfully, he didn't tuck me in.

As he sat across from me, his hands shook a little and his gaze darted all around. I wondered about how many dates he'd been on recently since he was clearly suffering from a bit of anxiety. I took in his appearance, straight dark brown hair, thin lips, and a little nick on his chin from shaving.

In a lowered voice, he said, "I have to apologize in advance, but I'm really nervous."

"I promise not to bite." I thought it was funny, but it

didn't work. His shoulders tightened up even more. "If it helps, I'm nervous too."

He sighed, a gentle gush of air escaping with a hint of mint with it. "It does. Sorry for asking so often if you were coming."

"Been stood up a lot?"

He nodded. "I'm not that good looking, and I think ladies see that and ditch me."

"Don't be so hard on yourself."

I wouldn't classify him as hot, or model worthy, but there was something subtly charming about him, more real. Maybe it was the way his hair had a side part and an actual style, rather than the haphazard look I'd seen many a fellow wear. Or the way his eyes held a little dazzle behind the tension. A man didn't have to be drop dead gorgeous to be considered a nice man. Look at Hudson. Another quick assessment of Cory, and I classified him as a cute gentleman.

"Thanks."

Our waitress arrived and took our drink orders. He chose a cup of coffee, and I ordered the same.

"I know it's hot outside, but it's never too hot for coffee."

"I haven't had a coffee in a long time, but it sounded like a great choice."

"So, you're Meghan."

"Yes," I said with a nod.

Colour flooded his cheeks. "I'm sorry. I'm really nervous." He looked away.

A small part of me felt bad for him because I didn't want this guy to get his hopes up. Our meeting was this lunch date and possibly the wedding date, but that's it. In my mind, there wasn't much to be nervous about.

"Cory, tell me about you. On your profile, you mentioned you had two children?"

With that, his eyes flashed, and a sparkle took centre stage. "Yes, a boy and a girl. My son is thirteen and my daughter is twelve."

"That's nice, although I don't envy the teenage years. I've heard they're terrible."

The waitress arrived with two cups of steaming hot coffee and set a mug in front of each of us, ending with Cory. She placed a tiny pitcher of cream between us and a quaint little bowl of sugar.

"I'll give you a few minutes and come back to grab your orders." She passed us each a menu. "If you need anything before that, just close your menu and I'll be right here."

"Thanks," I said looking up at her impressed. I'd be sure to tell the manager how she's doing.

"My kids are my pride and joy, and knock on wood, they're not too much trouble. Yet. My oldest is an honours student and the skip of his curling team. He plays clarinet in both the junior and senior bands and is just a great kid overall." His whole face lit up as he talked about his son. "My daughter is a b-student but is part of their Social Justice League and co-ordinates events for the school to participate in the community. She plays volleyball and basketball, and in her spare time, writes for the school paper." The smile never left his face, and he wore his fatherly pride like a halo.

"That's really great. Sounds like you have a couple of wonderful kids." I added some cream and a spoonful of sugar into my mug and quietly stirred, resting the spoon on the saucer.

He appeared as if he were relaxing marginally. The shoulders dropped a little and the tightness in his fingers as he stirred his coffee disappeared.

66

"Thanks. It's my hope they are well rounded and nice people. There are too many bad people in the world." Cory lifted the cup to his lips, and I did the same.

"I agree. The world needs more positivity." I put the cup down and looked around when Cory stared into the flickering candle in the centre of the table.

The place was marginally busy, not too bad given the time of day. Their location was great too, but not near enough offices in the area to have a true lunch hour peak. The newest location of Westside was situated in the heart of the Ice District downtown, and with proper planning would easily be able to cater to a busy lunch rush and a supper rush. The hockey nights and concerts hopefully would help increase business as well.

Cory stayed quiet, his eyes searching the menu.

I opened my own and ran my eyes over the selections. "Everything looks so appetizing," I said in hopes of getting him to speak again.

The air had grown awkward with each passing breath. I had nothing against someone being shy or nervous, but I felt enough time had passed for that and there should be a little less uncomfortableness between us. I couldn't—and shouldn't—be the only one carrying the conversation.

"The food here is amazing. Have you been before?" His deep brown eyes looked up from the menu for a brief moment.

"I have. My buddy knows the owner."

Gabe had mentioned several times how he was connected to this restaurant. Almost like a family business, as he knew all the employees and the owner. Maybe it was, although I never dug deeper into it.

"Ah," he said with a nod and closed his menu, folding his hands together on the edge of the table.

Following suit, as I knew what I wanted—what I always

got—I put mine down. Shortly thereafter, our waitress appeared and took our order.

The silence was deafening, and an image flickered into my mind. "You have a dog, right?"

"Yes, do you have allergies?"

I narrowed my eyes slightly at the quick way he jumped to that question. "No."

"Whew. Butter, that's my retriever, she sheds a lot and some people had told me her hair bothers their allergies." He glanced around again, and his focus stared over my right shoulder.

"No allergies here. What about you? Do you have any?" I suppose I should know in case there will be food products at the wedding that could set someone off.

"Just shellfish."

We're safe there. No way would Scumbag dish out money for everyone to dine on shrimp or lobster or crab. He was way too cheap.

"That's good." I took another sip of coffee. At this rate, and lack of conversation, I'd have it finished before our meal got served. Taking in a deep breath, I said, "I guess I should explain my ad."

He perched himself a little closer and his eyes fell to my hands. God this was awkward.

"I'm going to be totally honest and upfront with you. I'm only looking for a date to a wedding, and nothing beyond. There, all beverages and food will be covered, and I'll bring the gift. You are free to have a couple of drinks if you'd like."

"I don't drink," he said, shaking his head.

Oh lord, you should try. Might help loosen you up.

Right about now, I needed a drink. A strong one. Maybe two ounces of fireball.

"Fair enough." My coffee was halfway finished but the lunch date was a long way from that. "I'd ask you to join me about an hour before the ceremony so we can get acquainted, and that you stay until after the cake cutting. You're more than welcome to mingle and network."

He nodded. "I can do that."

"Do you dance?"

"Not very well."

Geez. "Well, we can dance if you like."

"Okay."

"I need it to look like we're a couple. Is that something you're comfortable with?"

He swallowed, almost hard enough that I swore I heard it. "Depends. What exactly?"

I fought the urge to roll my eyes. At this point, Hudson would make a better date. At least it would be interesting with him. "Hand holding, quick glances, that sort of thing." Against my better judgement, I reached out my hand to gently touch his. Underneath my palm, his hand quivered. "Like this."

"Oh-kay." He didn't retract his hand, but it firmed up the longer I touched him.

Enough was enough, and I wrapped my hand back around my mug of coffee. "Do you have any questions?"

Interviews for jobs went easier than this. Cory was a ball of nerves.

"I don't think so."

As sad as it was, by this point, I already knew Cory would not be joining me, and I felt it irrelevant to add anything personal about myself to the limited conversation we had going. However, I wasn't about to be rude either, I had to keep this lunch date to an amicable level. "Tell me, what made you decide to join Mingle More."

69

"My brother."

I nodded and waved my hand. "Tell me more."

"A year ago, I lost my wife to breast cancer."

Oh shit, he's a widower. Didn't see that coming.

"And we'd been together since we were fifteen. So, I was really lonely. My brother suggested I sign up, but I haven't had much interest. I've sent a few messages, but I rarely hear back from them."

I was starting to feel really bad for the guy. "That's rough."

"And then I saw your ad. Just a one-night thing, and I thought maybe that's what I need. Just a night out, no strings attached, to have a little fun, so I replied to yours." And once again, his gaze unhooked from mine and fell to the tabletop.

"Your children, are they okay with you going out with someone?"

"I figured I'll tell them if you picked me. I'd be obtuse if I thought I was the only one who replied to your ad."

"Fair enough." I drank the remaining coffee in my cup.

Our waitress set down our hot food and walked away.

Cory waited until I'd taken the first bite before he dug in. I'd give the guy his dues, he was a gentleman, however, he was a little too quiet for my liking. First dates were always painful, but this one was too much. After spending the rest of my lunch asking superficial questions and listening to a one-sided debate on Star Trek, I knew without a doubt, this was the last date with Cory.

I shook his hand and wished him the best, telling him I would let him know once I'd met with the others. There was no need to let him down on the curb to the restaurant, so I figured I'd tell him tomorrow. Besides I needed time to reflect on the whole thing. That, and I didn't want to be the jerk dumping a guy right after he insisted on paying for the meal. There was the coward's way of doing things—email, and I intended to let him down easy.

~Chapter Eight

*M*y inbox was full, and to be thorough, I actually went through each one, hoping this ad wasn't the worst thing I'd done in my adult life, maybe a close second or third. However, after seeing enough male parts to fill a porno magazine, I was ready to close my account forever when one email stood out.

> *Meghan,*
>
> *I'm sure you've received a hundred emails like this already and it's hard to make mine stand out from the pack when I've never done this (I'm sure you've also heard that a dozen times). I was stumbling through the site when your ad/profile caught my eye, and not for the beautiful picture of yourself, but for your reasoning behind the ad. I have a hard time believing a knockout such as yourself would have issues securing a date to your former fiancé's wedding, so it leads me to wonder what's holding you back? You mentioned you're a business owner, something I know from first hand experience it eats up a lot of free time, and thus, makes 'normal' dating something of an enigma. I'm going with that theory.*

I stopped reading and glanced around, ensuring I wasn't an unwitting guest on Candid Camera, before I carried on.

Weddings are a stressful time in one's life, and I don't know where you and your partner ended your relationship, but you being invited says two things:
a) either he genuinely cares about you being at this event, which would lead me to believe things ended amicably between you, and you bringing a date would mean you've moved on and you're just wanting a little company or, and I'm thinking I'm correct on this one,
b) he wants to see you cower and scurry, so by you showing up with a date, you're showing him your life is better without him.
If your reasoning leans towards A, then I wish you the best in your search as it's not important to show this guy up. However, if it's B, then I'm the guy to dangle off your arm. I have a soft spot for the underdog, which I feel you are in this scenario. That, and I highly suspect whatever happened between you and your fiancé, it came with enough hurt to last a long time and him inviting you to the wedding is putting salt on the wound.
Forgive me if I'm way off base.
I'm in and out on business, but have no problem meeting up before the wedding. I can easily meet the dress code requirement, and if you're up for it, we can communicate via email until the big day so we get a better feeling for each other. I suppose you'd like to know a little more about me first before agreeing to anything more than a reply. I'm 42, and have been divorced, but have no children. I'm not a 'player' and instead of thinking of me like a gigolo for this wedding, think of me like a big brother who's out to protect you.
If you are interested, please reply back.
Everyday Joe

I couldn't tear my eyes away, and read and re-read his letter. How can someone sound so charming in just an email? Had I moved over into uber desperate territory that a mere letter caused me to read more into it than was there? It was strange, and yet, reading it for the fifth time, I was intrigued. Very intrigued

Scanning through the remainder of the emails, I deleted most.

Except the one from Seth.

He'd sent a simple letter thanking me for meeting with him and to keep him posted on whatever my decision turned out to be – good, bad, or otherwise. In truth, of the three I met, he was the most down to earth normal of the trio. The part killing me was I liked him. Like liked him liked him. Even though I said I was only doing this for a single date to prove something to Scumbag, there was a connection with Seth and a curious feeling of possibly wanting more. Well... there was something about me that figured I could handle more of Seth.

I laughed to myself and put my laptop on the table.

It was wine o'clock and Gabe wasn't coming for dinner until after five, but I needed to start making the lasagna now if it was going to be tasty. My wine glass was filled three-quarters of the way with a merlot, and I started my afternoon quest of making the perfect dinner.

Gabe was out when I got home from meeting with Cory and surely was out cold when I stumbled home after eleven. Sometimes I missed working the day shifts, just because I loved the semblance of a regular life. There weren't many people in my circle who worked evenings – they all had regular nine to five type jobs. But I loved my job and being my own boss. I guess every job had a drawback.

Prepping and assembling the lasagna did zero for my thought process despite the two glasses of wine I'd consumed. I couldn't get two guys out of my head; this new *Everyday Joe* guy and Seth. Joe had failed to send a picture so I couldn't see if he was as handsome as his email was charming, where as I'd had a good look at Seth, and he warmed me from the inside out. I fanned myself just thinking about it.

How long had it been since I'd been with a guy? Way too long. Months would be short in comparison. Scumbag was the last guy, so over four years ago. That's a long time to be without physical contact. Perhaps that's why I was feeling so … hot and bothered. Hudson seemed willing to work me over, if I wanted. But I needed more than just hot sex. I longed for companionship, I just wasn't sure where to find it, or how to go about even looking for it. Mingle More wasn't the answer, but it was a start. Maybe my start was with Seth. Or could be.

I tidied my kitchen and washed all the dishes, and in the process downed another glass of merlot.

"Wow, that bottle didn't have much in it," I said to no one in particular. The empty bottle went into the recycling container under the sink. No point having it reveal its emptiness to my friend.

It was already after four, and I was feeling pretty darn good; loose, free and completely relaxed. I jumped onto the couch and retrieved my laptop, logging onto Mingle More once again. Seth's picture stared back at me, and images from our coffee date swirled in my brain. Our chemistry was decent, and we seemed to click right away. Would it be so wrong to connect with him and see if he was interested in a longer date, like a lunch or a dinner? Maybe it would help finalize my decision. Interested. I laughed. The word he used a few times over our coffee.

75

My fingers clicked over the keys as I typed back a response. I threw out a suggested meeting at the Burger Barn on Sunday afternoon. I was due to work by four, but a late lunch would give me plenty of time to meet and truly see if we connected, or if it had all been in my head. Without rereading it, or mulling it over, or checking for any possible spelling issues, I pressed send. Then I sadly sent a quick, cowardice email to Hudson and Cory, separately of course, to let them know I'd decided to go it alone. It was all lies, but there was no need to hurt anyone's feelings. I knew what it was like to have your heart set on something and have the rug yanked from underneath you. Twice.

Jerk. How dare he ditch on our wedding day. You'd think the Scumbag should've said something, even the night before, rather than embarrass me in front of our friends and family.

Oh god, his family. They would all be at the wedding as he declared his love to…

My heart plummeted into my gut.

Some friend. Some fiancé. And here I thought I'd be strong and go to his wedding holding my head up high and wishing him the best. Knowing his family was all there, the ones that left abruptly when he failed to show up, I'd be attending with my tail tucked between my legs.

It would be hard to be brave around his family and keep my tongue in check. They were the ones who put on a sad face when they looked at dejected me as the music halted and the bridal party searched out the annex rooms and halls, confusion reigning supreme. His family belonged to him, and as such they needed to go find out where he'd disappeared to and why. But I was the bitch because I kept the party going. After all, we'd paid for the food and drinks in advance, and the bridal party agreed

76

with me it should be used for those who wanted to stay.

There were no speeches, no toasts, no photographs taken.

I didn't eat the food I paid thousands of dollars for.

I didn't dance at my reception to music I'd spent many nights deciding.

I didn't drink the wine or the beer or the spirits.

I hung out in the back of the hall crying while the party carried on without me.

Without him.

There was no Mr. & Mrs.

My wedding day became the second saddest day of my life. And I was only thirty.

Tears I'd let out soaked my cheeks as I remembered that day. Anger surged forth, only to be replaced by sadness as each wave crashed over me. Each wave of emotion brought forth another feeling and by the time Gabe knocked on my door, I'd surfed them all.

"Hey, Meghan." His gentle rap sounded again.

"Give me a sec." In a flurry, I tossed the laptop onto the coffee table and wiped my face, drying my hands on the hem of my shirt. "Coming," I said as I hastily fluttered around, fanning my cheeks and eyes. As long as I'd known Gabe, I'd never shown him a tear, and I wasn't about to today.

He knocked again. "Are you okay in there?"

"Yeah, just a sec."

I scurried down to the bathroom and took a peek. My whites of my eyes were pink, and no amount of makeup would hide that. Gabe was going to see a new side of me, one I'd promised to not let anyone see. With a heavy heart, I walked to the door.

The chain bolt slid from its protective casing, and I slid the door open.

"Sorry about that." I kept my head tucked down.

I turned towards the kitchen and fired up the oven, my eyes only made contact with the green numbers as I punched in the oven temp.

"Everything okay?" Gabe asked, the sweetest voice coming from him. It saddened me to hear it.

"I'm fine. Just having a moment." I opened the fridge and inhaled the cool air, pushing my head in more than necessary in hopes of reducing the painful burn in my eyes. It failed.

"Anything I can help with?" He stood only a couple of feet away, and I kept my focus on his feet, with his weird socks sporting a bacon and eggs pattern on them.

"No, I just need to throw this in, and we'll wait for forty-five minutes."

The oven hadn't yet pre-heated, but I tossed the lasagna into it anyways and added an extra three minutes to the timer. *That should do.* I wasn't the greatest cook, but I wasn't the worst either.

Gabe shuffled around the kitchen. "Look at me."

"Not just yet." I closed my eyes and turned in his direction.

"Meghan." It was the plea in his voice and the concern wrapped around it. It made it difficult to keep my guard up.

Inhaling a sharp breath, I opened and took in the sympathetic half-smile on his face. Five o'clock shadow peppered his cheeks and chin.

"There you are." It was so soft and sweet, and it made me giggle. "Tough day?"

"No, just a moment of self-pity."

Those grey-blue eyes held mine for a second. "Well, we all have those. Sounds like you need to have a glass of wine." He wiggled the long-necked bottle in front of me, breaking the gaze.

"And what's tonight's flavour?" I grabbed him a fresh glass from the cupboard and set it beside mine, giving my face a solid wipe.

His eyebrows arched with delight and his face lit up. "It's Grenache, from Spain. According to my sources it pairs nicely with your lasagna." He twisted the cork out with relative ease and poured an ounce into my glass. "Swirl it and smell it."

I did. It didn't smell any different to me than a normal wine. "It's good."

He laughed. "No, really smell it. Close your eyes."

"But you just told me to open them."

"Close your eyes." His warm hand wrapped around mine as the wine glass danced under my nose, a gentle swirl going on. "Now, what do you smell?"

I braced my free hand on the counter and inhaled deeply. "Something fruity, but not a grape smell. Maybe a spice of some sort." It smelled heavenly.

"There you go."

"Can I open my eyes now?" I tipped back my head.

"Of course." Gabe let go of my hand and stepped back. "Now taste it. Slowly."

These wine lessons were all for naught as I just wasn't into it like he was, but it was amusing to watch him get so much out of it. I lifted the glass to my lips. It wasn't as deep a red as the other wines. The liquid touched my mouth, and my taste buds did a jig. The taste was incredible. This was a sipping wine, not a gulp it down kind.

"Oh my."

"See?" He clinked his glass against mine.

I had another taste. It was sweeter than the merlots I was used to, but not an overpowering sugary taste. "It's good, real good." I nodded in agreement.

"So, tell me, what's going on? Why the face?" His pointer finger encircled my head.

A soft sigh escaped me. "It was just a moment. I assure you it's already gone."

A quick mental check confirmed what I just vocalized. Indeed, the moment of self-pity had vacated like a fart in the wind. Wine glass in hand, I walked over to my sofa.

Gabe followed and sat beside me, his ankle sitting atop his opposite knee. "No, it's still there."

"I promise you, I'm fine."

"Okay," he said, his tone betraying his words. "You know, my friend Charlotte used to lean on me a lot a while back. Said I was a good shoulder to cry on." He patted it for extra effect. And it did look comfortable. Friendly. But that was it.

"Used to?" I laughed. "Did your magical powers dry up?"

He grinned. "No, now she leans on her husband."

"Oh, well, I guess that's okay."

"I hope so." He winked. "She's very happy with Andrew, and they deserve that. Especially her. With everything she went through, with what we went through…" He drifted off.

"Charlotte?" An image of a red-head sprang into my mind. Her picture was one of the many photographs in Gabe's apartment. "She's your sister-in-law, right?"

"Former. She was married to my older brother."

I nodded, trying to remember. The little bits he shared with me were very confusing. Charlotte married his brother, but he never mentioned him by name, usually called him Asshole or something. Guess the sibling rivalry between them was high. Maybe he had a thing for Charlotte and the brother stole her away. That could cause a lot of animosity. Poor guy.

"It's okay, you don't have to talk about it."

"I couldn't even if I wanted to. There's still so much hatred and anger."

Maybe Charlotte's the ex-wife he doesn't speak about. No, that wouldn't make any sense. There are pictures of her in his apartment. Hmm. It's like a mystery soap opera. Maybe Charlotte married the asshole, and that's why he's always so angry when he talks about his past. That must be it. Could be an interesting story though.

"Not towards Charlotte?"

The sipping wine disappeared beyond his lips fairly quick. I hit a nerve.

"Never towards her. She was the innocent, just as much as I was."

Well, if I wasn't confused about the whole thing before…

"You know what, I don't want to talk about it. I thought I could. I kept thinking I had moved passed it, but nope. It's still too fresh."

Was he talking about the ex-wife or Charlotte? How much wine had I consumed that I wasn't able to straighten this all out? Not knowing what I was doing, I reached out my hand and rested it on top of his. The softness surprised me.

"How long has it been?"

"Long enough that I should have moved beyond it. But every time I get dumped, it just slaps me in my face again. Like I'm not good enough for anyone."

"I'm sorry about Jordan. I really liked her."

He'd dated a few of women in the time I'd known him, but Jordan was the nicest by far. She was down to earth and enjoyed a good pun. But whatever kept two people together apparently had other plans for them.

"You'll find someone. Someone who appreciates you for you, and your weirdness for a fine wine." I let a snicker out.

"Weirdness for wine? Is there such a thing?" He rose, empty wine glass in hand. "More?"

I looked at my glass, still half full. "I'm good for now. Besides I finished off a bottle before you got here."

"Ah, so you had a tipsy cry."

Damn, he was good at cycling back to the original problem. "No, I had a moment, but it's long since passed."

He gave me a solid stare, bordering on the edge of uncomfortable, but it faded as quickly as it arrived. "I'm not sure I believe that, but okay. I'll let you off the hook. For now."

"Thank you."

"Tell me, how was your date with number three?" He sat back on the couch and wiggled himself into a comfy position.

I launched into the details, and ended with, "He should've had a taste of this wine. It may have loosened him up substantially."

"We all have issues getting back on the horse. Think about the first date after you and–" He kept the name from rolling off his tongue. It was like saying *He Who Must Not Be Named* instead of *Voldemort*. Somethings were better left unsaid. "That first date must've been very weird. After all, you'd pledged to live the rest of your life with him, and there you were tossed back into the dating game again. You should cut this Cory a little slack."

Gabe made an interesting point. The first date post non-wedding was a disaster, and the subsequent ones that followed. They were all weird, and I gave up trying a couple years back. It was clear I wasn't ready to move on.

"You haven't been on a date-date in a couple of years?"

My cheeks caught on fire with the heat burning through them. "What? Did I say that out loud?"

Gabe laughed. "Yes, you did." He turned serious. "For real? You haven't been on a date in that long?"

"Excluding the three dates in recent days, yes." I shrugged. "There was no point. I harboured too many ill feelings."

"Like what?"

I wasn't doing this, not in my living room. I'd talked with a few psychologists a couple of times, but it always turned out to be some hippy-dippy problem and if I would just look inside myself, I'd see the answer I wanted and could make the changes. It was utter bullshit. Scumbag left me, embarrassed me, and expected me to pick up the pieces of the shattered life we'd planned on living together. Yes, maybe it was mostly my problem, but it chipped away at the fragile ego I already held onto with slippery fingers. To find out I wasn't worthy enough to be with someone forever, yeah that hurt.

"I can't." I shook my head. "I can't talk about it."

This time, I stood and paced about the apartment.

Gabe jumped up and stopped me by placing his hands on my shoulders. "What are you afraid of?"

My vision blurred as I looked at him. "Of being hurt. Of not being good enough."

He wrapped his arms around me and pulled me into a comfortable embrace. "You are good enough. He just didn't see that. He's the bad guy, not you. Don't give him that power over you. Anyone can see you are a wonderful person."

83

As much as I enjoyed the closeness, I pushed out of the hold. "Ask my staff."

Sympathy crossed his face. "As I've said before, you're their boss, you're not supposed to be friends. Clearly, they respect you and you don't have a high turn over rate, so you must be doing something right. Don't be so hard on yourself."

"Does your staff like you?"

"Some days. The thing is though, we don't have to like each other, but we do have to respect each other. And we do. So, I keep them around." He patted my shoulder. "You're way too hard on yourself."

"I'm not hard enough."

The timer beeped on the oven, and I pulled the lasagna out.

He sighed and leaned on the counter. "So, what are you going to do about the wedding?"

"Well, I was thinking I'd take Seth. He seems to be the most normal of the three, although..." I drifted away as I thought about the latest email in my inbox. "There's this other guy, who signed his letter *Everyday Joe*, who seemed to get me. He emailed me via the website."

"Ooh, a mystery guy?" Gabe grabbed a hot mat from the cupboard and tossed it onto the table before he retrieved my wine glass. "Tell me more." He topped up my wine.

"I don't know how to explain it. Here, just read what he wrote."

With a few clicks I had the email on my screen. While Gabe read it, I set the lasagna on the table and whipped up a salad, thanks to the ready to serve varieties. Whoever invented those was a godsend. I placed the salad on the side.

"Wow," Gabe said, closing the laptop.

"Am I right?"

"I don't know, but that was a pretty intense letter."

I nodded and sat at the table. "So now I don't know if I should say yes to this *Everyday Joe* without anything to go on, or if I should stay with Seth." A wave of my hand towards a chair, Gabe joined me.

"Well, this guy did say you could communicate back and forth. Maybe you'll be able to do some digging." Gabe helped himself to a healthy amount of greens.

"People hide behind their anonymity online. Behind their screens, everyone is a better version of themselves."

Gabe passed the bowl of salad. "Not always."

"Most of the time, it's true. However, I am morbidly curious, so I'll email him, even though I've already emailed Seth. We're going to go for lunch on Sunday and see what things are like."

Hopefully hot. Smoking hot. Maybe I won't be so restrained next time.

"I still think you are better going by yourself rather than bringing a fake boyfriend."

"I still disagree. This is something I can't do on my own."

Showing up at this wedding was more than just showing up. If his intentions were malicious, then mine had to be sincere. I had to go and prove he didn't truly break me. That I moved on. That I'm better off without him because I'm sure he wanted to see me fall and fail and come back grovelling, which was never going to happen. I'd moved on, for better or worse.

Although as I watched Gabe dig into his lasagna, maybe going alone was better than a fake boyfriend. Giovanni the Scumbag would see right through me. What I needed was a real, bonafide boyfriend.

Perhaps Seth was the perfect one to take after all.

Chapter Nine

$\mathscr{S}$aturday morning greeted me with a smile, and I woke up feeling great. Gabe and I had a great evening, even though we danced around the touchy subjects we both kept under lock and key, we enjoyed the other's company. We always did. There was such an easy feeling with Gabe, I didn't need to hide who I was. When I was with him, I was me, the truest version. And I got the feeling that's how it was for him too. I wondered if he ever thought about me in a more than friends way? Probably not. We're just good friends with similar interest. Someone to bounce ideas off.

Any possibly romantic feelings seemed to be Seth-centric lately. I hadn't felt that for a long time, and it made me even more eager for lunch with Seth. Only twenty-four hours to go. The more I thought of the dark-haired man, the more I wanted to be with him. I hoped it wasn't just the idea of a man in my life pushing me forward, and that it was an honest-to-God sincere thing.

But first, I needed to go shopping for a dress to Scumbag's wedding. I needed something new, and highly attractive, but not slutty. Only one person would have a keen enough eye to help me find perfection; my mother.

An hour later, I met the older version of me standing outside Le Chateau, window shopping.

"Hi, mom," I said as I approached.

"Hello, darling."

I wasn't a hugger, but I allowed her to wrap me in a motherly hug, complete with a gentle squeeze.

"How's my girl?"

"I'm good."

"You never phone me anymore." A hint of sadness coloured her guilt-trip. It always did.

"That's not true. I phoned you this week."

"Well, it's not often enough if you ask me."

I laughed. "I could phone you every day and it still wouldn't be enough."

She softened and relaxed a tad. "This is true. So why are we meeting here?"

Our phone conversation had been brief, just long enough to see if she had time to meet with me. She was in town for the day, and I didn't want to monopolize her time. She was meeting her old sorority sisters to plan for their fortieth reunion.

"A couple of weeks ago, I got an invite to Giovanni's wedding."

Her mouth dropped open. "He didn't."

I nodded, slowly and deliberately. "Addressed to me *and* guest."

"I take it you're going?"

"I wouldn't be shopping if I wasn't."

She peered up as she stood a few inches shorter than me. "Who's the guest? Someone from work?"

I shook my head. "No. Robin's working that night. He's going to cover my shift." My mom liked Robin and when she'd come in, prior to his promotion, he always served her.

"What about your neighbour friend?"

An image of Gabe projected on my brain. Too bad he'd turned me down.

"He's busy." Although I couldn't remember his original reason for saying no, it had something to do with Jordan.

"Is your guest one of your staff?" She said with such disdain, not that I blamed her.

The kitchen staff were not my type and the front-end staff were mostly young kids. Besides, you either take someone you know *really* well to a wedding or you take a complete stranger. You don't take an employee, it's just bad for business, no matter which way you look at it. Plus, I didn't have anyone I felt I knew well enough to accompany me. No guys anyways. And if I showed up with a gal pal, well, I could only imagine the things Giovanni the Scumbag would say. He was a closet homophobe.

"Too bad."

"It is what it is." I led her into the store.

"Who's the guy then?"

A small smile bubbled out from inside me. "His name is Seth. He's a marketing director who's new to town and kind of reminds me of someone, I just can't figure out who."

My mother stopped her search through the rack and stared. An expression of pure happiness on her face. "He sounds delightful."

"I hope so. We're having lunch tomorrow."

"Aw, darling. It's so nice to see a smile on your face again." She cupped my chin and gave it a little squeeze. "I can't wait to meet this guy."

I turned away, the sting from the loving gesture tingling a bit on my chin. I pushed a dress out of the way. A shade of amber only a star like Claire Danes could pull off.

"Slow down, Mom. This is all very brand new. I need a chance to get to know him better before I introduce him to the rest of my world."

"Yes, I know, everything moves slowly. You and Giovanni took years to get your acts together and now look at you."

"What do you mean by that?"

"Nothing." She continued to flip through the rack and pulled one out. "This would look lovely on you. A nice deep green." The dress was pressed against me and her gaze ran up and down. "It's long and needs to be hemmed. When's the wedding?"

"Two weeks."

"Well, that won't work." In haste, she hung the gown back up.

I tapped her on the shoulder. "What did you mean by that 'look at you now' comment?"

"It was a slip of the tongue."

"Tell me." I hated the pleading in my voice, but I wasn't a child. I deserved to know what she was thinking.

"It's been so long, I figured you'd be married by now, but you never make a quick decision. Every little detail takes so long in your decision-making process."

"That's not fair."

"Look at your college apps. You applied to how many schools?"

"Two."

But in my defence, of all the schools I could've applied to, they were the right ones. Each had their own perks, and both came highly rated and offered what I needed in terms of extra-curricular activities.

"And you nearly missed the acceptance deadline."

"But I made it."

"Barely. I just don't want to see you weigh every decision so harshly."

"Right." I nodded, a growing seed of anger sprouted in my gut. "Because choosing a lifetime partner should be a snap decision."

She sighed, one of those long motherly sighs suggesting I was way off base. "That's not what I mean."

"Explain it to me."

"Giovanni was the only guy you were ever serious about. I'm just saying, you hummed and hawed over that relationship for so long; together, apart, together again. And it didn't get you anywhere. Sometimes you need to listen to your heart more and your head less. You're very good at talking yourself out of things."

I couldn't believe what I was hearing. "Is that what you truly believe?"

"Darling, you're not getting any younger, and I'd like to be holding grandchildren before I'm in the grave." She resumed her search through a rack of poufy, prom-style dresses that belonged on a Barbie-doll, not on a real person.

"Yeah, well, you can thank Giovanni for that one, because if he hadn't left me, there'd be a grandchild here now, and I wouldn't be having this conversation in a dress shop of all places." I stormed away from her, out into the mall corridor. Internally, I screamed at myself for having let out the biggest secret I've ever hidden from my family.

The click-clack of her heels on the tile floor announced her arrival. "Of course, you two would've had children by now, everyone knows that. One for sure, maybe two."

She didn't get it, and just as well. Only a handful of

people knew the truth.

"All I'm saying, darling, is to not be so picky the good ones slip by."

"I'll keep that in mind." My tongue was heavy with sarcasm.

She wrapped her arm around my shoulders, oblivious to all I'd let slip. "Now, tell me about this guy you're taking to Giovanni's wedding."

My great mood and planned fun date with my mom were totally crushed. Instead, I battled a mother who firmly believed I'd let her chances at grandmotherhood pass by. Because that was important, how she'd become a grandmother. It was what many people cared about – how the breakup affected *them*.

In the days following the non-wedding, my friends scattered to the wind like dandelion seeds. No one asked how I was doing. No one checked on me. No one called to see if I wanted to go for coffee. Maybe if they had, they would've learned I had used my honeymoon time and got away. I didn't go on the trip to the Pacific Ocean and cruise down the coast in our rented convertible. Instead, the heartache at being dumped took its toll on me in a physical way I'd never expected.

I landed in a hospital four hundred kilometers from home listening to the doctors tell me I was lucky. They couldn't save my baby—my wedding gift to Giovanni—and they couldn't save the ruptured tube, but after a few months of healing, I could try again for a baby. Because that was supposed to heal the double blow of unimaginable heartache.

Not only was I not fit to be a wife, it seemed I wasn't fit to be a mother either.

I'd lost my heart, my baby, and a fallopian tube all in the span of a week, and that wasn't even the worst week.

#

The walk down the hall to my apartment was never ending, like the scene in Poltergeist where the mom was trying to rescue her baby. I felt the same way about getting home – I couldn't get there fast enough. I was just about at my door when he called out my name.

"Hey, Meghan."

"Gabe." I flung the dress over my shoulder as I rifled through my purse in pursuit of my keys.

He walked towards me, looking like he was heading out for the day, dressed in a nice pair of shorts and a fitted tee.

"Got yourself a new dress?" He touched the plastic encased garment with *Geraldine's Dress Emporium* logo on it.

"Yeah, for the wedding." I put my key into the door and grunted as it stuck in the lock. One day I was going to have to call the locksmith before I broke my key in it. My frustrations from the day were coming out on the silver key, and it would serve me right if it snapped off. I took a long, deep breath and twisted. My door unlocked.

"Are you okay?"

"I'm sorry, I'm not in the mood for friendly chatter today."

"What's up?"

I shook my head and pushed open the door with my foot. "I went shopping with my mother and it just wasn't as fun as I'd hoped."

It was light years away from what I'd hoped it'd be. As I walked into my apartment, I placed the dress over the back of the kitchen chair.

"I'm sorry."

I gave him a solid once over as I desperately needed to

change the topic. "Where are you off to?"

"I'm meeting the guys for a round of golf."

"It's a little late in day, isn't it?" I always thought they headed out in the early morning to beat the heat.

He gave me a shy smile. "It's actually quite nice. We tee off at three, finish around seven thirty and have a nice dinner while the sun sets."

The vision of four guys dining in such a way made me giggle. "Sounds romantic."

He suppressed a grin.

"Well, have fun." I tossed my purse into the closet and kicked my shoes in even harder.

"You know," he checked his watch, "I'm not meeting them for an hour. I have time to chat."

"Not today. Besides, I work at four, and I have a ton of stuff to do." I searched his eyes to see if he understood I didn't want to open up and discuss the horrible parts of my life that kept resurfacing. I just wished they'd go away. Forever.

He stood close, but not close enough to breach any barriers. His grey eyes bored through mine. "Some day, maybe."

"Not likely." I busied myself by getting a large glass of water and downing it.

"You working tomorrow?"

"Yep," I said, wiping my mouth with the back of my hand.

I fluttered my shirt to cool down as an unresolved rage flowed through me. I was impressed how fast it built, and I knew deep in my soul, it wasn't because of Gabe. "I'm sorry, but you'll need to go."

"Monday night? Can I make you dinner?"

The rage was building and if I didn't get him out ASAP,

he'd witness a meltdown, and I didn't want that for either of us.

"Sure." I held open the door.

"Five work?" He was looking me over with a great deal of curiosity and concern.

"Perfect." My knuckles whitened as I gripped the doorknob. The tiny piece of self-restraint was being tested. I didn't know how much longer I could hold out.

He tipped his head and studied me. "See you Monday."

Fast little head bobs sprang out of me. "Great. Have fun golfing." I closed the door just in time.

The flood gates broke free, and I slid down the door, crumpling onto the floor.

~Chapter Ten

*I*t's rare for me to feel nervous, but as I sat in my car outside the Burger Barn, it was a feeling I couldn't ignore. I was meeting Seth. *Seth Morrison.* A laugh bordering on maniacal released from deep inside me as I recalled how he introduced himself, as if he was James Bond. Looking back, it was endearing. My hands tapped wildly against the wheel as I scanned the parked cars and the people who dotted the strip mall where the restaurant was housed. Not sure what I expected to see since I didn't know what he drove, and he wasn't amongst the people mingling in the immediate area.

A gentle, anxious sigh escaped. But why was I nervous? I could handle this. I was the one who had agreed to this. Still… my hands vibrated, and my heartbeat zoomed.

A deep rumble from a car caused me to look to my left, and I ducked down into my seat as Seth pulled in, two spots over. The car was an older model needing some exterior work as it was a little rusty, and the rumbling was likely due to a hole in the exhaust pipe and not some after market add on. In some ways, I related to the car. How sad.

He climbed out and without a glance around, bounded

up the five stairs into the entrance way of the Burger Barn, a lanyard loop bouncing along his hip. Sharply dressed in a pair of khakis and a greyish-green shirt, he looked fine, at least from the back end. His tanned and muscular legs had a gentle bow-like quality to them I hadn't noticed before.

Steeling myself, I hopped out of my car and brushed down the length of my sundress. With its flutter sleeves and long skirt, I assumed it would be more than appropriate for a Sunday afternoon lunch. Doors locked and shoulders back, I strode up the stairs and into the restaurant.

Seth was looking right at me as I opened the door into the brightly lit area.

"Hey there." He bridged the distance between us.

"Hey," I responded back, feeling a little breathless at being so close to him. Which I found bizarre because I hadn't felt I was *that* interested when I met him last, although given the other options I'd met, he was a super nova in comparison.

"I'm so glad you decided to give me a second interview, if you will." There was a twinkle in his eye commanding my focus.

"Well, I figured you were the best candidate, and I needed to follow up." A giddy grin threatened to burst out, but I managed to rein it in before it embarrassed me.

"Shall we?" He gestured out as the hostess led us to our seats.

She went over the menu and highlighted the specials before taking our drink order with a promise to return.

The moment she was out of earshot, he asked, "The other interviews you conducted, they didn't go well, I presume?"

"Ah no." I debated if I should generalize how bad they were or just leave it in the past. Figuring it would only reflect poorly on me if I shared, I refrained from throwing either Hudson or Cory under the bus. "It is what it is."

"Indeed," he said, the smile never leaving his face. "At any rate, I'm glad you're giving me a second chance."

I didn't know how to respond, so I sat with my hands together.

He chuckled, a low throaty sound that stirred something in me. "Are you nervous?"

In an instant I flashed back to my lunch with Cory and remembered how he acted. I wasn't far off. I took a couple of quick breaths and cleared my throat. "Can I be honest?"

"It's always the best policy."

"I am nervous, and I'm kind of weirded out by that." I hovered over the edge of the table.

He leaned closer and locked onto my eyes. With a voice low and deep, he whispered, "I get that, truly I do. You were calm, cool, and collected at our last meeting so what's making you nervous? Maybe I can help."

My mouth dried out like sun-soaked skin. Sure wish I could channel that calm collected feeling now. "Well... It's been a while."

"We won't be having intimate contact, remember? So, you're safe there." The grin faded a touch, but there was warmth and sincerity on his face.

Heat burned my cheeks. "It's not that." Although I did wonder if I would fail with sex since it had been so long. "Truth by told, I haven't dated in a long while."

"Like a few months?"

I grimaced and he pulled back.

"Longer?"

"Well...not since... Him." And there it was, completely out in the open. I had just announced I was a total loser.

97

"Him?" Realisation blanketed his face. "Oh, *him*. The one who's wedding you're going to." He leaned back and stroked his beard.

The air changed and the easy-going nature I'd felt just a few breaths ago was gone out like a candle in the wind. Instead, as I flittered a quick glance over him, I felt the rising judgement rolling off him. I was ready to ditch the date when the perfectly timed interception from our waitress stopped me.

"Have you had a chance to look over our menu?"

Seth spoke. "We need more time, please."

"Fair enough." She walked out of sight.

"For real? You really haven't dated since him?" He cleared his throat. "You're a knockout, and I find your statement really hard to believe."

"I know it sounds horrible but–"

"Are you an axe murderer?"

I narrowed my focus at him. Was he joking? "Absolutely not."

A grin tickled at the edges of his lips. "And you don't harm small animals?"

I shook my head, a small smile leaking its way out. "Never."

"That's what I figured." He stroked his beard again as his grin broadened into a smile. "It's so interesting to me how you haven't dated in a long time. I don't buy the idea it's because you work a lot of hours, because there's always a lull in the day for a bit of a break, so it's something else. It's a trust thing, right?"

My eyes grew wide as I faced him. How could he know? I pulled my hands off the table and dropped them into my lap.

"Sorry. I've overstepped. It's a bad habit."

I looked over his shoulder, my focus on the people lingering around the entrance, laughing, and enjoying themselves. Swallowing down my moment of self-pity at the nervousness nipping away at what could've been – should've been – a positive dining experience, I took a couple of quick breaths.

There were two choices; I could leave and put this experience behind me, or I could change the conversation around and take the claustrophobic pressure off me. Seth was a nice guy, intuitive for sure, but I sensed a genuine good guy in him. One I did want to know more about. The choice suddenly became very easy.

"Tell me about your life in Thunder Bay. Quite a different city than here."

He chuckled and a hint of tension released from his shoulders and jaw. "Truly, they are light years apart. The air is so dry here, my skin feels like it's in need of constant moisturizer."

"You'll get used to it." I only noticed how dry it was when I returned from tropical vacations, which were as few and far between as dates.

"And the change in my hair?" He leaned in close, his chest pressing up against the edge of the table. "I'm sure this will come off wrong, but I miss the silkiness it used to have."

A small smile bloomed out of me. "I can't help you with that. My hair is never soft, but I blame the chlorine."

"A swimmer, are you?"

"Occasionally. Do you swim?"

"Not since I was a kid. But I play racquetball."

I gasped mockingly. "Is that still a thing?"

"You say it like it shouldn't be."

The tension was definitely ebbing out of me. Staying

99

instead of running was so far a good choice. "Nah, just my dad used to play it all the time, and I've just never heard of people our age playing it."

He ran his hands through his thick hair, and as he did, I wondered how rough it really was since it looked soft. It had a nice sheen to it and matched the beard perfectly.

"It's part of the code." He winked and pointed a finger in my direction. "But you have to keep a lid on it, otherwise everyone would join, and we'd never get a court time."

"Your secret's safe with me." For good measure, I even crossed my heart like a child's promise.

"Courts are few and far between here."

I imagined they would be. Racquetball wasn't a sport that came up in conversations. "Do you miss it? Thunder Bay, I mean."

"Yes and no. It's good to get some distance. My ex-wife lives there, and I saw her all the time."

I scrunched up my face in confusion. Guess I was lucky. Since the last meeting I had with Giovanni, I had yet to run into him. Although Edmonton has a small-town feel, it's still a major urban centre.

Seth played with his cutlery and gave the knife a polish. "She's a realtor, and her picture is everywhere."

"Oh," I said, understanding coating my reply. "Did you part on good terms?"

The knife clattered against the fork and spoon, and he wrapped his cloth napkin around it. "Not at all. She got half my pension, the dog, and the house, ironic given she could've picked any house in town. It turned out we were great at dating each other but terrible at being married. That piece of paper seemed to have changed our expectations of the other."

"How long were you married?"

100

"Seven months."

Not long at all. Had Giovanni and I got married; had he actually showed up, would we have ended in divorce? It wasn't until we had some distance when I started focusing on my life goals and succeeded at attaining them. Too bad I didn't have that focus before the wedding. Then again, there was a time I thought Giovanni hung the moon.

"I'm sorry."

"You're apologizing for what? My marriage breaking up?" He chuckled.

"No, because I didn't know you then, but I'm sorry you went through that. It's no walk in the park. Breakups are hard."

"Yes, they are. Let me ask you something…"

Curiously, I leaned in closer. "Go ahead."

The soft expression on his face tightened just enough to notice. "Do you always have to be in control?"

"Of my life?"

"Of everything? You picked this place, this time. You picked me. Do you ever relinquish control to others?"

I studied the flicker in his eyes and the subtle twitch in his lips. He wasn't asking to be mean, he was truly curious. Pictures of my life passed before my eyes, ones where yes, I did have all the control. It was comforting.

"I like making my own choices and being responsible for them."

"Which is noble, I won't disagree. But sometimes, do you ever wish someone else did all the planning?"

"Are you talking about dating?" Because I wasn't sure at this point anymore.

"We can start there, sure."

The waitress popped by and before she spoke, Seth looked right at me. "Do you want to get out of here?"

101

"What?" I glanced between him and the waitress.

"I have an idea. Let's go someplace else."

"Sir, did I do something wrong?" There was confusion in her voice.

"No, it's not you. It's us. I think we need something different." He rose and pulled out some cash from his wallet. "For the drinks and sudden departure." Extending his hand to me, he said, "Come on. Let me have control. For a little bit."

I stood slowly, my eyes darting between her and Seth. "I... I don't... know."

It was much more comforting for me to have this all planned out. A kink in the plans?

"Tell you what." He glanced at the waitress. "I promise to return you back to this spot for three o'clock in the exact same condition I'm leaving with you in."

"What?" I wished more intelligent words fell out of my mouth, but it was all my brain formed.

"I promise, you will be safe."

The waitress, put into a terribly uncomfortable position, backed up. Part of me wanted to join her, but another part was curious as to what Seth had in mind. I searched my gut, hunting for any kind of alarm bells. They went off far too easily lately and yet, in this moment, they were quiet.

The patrons around us had stopped their conversations and were watching us intently. If it was one thing I hated, it was being the centre of attention. I just wanted to disappear. And under the table beside me looked like the perfect spot.

"Okay," I said to Seth, watching my loss of control breeze around the room.

His whole face lit up as I placed my hand—and trust—in him and left.

~Chapter Eleven

eth held open the car door for me as I slid in. The interior was in better shape than the outside led me to believe, even if it was a little dusty.

He slipped into the driver's seat and fired up the engine.

"I assume you know where we're going?" My purse tucked into my abs as I clicked the seatbelt in place.

Adrenaline pumped through my veins and raging curiosity filled my brain. It was like a trial adventure or something. A chance for me to see the real Seth, and probably a chance for him to see a part of me I never showed because admittedly, I was excited with the sudden change in plans.

"Yep. Since moving here, I've found this really amazing spot where I like to think and unwind. Maybe it'll help you too." He drove like my grandma as he pulled out of the parking lot. "It's not very far away."

I nodded, checking once again for any signs of alarm. There were none, but still, as a precaution in case things changed fast, I sent a text to Gabe. Even going with the unpredictable, there still should be a safety net of some sort. "Since you promised the waitress, I'm just going to let my friend know I'm no longer at the Burger Barn."

"Fair enough." A smile spread across his face.

The light turned red, and he slowed down a good three hundred feet away. At this rate, we wouldn't even make this special spot by three.

Gabe typed back. *And you're going?*

Totally out of my comfort zone, but I'm not worried. Something about this feels right.

I hope you know what you're doing.

I don't and I think that's the best part. Anyways, I'm just letting you know.

So if I don't hear back from you by three, I should worry?

Something like that. I added a winky face.

Be safe.

I plan on it. I slipped the phone into its pocket on the front of my purse.

"All good with your friend?"

"Yeah. He thinks it's weird, but as long as I check in with him upon my return." I shrugged.

Exhilaration flowed through me. I could only imagine the look on Gabe's face, a mixture of shock and surprise. Doing things on the fly wasn't my style. It wasn't Gabe's either. One of the reasons we clicked so well. Everything was nicely planned out. Boring as some would say. But I preferred comfortable. I was always comfortable around Gabe.

But Seth. I wasn't scared. There was no part of me fearing him, and I trusted in that.

Seth turned on his radio and popped in a cassette he grabbed from between the seats.

"Seriously? A cassette? How old is this vehicle?"

"It's a late model."

"You don't know?"

Isn't that a guy thing? Like when they pop the hood and stand around gawking at the engine, making comments about size and length and all that testosterone fueled jazz? Even I knew a late model was a more recent version of a car and this one was definitely from the late nineties.

"No. Not into cars. All I know is that after the divorce, this was all I could afford, and this little engine drove me all across the country. She's not pretty but she's reliable." He patted the dash for good measure.

Neil Diamond's sultry voice played from the front speakers, singing about his Shiloh. I cocked an eyebrow. "Is this for my benefit or do you really like him?"

Hands firmly placed at ten and two, he said, "I drove eighteen hours in terrible wintery conditions to see him play live at Air Canada Centre. Trust me, I like him."

Wow. When I placed that tidbit on my profile, I didn't think anyone would seriously get it, let alone actually like listening to the music. Figured, at best, I'd get someone who did a little research, which was okay too. The music playing in his vehicle was completely unexpected.

He tapped his wheel to the beat and his lips mumbled along to the lyrics. *Sweet Caroline* was a song I knew well, and I bobbed along to the music.

The chorus came on, and I turned the knob up to drown out my off tune singing. Seth joined in and the two of us belted out the words adding in our own little sounds. I increased the volume and sang it with all my heart, a serene feeling blooming in me with each beat. Never in my life had I sang aloud with someone. It was the strangest thing and yet, somehow, it was like I'd done this all my life with him. How did that work?

The song ended and the biggest smile I'd seen on Seth cracked his face in half. "That was fun." He reached for the dial as another one of my favourites started – *Red Red Wine.*

"One more?"

He sang and I joined in, trying to blend my pathetic melody with his slightly off beat sound. It didn't work and we sounded terrible, but it was still fun. Parking at the bottom of a hill, he announced, "We're here."

"Where are we?" I'd lived in Edmonton my whole life, but this was unfamiliar.

"The Fort Edmonton Foot Bridge."

"Where is it?" All I saw were trees and a variety of parked cars in a tight looped area. It wasn't even really a parking lot. If this was a bridge like he claimed, there should be a river or something within sight.

"It's a short walk from here."

I looked at my shoes. To match the feel of the dress, I picked pretty shoes, not practical ones. They weren't built for long-distance walks.

"You'll be fine."

Nodding, I stepped out of the car and walked a short distance until I saw the sign for the bridge, and a nicely paved path.

Seth stayed close, but not too close as to infringe on my personal space. "Someday I'd love to have a house down here by the river. It's so pretty and quiet and yet you're only minutes away from grocery stores and that kind of thing."

I pointed to the hill we just drove down. "And that hill I'm sure is a bitch in the wintertime."

He shrugged. "Doesn't the city plow and sand it?"

"You haven't lived here through a winter yet, have you?"

You'd think for a city that gets upwards of six months of wintery cold we'd have the best roads, and you'd be wrong. The street outside my apartment got plowed twice all of last winter.

He shook his head.

"You'll change your mind about staying here." It's cold, brutally cold, and it can hurt to go outside and breathe.

"I doubt it. Everything I've encountered so far, is quite beautiful."

I know he didn't mean me, but when he said those last three words, he was looking right into my soul. It warmed my heart, even if it wasn't geared towards me. We walked in silence down the tree-lined path as a breeze blew past us. We continued passed a large backyard where children bounced on a trampoline, their screams of delight slicing the peacefulness.

Once the trees broke apart, the sun danced on the path, and we stepped out of the little forest-like sanctuary while rounding to the south.

I gasped.

Two giant black pillars rose up from the bridge deck and supported a massive concrete top through which black cables hung. It was huge and beautiful.

"Wow."

"See."

We walked the length of the lead up onto the bridge deck, and I surveyed the view from the edge. "I can't believe I've never been here before."

The river streamed underneath my feet, moving at a good clip. The breeze had increased to a light wind, and I fought to keep the bottom portion of my dress from billowing up.

"Hey look." I pointed out four canoes in the distance, heading our way.

107

"I'd love to do that. Would be a great way to see the city."

"I'll bet," I said, my eyes focused on the yellow canoes.

It would be a hoot to paddle down the river. I wondered how far they travelled and made a note to do some research on it. As the canoers approached, I read the name on the side and added it to my mental file. They floated under the bridge and eventually around a bend and out of sight.

Seth wandered away from me, over to one of the black posts. Encircling the support was a black metal bench. I climbed the steps, tucked my dress under me and sat beside him. We were the only people on this side of the bridge. Further down, beyond the halfway point, a couple walked hand in hand, their children riding bikes in front of them.

"I can see why you come here. It's very peaceful." Aside from the wind bellowing through the cables on the bridge deck as if it were whistling its own tune. But even as I twisted my head to listen, it was a soothing sound.

Summer was still in full bloom as the banks of the river were bathed in the brightest greenery from coniferous and deciduous trees. Higher up, the odd house dotted the edge, their expanse layout belonging to prestigious and wealthy homeowners. Far below, the rushing water had flickers of gemstones where the sunlight caressed it. It was amazing the solitude I felt, how it was peaceful and relaxing. Sitting here, you'd also be hard pressed to think you were in a city, a major urban one at that.

"You can see why it's a great place to think?"

I nodded and pushed the blown hair off my face. "You do that a lot, do you?"

"Sometimes. I've come running through here."

"Seriously? Where do the paths go?" Clearly it was

high time I explored my own city more.

He leaned closer and the wind breathed his cologne under my nose, a light woodsy smell. "Well, I've parked where we did and crossed over the bridge. On the other side, the path splits. See those stairs off in the distance?"

I followed the point of his finger, getting closer. In the far distance along the other side of the riverbank I spotted an enormous set of stairs carved into the hill. "There?"

"Yeah. I'll run up those stairs, stretch at the top, take in the view, which is incredible by the way, and return."

The stairs seemed plentiful from here. "How many stairs?"

"Two hundred and one."

"Shit." I covered my mouth as I swore. "Sorry." I stared through the dark sunglasses shielding his eyes from me.

"Don't be. It's nice to see you be yourself. Dating is hard enough without all the extra pressures."

"I suppose it is." A cool gust of wind tickled my shoulders, and I shuddered.

Seth moved a little closer and the distance was nice.

"How long after your divorce did you start dating again?" Surely Gabe and I weren't the only ones that hadn't let go, or at least in Gabe's case took a while to *mostly* let go.

"Well, she was dating within six months of our separation. I waited until the divorce was final."

"Why?" When he winced, my words stumbled out. "Sorry, you don't have to answer that."

"It's okay. I waited to make sure."

"To make sure the divorce was final?"

"To make sure I wouldn't take her back."

"Oh." That thought hadn't crossed my mind. "Do you still love her?"

He turned away from me, and his posture went rigid. That was a yes.

But I understood the feeling. As nasty as the ending was with Giovanni, a part of me still loved him. He was my first everything. There's something special about that type of love. Sort of like how everything else after it compares to the first one. Just like my foray into the online dating world. Seth was the first, and the others were measured against him. Sort of.

I looked down at my feet, the bottom of my dress billowing up and exposing my knees. I tucked it tighter underneath me. As I did, my hand brushed along his bare knee and his head snapped back in my direction. "Sorry."

His skin was soft, given his complaints about how dry it was. The hairs were lighter than his head but there wasn't so much I'd consider him a hairy man. It was just the right amount in my mind. Giovanni had been part bear.

The weight of his stare balanced on what I was about to do. I had two choices as I saw it; do nothing and let the moment pass, or dive headfirst into it. Without another moment's hesitation I reached for his hand and threaded my fingers through his. They were chilly, a total opposite to mine which felt like they were on fire.

He looked at our clasped hands. "Are you okay with this?"

"I wouldn't have done it if I wasn't."

"Want to walk the length of the bridge?"

Suddenly I did, and very much so. It was like being sixteen all over again. Youthful emotions swirled inside me as he rose and pulled me beside him. When he stepped down the first stair, we were eye level, and I couldn't break my focus on him.

A shy smile crept out the left side of his mouth as he

took me in. The light hit the side of his face and his eyes had locked onto mine. If there were others around, they faded away. It felt like we were the only two people around; both mesmerizing and scary all wrapped into one. And for a moment I wanted to push things just a bit. See if what was twisting and building in me was real or based off an idea my mom had said – I was in love with the idea of being in love.

Thankfully, he stepped down another step. Another mesmerizing moment like that, and I would've caved and given into the stirring emotions inside.

Hand in hand, we silently walked the length of the bridge. It was a newfound form of serenity I hadn't experienced with the comfort of a man in a long, long time. I figured there should always be a conversation going, but it wasn't the case with Seth. It was comforting between us, natural. Like with Gabe, except there was more than friendship here. I was sure of it.

My toe hit a pebble, and I bent down to pick it up. With a solid throw I tossed it over the edge and watched as it fell and made a minimal splash in the river below.

"Well, that was pathetic," I said with a laugh. I turned and leaned against the metal railing, the heat from the summer sun on my upturned face fighting with the cool blowing breeze.

Seth stepped closer, becoming my own personal eclipse. His hands braced on either side of me, his face inches from mine.

My heart pounded loudly in my chest, its roar louder than the wind's song over the bridge deck. I was sure Seth could hear it too.

He leaned closer, his mouth hovering above mine. "I want to kiss you, but I know you said there would be no intimate contact."

111

Yes, I had said that but what I was feeling right now was growing and changing. And I could adapt to it to. He was giving me control and putting me in charge of this. Hard to not respect that.

"Kiss me," I whispered without thinking.

The smile on his face grew, but only for a moment. The next second his full lips brushed over top of mine, igniting a fire deep within my soul. He pushed a little harder and the swirl of emotions grew like a tornado descending out of the storm. An arm wrapped around my waist and the urge to run my fingers through his hair became reality as the kiss deepened, his tongue flicking for my tonsils.

Like Giovanni did.

Suddenly, an image of the jerk exploded in my brain and like a movie on fast-forward the pictures from our life together zoomed on by, ending with me crawling under the covers of our bed after he told me I wasn't worth it, and my life would never amount to anything.

"Stop," I yelled, putting my hand on his chest and pushing him away. "Stop. Stop. Stop." I lowered my head between us and slammed my eyes shut.

"Okay, I've stopped."

"I can't. I just can't." I crouched down and sat on the bridge deck, wrapping my arms tightly around my legs, and rested my forehead on top. It was a bad idea to give in to my feelings, nothing good ever came from that.

He lowered himself beside me, quiet for a few breaths. "What happened between you and your ex?" His voice was full of concern. "Clearly something beyond a normal breakup happened."

I kept my head down and hoped the building nausea faded. "I'm sorry."

And it was for more than stopping what was arguably the best kiss in the past few years until the tongue part, it was for agreeing to another date when I clearly wasn't ready. The closer the wedding date got, the worse my reaction to it all. What was wrong with me? Why couldn't I get beyond this?

Twisting my head, I faced Seth – this wonderful man who by all accounts should be running the length of the bridge, hopping into his car, and speeding away from me as fast as humanly possible. Giovanni was right. I wasn't worth the trouble. I was a mess of epic proportions and Seth deserved someone better. Stable. In control.

"I'm sorry."

"You've mentioned that," he said in a tone I had trouble discerning. Was it concern? Or disbelief? "Are you okay?" He raised his sunglasses to his forehead.

A quick roving check followed by a slow nod. "I'm okay."

He tapped on his watch. "I promised the waitress I'd have you back by three so we should get going." With ease, he pushed himself to a standing position and helped me to my feet.

I didn't let go of his hand and he didn't attempt to break free of it, so I considered it a small victory. The howling wind continued to hum its melody and cooled my flame red cheeks as I concentrated on the way Seth's hand felt in mine and how he stayed in step with me. It was a long walk back to the car and didn't feel quite a natural as before. I wondered how much my small hand holding victory cost me and all future potential.

Chapter Twelve

*D*ear *Everyday Joe…*
I crossed it out and started over.
Hey there, Joe…

That didn't sound any better, even if I was trying to keep things casual. I gave my head a scratch and leaned back on my office chair, letting it bounce to the faint Lady Gaga playing from the stereo in the living room. Originally, I was working in the living room, computer on my lap, but decided I'd focus better if I was away from any distractions. When I sit in my home office, it's like my brain understood I meant business and it was easier to focus on the task at hand. Replying to this mystery guy's email threw that into a tailspin.

Screw it, I'll just write what I feel.

I typed a bit, picking up speed and hearing the clicking under the pads of my fingertips. It felt good to write at a decent clip. It didn't take long, and I finished up the short reply. The wedding was less than two weeks away and assuming Seth was still a go, he'd be my date, although I hadn't yet told Everyday Joe that… I was still trying to dig a little more information out of him and hoped my email worked. The cursor moved over the

114

submit and hovered. Too many questions lingered in my head. What ifs a plenty.

A solid bang on my door made me jump and click the send button. *Damn!* I hadn't even checked for spelling and grammar errors. Crap.

"Just a sec," I yelled down the hall, not that I expected anyone to hear me.

The building was solidly constructed and had high sound proofing, or so I was told by the realtor. I stared at the screen hoping the death glare I gave it would undo the transmitted email. No such luck, the word 'sent' flashed on the screen.

I pulled on my hoodie and padded to the front door. Eye against the peep hole, Gabe was on the other side. Sliding the chain, I opened the door.

His hand ran through his hair, and he tapped his socked foot on the carpet.

"What's up?"

"There's a bad storm rolling in." It was said in such a way it made me wonder if he was afraid of it.

"I know. I heard the thunder rolling and was going to sit on the deck and watch. Care to join me?"

He hesitated for a moment but shrugged and entered. "Working late again?"

"Actually no. I was responding to an email. That mystery guy I told you about."

He nodded. "How was your date today? You never expanded more than 'I'm back'."

"I know, sorry. I had to come home and get ready for work and the evening just disappeared."

It had been incredibly busy over the supper rush but after eight it died down to a tiny trickle. I left the restaurant at nine-ish leaving behind a bare bones staff; a shift manager, a server and a cook. Just enough to manage the final hour.

My phone pinged with an alert, and I swiped it off the table. The alarm over at the restaurant had just been set. I loved how the company set it up, so I got constant notifications about it being deactivated or set. The alarm going off was a given, so the extras were a plus.

"Work." I set the phone back on the table. "Let me just close out of my email and I'll be right back. Help yourself to anything to drink. There may even be a decent red in the cupboard."

I raced down the short hall and into the office. With a couple of clicks I'd exited the website and sent the beast off to sleep.

A quick check in the mirror in the bathroom. I was totally fresh-faced and free of makeup. Dang. My hair was a little flat but after running my fingers through its length it had a little more zip. However, I was dressed in my finest lounge wear and if I changed now, it would look weird. Pajama bottoms and a hoodie it was. At least I had a bra on.

When I came into the kitchen, Gabe had two glasses of red wine poured. "I'm really going to have to educate you."

"Oh stop," I said playfully.

Clearly, he hadn't looked very hard. There was a bottle of red from Australia I'd purchased for our get togethers.

He held out one for me. "Wine from a box? How low." There was tsk on his tongue, but it stayed away.

"Well, you should know, wine from a box is a very affordable way to get my antioxidants and all the good stuff that comes with wine. Like flavonoids."

The wine swished in his glass with his laughter. "Flavonoids *are* antioxidants. I swear you haven't been

116

listening to any of my wine-ucations."

I took a long sip of my cheap boxed red. "Hey, at least I knew the word and wasn't throwing it around all out of context."

"That's good to know." Glass raised in cheers, he lifted it to his lips.

Wanting to judge his level of fear, I pointed to the deck. "Let's go outside and watch the storm."

I pushed open the patio door and stepped out into the humid air ripe with the scent of ozone. On the western horizon, a small flash of lightning sparked. I set my glass on the tiny table and rearranged the two plastic Adirondack chairs.

Slowly, he emerged and settled into a seat. "You know for a Home Depot find, these are amazingly comfy," Gabe said. "Needs a pillow though."

"I can grab one from the living room."

"Nah, I'm fine."

I lit a couple of flame-less candles and hung them on the deck railing hooks. It added a nice ambiance without being overpowering. Kind of romantic, if an outsider looked at it. But it was Gabe. And he didn't see me that way. Besides, I figured he was still getting over Jordan.

"Tell me, how was date number two with Seth?" He focused on my eyes and it was hard to look away.

Gabe was a good friend and confident. Was it easy for him to see how things went down? I debated though on what to share. How things had been so easy between Seth and I, like they were with Gabe and I, or how Seth's probing tongue instantly brought up images of Giovanni the Scumbag and ruined what was a romantic moment.

I spared him the details. "He said it wasn't the worst date he's been on."

Gabe sat up straighter. "He said that? Who does that?"

My body sagged into my chair, and I offered up a polite smile. "But I'm sure it was true."

"Why?"

"Because..." I paused and reflected on how to phrase my words. "Things were going so well. We had a walk on a bridge and enjoyed the other's company. It was when we kissed that things went south."

"He kissed you or you kissed him?"

Seth had been so sweet to let me have the metaphorical reins on that. He'd given me back control, and I blew it. Or he did. I shook my head.

"Does it matter?"

"It does, especially since you said things went south."

I looked away from Gabe out to the horizon. "He kissed me, and I kissed him back, but he stopped when I freaked out."

Gabe's chair scraped on the patio as he inched it closer. "You freaked out? About what?"

A car pulled into the parking lot below and the driver slowly sauntered over to the other building.

"I don't want to talk about it."

Instead, with the parking lot devoid of people to watch my focus returned to the lightning storm dancing in the west. A cool breeze blew over my arms, igniting the hairs and a nasty case of goosebumps. I shivered.

"Where'd you go?"

"A footbridge spanning the North Saskatchewan."

There were at least a dozen foot bridges... I thought anyways. I really needed to explore my city a little more.

"The Fort Edmonton one, I think. But I don't remember seeing Fort Edmonton Park." I faced him since it was a curious question to ask. "Why?" Even in the dim of the evening, it was clear how much Gabe paled. "What's wrong with that bridge?"

An array of emotions swirled across his face, and he gulped down his wine. "I don't want to talk about it."

Following his actions, I too drank up the rest of my wine and rose. I returned a minute later and plunked the whole box of red on the small table separating Gabe and me. We each refilled our glasses. It felt like a night to drink away the past.

To drown out the odd feelings coming out of me, and clearly Gabe about this bridge. It was best to forget it, and another glass of cheap flavonoids was the best way.

"Tell you what," Gabe said, wiping the spout on the rim of his glass. "We can't dance around things much longer. I want to tell you about my past, and I think on some level, you want to talk about yours. We've been friends long enough that maybe it's best we know. Who knows, maybe by talking about it, we'll be able to figure out why we're stuck."

I laughed and almost choked on my red. "You sound like a therapist I used to visit."

"If it gets to be too much, we'll end the discussion and shut it down faster than this storm could."

The lightning flashed and a rumble of thunder greeted us shortly after.

"Does it scare you?" I tipped my head to the west.

He swallowed and looked away. "Very much."

Aww... how cute was that? Gabe was scared of the storm. My heart swelled just a bit. Guys were supposed to be tough and fearless, and women were supposed to cower and want to be protected. But right now, all I wanted to do was pull Gabe into my arms and hold him tight. It was just a storm and it wasn't even getting much closer; just skirting around the edges of the city.

"Shall we?"

"Shall we what?" I'd totally forgot what we were discussing while I pictured snuggling into Gabe's arms. What was the matter with me? He was my friend, not a romantic interest.

"I want to share something with you. I want you to know about my past, and I want to know about yours."

My heart skipped a beat, and I took a long drink. If I was going to share anything about Giovanni with Gabe, I'd need to be way more relaxed and drunk than how I was. At least another glass needed to pour into my system... after I finished this one. But I didn't want to be so wasted I didn't hear everything he wanted to tell me.

I pounded back the rest of my glass, the taste of it jumping over my tongue and crashing into the back of my throat. An old college trick of drinking a lot without tasting it. Like chartreuse. Yuck. The glass empty, and I held it up to the flickering candles to double check before I refilled it and took another sip.

"Easy there," Gabe said, removing the glass from my hand.

"It's easier to discuss deeply personal things when I'm bombed and will have no recollection of what I said." After another glass, that feeling of not giving too many damns would arrive, and then I could talk. Maybe.

"Nice try." He downed a sip of his and shuddered.

"Are you cold?" I asked.

He shook his head.

"It's the wine, right?" I rolled my eyes. That horrible, boxed wine.

A slight nod of agreement. "I'll go first." He inhaled a sharp breath and crossed his legs. He took another sip and re-crossed his legs. "God, I haven't told anyone outside of the

120

people it affected." Another shudder moved him, and an overwhelming urge to pull him close and into my arms crashed over me. I blamed the storm and wine. "Remember how I've mentioned my friend Charlotte?"

I twisted in my seat to get a better look at him.

"Well, she jumped from that bridge."

"Like a suicide?" I thought Charlotte was alive and well.

In a slow voice laced in haunted breaths, he finally said, "Yes." His eyes darted everywhere but in my direction. "She survived, thank God, but I watched her jump. I was helpless to stop her."

A massive shudder rippled through him, and he dropped his head into his hands.

My eyes were as big as saucers and my heart as achy as ever. To watch someone you know jump to their death, what does that do to a person? What made her think there was no way out, and suicide was the only answer?

"Oh my gawd, I'm so sorry." I reached beyond the wine I desperately wanted a gulp of and squeezed his arm.

"Thanks." A sigh of relief as if he'd been holding his breath came from him. The wine glass lingered at his lips but hardly any wine tipped out of it. "Your turn. Why did you freak out when Seth kissed you?" His face stayed somber, but an intense curiosity played behind the pain.

I didn't feel drunk enough yet to spill all the details. So, I waited. The lightning flashes intensified, and the storm moved a bit closer. The booms were as loud as the flashes were bright. Although there were still a good twenty beats between flash and sound.

"It's complicated," I said after a few minutes. Reaching for my wine, Gabe held it up and away.

"I am the Professor of Complicated Relationships."

I sulked. "Fine. When I kissed Seth, images of my life with Scumbag surfaced." So many images. There was happiness in there somewhere, but it ended abruptly.

"That must've been awkward."

"It was bad timing. I mean for the images to show up." Because for a moment, I truly enjoyed Seth's lips on mine. Absentmindedly, I ran a finger over my lips, remembering the brevity of it all and the small fire lingered, wishing the kiss continued. Damn brain!

In the distance, the thunder rolled.

Talking about Giovanni wasn't pleasant, and I needed to stop seeing his face in my head. "Tell me about Charlotte."

"Not really my story to tell." He shrugged and passed me my wine glass.

Like a thirsty man in the desert, I drank up greedily. "What were you doing with her on the bridge when she jumped?"

We were going all in tonight, and I wasn't going to hold back. If he was going to question me about Giovanni, I was getting to the bottom of the whole Charlotte situation.

He leaned back in the chair and crossed his legs, trying to find a comfortable position. With the amount of movement, it was clear finding a sweet resting spot wasn't going to happen.

"I don't even know where to start with that." He shook his head. "That day, her best friend died, and her head wasn't in a good space." There was a long pause and his lips mumbled as if he were speaking, but no sound came through. "I should back up a little more. Charlotte was married to my brother."

"The asshole?"

"Right." He downed his glass in a record pace. Guess he needed to feel tipsy to share too. "He was mean to her. Very

122

mean. I had a suspicion there was more going on than meets the eye, but she kept it all hidden from us, until a few days before Joe died. She'd been planning her escape but when that tragedy happened, she lost a part of herself and took off. Andrew, her now husband, followed her and informed me. My dick-head brother and I raced to her, desperate to stop her. A fight between Andrew and my brother happened, on the bridge of all places, and Charlotte either couldn't take it anymore or didn't want to. I've never figured that out and I've never asked her."

It was subtle, but he wiped a tear from eye. It had to have been traumatic witnessing something like that.

"I watched her jump into the frigid water. I couldn't stop her." And like an after thought, he added, "I couldn't save her."

I was on the edge of my seat. "But she survived?"

"Barely. Thankfully a police boat was already on the river for another call, and they picked her up." He looked away and my heart cracked open for him.

Oh, the pain of watching a friend jump to her death. Or attempted death.

A lump formed in my throat, and I swallowed it away. In a quiet voice, I asked, "What happened? After?"

"They got a divorce, and she got a restraining order against him." A violent shudder coursed through him as he twisted on his seat. "In the hospital, everything surfaced. *Everything.*" The word spit out from him with such venom it clearly held more meaning to him than he let on. "Charlotte wasn't the only one Asshole hurt." That faraway look flowed back into his eyes, and a voice flowed out of him that was even further away. "Asshole had been screwing my wife since before we got married."

I gasped. "What?" And here I'd thought my Scumbag

123

was the lowest order of man.

"And she was pregnant with his child."

"Oh, dear Lord." Exasperated, I fell back into my chair. "I'm so sorry it all happened to you." I reached out and touched his hand. It was cool from the air, and maybe from the disclosure too.

Underneath my hand, his squeezed into a fist. "Not going to lie, it took a long while to get over that."

"I'll bet, and rightfully so." I allowed my thumb to rub the top of his hand in soothing strokes. "I'm really sorry."

The faraway look in his eyes turned into a haunted expression. "You know I haven't spoken about that in years. None of my former girlfriends knew the truth." A tear fell from its hold.

Tenderly, I reached over and wiped it away. "I promise your secret is safe with me."

This sweet man had been through so much hurt and betrayal. No wonder he had a hard time with past girlfriends and things moving too fast. Probably needed to check and double-check the person was who they claimed to be. Something I could relate to a little too well.

Gabe's blue-grey eyes locked onto mine, and he turned his hand upright and linked his fingers through mine. The gesture was so natural and comforting, like two puzzle pieces finally connecting.

I tipped the rest of my glass, emptying it in my throat. "Guess it's my turn, eh?"

~Chapter Thirteen

Four years earlier

"**I** can't believe that by this time tomorrow, I'll be a married lady," I said to my best friend, Samantha. "You're going to make a beautiful bride."

My wedding dress hung in all its glory in my old bedroom at my mom's house, and Sam and I were staring at it. Again. Her bridesmaid dress hung in my old, empty closet.

I squeezed her shoulders. "Tomorrow. It's happening tomorrow."

"I know," she said, but she wasn't echoing my joy.

"Are you excited to walk arm-in-arm with Colton?"

Colton was Giovanni's best man, and we were thrilled to match him up with Sam. We hoped our wedding would sprinkle fairy dust on them and perhaps one day, we could be at their wedding.

"He seems nice."

"Seems nice?" I laughed. At my mini-bachelorette party he was all she could talk about.

Sam sat on the edge of the bed. "Are you sure about this? About marrying Giovanni? You two have been fighting an awful lot lately."

"It's just because we're stressed with the wedding. All the details, and his mother voicing her opinion on every little thing."

They say when you marry into an Italian family, you marry the whole family. That sentiment could not have been truer with Giovanni. His mother just didn't know when to butt out.

She twisted the family ring from her grandmother on her finger. "Are you sure?"

"Samantha. If there's anything I am sure of, it's wanting to marry Giovanni, despite the fights. I'm in love with him."

"Okay." She stood and paced around the room, finally sitting at the vanity, and running a dry blush brush over her cheeks.

When I moved out years ago, my mom kept my room exactly the same, for whenever I wanted to stay over. It rarely happened as I lived only fifteen minutes away, but still, my old bedroom remained frozen in time. Bed, vanity, and dresser—all currently being used like I'd never moved out.

"What's on your mind?" I sat on my bed, careful to not touch my gown, and faced Samantha.

"Nothing. It's just something Colton said that stuck with me."

"Which would be what?" Suddenly deep-seated fear took root in my gut.

Her expression changed from sadness to a glowing smile. "I'm just messing with you. Colton says Giovanni can't wait to marry you either."

I playfully smacked her on the shoulder. "That's a mean trick to play."

"I wanted to make sure you knew what you were doing."

"I do."

"Great, but save the I do's until tomorrow." She rose and smoothed down her satin dress. "Are you ready for the rehearsal dinner?"

I checked my reflection in the mirror. My long brown hair hung in loose waves beyond my shoulders. It needed a cut desperately, even though the stylist trimmed it last week. I've itched to cut it pixie short, but my hairdresser, encouraged me to keep it long as it would give her more to work with on my wedding day. After the honeymoon, I planned to chop it off regardless of how much Giovanni wanted it to stay long.

My nose got a good powdering, and I rooted through my suitcase. I wanted to double-check on the Giovanni's present. Samantha excused herself to go round up my mother, while I opened the black pen box with a red bow on it. Lifting the lid, I looked at the positive pregnancy test I'd taken that morning. I already knew I was pregnant, as the test in the box was the fifth of the week. My big plan was to gift Giovanni the news at our hotel tomorrow night after the wedding. Then he'd know why I wasn't going to drink any alcohol when we jetted off for California and cruised back home along the coastline.

I was thrilled to be a mom. The timing was perfect. I was newly thirty, almost married and just been promoted at the restaurant. Rumour was the owners were selling, and I'd hoped to get in as a new owner, until the pregnancy news. I can't be trying to run a business and adapting to motherhood at the same time. I closed the lid on the box and tucked it under the sexy chocolate-coloured negligee I'd picked out for our first night as husband and wife. It was his favourite colour and it had been tough to find that specific shade of brown.

Secure that my life was going to be perfect, I meet Samantha and my mom at the door, and we headed over to

Demetri's for dinner.

"There's my husband," I squealed and sped over to where my knight in shining armour stood.

"Not yet, don't jinx it." He stood there; hands deep in his pockets.

Tall and lanky, he was the opposite to my short and curvy stature. Not that I was short-short, just compared to his 6'3" frame, everyone was short.

"Oh, I'm not jinxing anything. Tomorrow at this time, we'll be happily married." I wrapped my arm through his and squeezed tight.

In twenty-one hours, I would be Mrs. Meghan De Luca.

We sat at the table with Samantha, Colton, my mom, and Giovanni's parents and siblings; our small but cozy family. It wasn't a big wedding, less than eighty people total. Neither of us had big families or many friends. It helped to keep the expenses to a minimum – for a wedding.

"So, Meghan," my future mother-in-law began in a way that pre-warned of a venom-laced attack. "Now that you're going to be a De Luca, what are you going to do for a job?"

My career as I'd told her many times was in the restaurant business, something she clearly despised. "I'm staying at Westside."

"Oh really," she said, giving me the evil eye.

"Yes, I really enjoy it there and just recently got promoted to shift manager."

"My daughter-in-law is going to be a restaurant manager?" Such disdain rolled off her tongue.

Like her son was so much better than I, jumping from job to job. At least I had selected a career path. Giovanni switched paths like I changed underwear.

"At least my son brings home decent money." She put her hand on his arm in a motherly fashion. In her eyes, he could do no wrong, and I secretly wondered if he lied to her about his take home pay, because decent wasn't a word many would use to describe that paltry amount.

I scoffed.

His latest endeavour was repairing bicycles… in our living room, hardly a five-figure income, which surprised me given his high IQ. If he applied himself and focused a bit, he could get a better and more secure job. Something we'd need to discuss after I gave him his wedding gift.

My mom, always one to *usually* bite her tongue, spoke to Mrs. De Luca. "Your son is not the shining star you think he is."

"Mom," I said through gritted teeth.

"No, darling, you two are about to be married. There should be some balance between you. You're working all the time so he can stay home and fix a bike once or twice a week. That's hardly what I wanted *for you*."

My eyes opened wide as saucers, and I kept my voice low. "What are you doing?"

"Listen, I've kept my mouth shut for about as long as I can, but I'm not going to sit here and let that woman put my daughter down. You work very hard, and you have a great job, with fabulous benefits. A nice *steady* job." She glared in Giovanni's direction. "And someday you will bless me with grandchildren, and I know enough to understand that 55% of your salary on maternity leave will not pay the bills."

I wanted to die, or at least crawl under a rock.

She turned her venting in Giovanni's direction. "You're a sweet guy, and I love you like a son, but you need to get your

129

act together and get a proper job. Just like your mother expects great things from my daughter, which she's already doing, as the man marrying my only child, I expect better from you. Call me old-fashioned, but as the man, I expect you to be the breadwinner and to support my daughter. Not the other way around."

Giovanni sat there in stone cold silence.

There was no rock big enough to shield me or hide me from the burning shame colouring me red. I needed to be beamed out of there, or a time machine to go back in time and prevent my mother from speaking. Not that she was wrong, but the rehearsal dinner was hardly the right time and place to discuss it.

She lifted her glass of champagne to the others. "Cheers."

After a tense supper, where the loudest sounds were those of the cutlery rubbing against the plates, Giovanni walked me outside. Mom and Samantha waited in the car for me, and Colton hung out by his vehicle. Mr. and Mrs. De Luca had left before dessert, citing a headache she wanted under control before morning, although the sharp use of the word *headache* was intended for me. Even Gio's siblings left shortly after the matriarch did.

He held my hand and pulled me off to the grassy area, away from the parking lot. "Let me ask you something. Do you share your mom's views?"

I did but this wasn't the place to discuss them as I sensed the tension. "Do you echo your mom's feelings? Do you think I could do better?"

He trailed a finger down my face. "To a small degree, yes."

A physical slap would've hurt less.

"I love the control that comes with being my own boss and deciding what projects I'm going to work on. And I honestly think you could do better than being a manager at a trashy restaurant."

Trashy? If I didn't bring home food we would've thrown away, there'd be nothing to eat some days. Instead, I looked up at him and pushed down the horrible feeling building in my gut.

"If you insist on working in that disrespected field, I just wished you had more discipline to find a higher paying job. There are so many other restaurants that would be better."

"But I'm happy there. It gives me a sense of purpose and big changes are coming soon."

With new owners, no doubt changes were front and centre. I stepped back just a little and sighed.

"That's like me and the bike shop, I'm happy to be doing that."

Bike shop? Is that what he called our living room?

A loud gush of air blew out of me, unrestrained and without caution. It had become the norm as of late and talks always turned to my career aspirations rather than his lack of one. I blamed the exhaustion of planning our wedding.

Deciding what food to serve to people with a variety of food intolerances and allergies.

What music we wanted for our first dance, as our music tastes were as opposite as it came. There would be no death metal playing that night.

The location for the ceremony and reception.

Where we wanted to go for a honeymoon.

It wore us out and down. I hoped the night after the wedding, things would return to our normal; the quiet peace that preceded our engagement. For now, I needed to bite my tongue and remind myself of why we were going through such hassle.

"I love you so much, Giovanni. I can't imagine being married to anyone else. You are the reason I get up to work. If you're happy, then I'm happy. That's all I want for us."

Love was all that mattered, and we had it in spades. I'd never felt more loved than being in his arms, and maybe he didn't care for me financially, but he took care of my mental and emotional needs. Sometimes. He was a sounding board for me on the rough days, and the only person I wanted to share my feelings with. He was my whole world, and I couldn't wait until I carried his name and had his child.

The horn honked, and I turned in the direction of the car.

"Your mom is calling you."

I placed my hand on his chest. "She can wait."

He bent down to kiss me, but it was light as a feather.

My lips chased after him, wanting more than he gave.

"Now, now, now," he said, mockingly waving a finger at me. "Remember our agreement."

A shitty one I reluctantly agreed to after a wild, satisfying night of heated passion, that culminated in the conception of Baby De Luca. In the month leading up to our wedding, no deep kissing, no sex, and no physical contact until we said I do. It had been a long, lonely thirty days. I couldn't wait to kiss him like I wanted to and to rip the tuxedo from his body and make glorious love to him.

Nineteen hours until our vows.

Our wedding night I stayed up until the sun shone through the windows and reflected off the porcelain edge of the in-suite jacuzzi. Giovanni didn't show up, he didn't call or text, nothing.

I went to the hotel room, hoping he'd make an appearance or explain himself. The black pen box with his wedding gift stayed on top of the bed, untouched.

My phone rang, the display showed it was my mom.

"Hello," I said, my voice exhausted as it cracked.

"Darling, why don't you come home?"

"I'm waiting for him."

"I don't think he's going to show."

"Do you know something?" My voice pitched in hope.

"I'd be the last person he'd call." Maybe not the last, but close. At this point, I think the last person would be me.

"Come home."

"I need to work this out, mom. Find out why he changed his mind." Fresh tears streamed down my cheeks, and I wiped them across my mascara stained cheeks. "What kind of a man abandons his future wife without an explanation? Don't answer that, it was rhetorical."

My mom would no doubt have a slew of unflattering words to use. I'd heard some of them yesterday in the church.

"Look, I'll call you later."

I lifted my wrinkled wedding dress off my legs and stood up. Time to take it off and put it back on the hanger. As I slid down the zipper, a new wave of tears burst from me. It shouldn't be me doing this, it should be Giovanni.

As I packed up my dress and selected a pair of shorts and a tank top from my suitcase, I left our honeymoon suite behind. The black box still sat upon the bed.

When I got back to our apartment, stunned would not have been the right word. All of his things were gone. Anything he'd brought into our shared home was missing. Two kitchen chairs and the kitchen table. He'd left two behind because they were mine; an inherited partial set from my grandmother. The couches gone, but the end tables remained. Everywhere I went, whatever had been his, he took. Anything we bought together he left untouched.

The bedroom was a like a ghost town. He stripped the bed of its coverings and emptied his side of the closet. The dresser was gone, my things neatly piled up on the floor beside the wall. Even the two-dollar shower curtain in the bathroom was gone, but the fancy ruffled decorative curtain stayed, even though I thought it was his.

Someone had to have helped him, so someone had to have known. One didn't make a rash decision and pick and choose what furniture to leave behind. It had to have been planned. But when? Why?

I raced to my laptop and opened up to our banking site. Logging in, I checked the balance. It had enough money to pay the last installment on the photographer, which I didn't think we needed to pay. She didn't hang around after the ceremony and there weren't going to be any happy wedding pictures to touch up and send out. As I scrolled through the back account, nothing seemed out of place.

Until I went into my profile. I was the only listed name. He had removed his name.

More questions flew through my mind. He'd known some time ago he was leaving. Everything had been planned. Everything.

Angry at how I'd been duped into believing he was my forever, I grabbed the item closest to me – a coffee pot. He'd taken the coffee maker but left the pot behind because I had bought the replacement. I threw the pot with all my might against the patio door, glass shards flying in every different direction, and a giant, maddening crack streaking across the door.

I called him. And called him again when he refused to answer. I swore into the phone, leaving message after message.

Composing myself, I marched down to the rental office and demanded they change my locks. They were kind enough to inform me they would at the end of the month when I moved out. Apparently, Giovanni had given our notice that we'd be leaving two days after we got back from our week-long honeymoon.

Deflated, I walked out to my car and hopped in. I drove to his parent's place, hunting for his car, and off to his brother's house. My vehicle went through two tanks of gas as I tried to locate him, but it paid off.

In dingy strip mall, I grabbed a cup of coffee to fuel me for another drive. Out of the corner of my eye, I spotted him walking out of the vape shop, a brown paper bag in his hand. I sped out of the drive-thru and threw my car into park, and ran out, calling his name from the tops of my worn-out lungs.

He stopped and slowly turned in my direction.

Whatever anger I'd felt a moment ago disappeared as I saw his handsome face. He had aged in the past few days, as much as I had. Breathless, I ran up to him.

"Giovanni." I lifted my hand and reigned it back in.

Like I was a bug to be squashed, he looked at me with a furrowed brow. "Megs."

"I've been so worried."

Confusion replaced his displeasure. "Why?"

"I didn't know what happened to you. At first, I was concerned something had happened, and then..." I didn't bother to finish. His tightened body said it all. "Can we talk? I think you owe me that much."

"I don't owe you anything."

"Please." I hated the pleading, desperate sound in my

135

voice, but I had to know. "What happened?"

His face darted around the parking lot, and he grabbed me by the shoulders and turned me around. "It's over. Go home."

I pushed out of his less than friendly gesture. "To what home? You gave our notice."

"Well, I was tired of paying two rents, and I needed the money."

My eyes bugged out of my head. "What?"

"Look, Megs, it was never going to work. We're two different people. We want different things. We rushed into this."

"Rushed into this? I disagree. We've been together for years, not a few months, but if you need more time, I can wait."

"I don't want you anymore."

A band around my chest constricted and cut off my air. It hurt to breath. "What?"

"I fell out of love with you and knew I couldn't spend the rest of my life with you anymore."

My breathing hitched and my heart bounced right onto the ground. I fought the tears as they built and tried to blink them away. "When?"

"A few months ago, when you accepted the shift manager's position."

"Oh." I leaned against the concrete garbage can, my manicured fingernails digging into the embedded rocks. My nails broke the harder I clamped on for support. "All that time you knew?" Anger grew and pulsed within my limbs, giving me strength. "You planned on moving out, took your name off the lease and gave notice, removed your name from our joint bank account and went ahead with the wedding, and you knew?" My voice rose in volume. "You're a coward."

He whispered, "I didn't know how to tell you."

136

My voice rose. "Any other way than jilting me at the altar would've been preferred."

"I'm sorry."

"You're sorry? You're sorry! Your family, did they know?" I glared as I screamed.

"Not until the day of."

"Someone knew. Someone helped you move."

"Just Co–" He slapped a hand over his mouth.

I punched him in the shoulder as hard as I could. "Colton? Son of a bitch."

I thought back to the conversation I had with Samantha. My best friend knew the day before too, and she didn't have the courage to say anything.

My voice cracked. "Everyone knew? Everyone but me."

He placed his hands on my shoulders. "No, not everyone. Your mom didn't, my parents didn't."

I broke out of his hold with hardly any effort. "How could you?"

A small crowd started gathering around us.

He should've whispered but he didn't. Instead, his "I'm sorry," came out like a child who really wasn't.

"Fuck you." I pushed him as hard as I could, hoping he'd stumble and fall. "Fuck you and your cowardice, you fucking liar."

Everything I had believed in was a lie.

I thought I knew who my best friend was.

I thought I knew who my fiancé was.

I thought I knew who I was because for some strange reason, despite what Giovanni did, I still loved him, and I shouldn't have.

~Chapter Fourteen

he lightning crackled and a shiver raced down my spine.

"So, that's my sad little story," I said, refilling my wine glass and guzzling it down, barely taking a breath as I swallowed.

"And..." He inhaled sharply. "What about the baby?"

A sensation of dread quickly washed over me, but I was done hiding. "He left me and soon afterwards, so did the baby." My hand instinctively fell to my lap, as did my gaze.

"I'm so sorry. Did he ever know?"

I shook my head. "No one did."

"Not even when you..."

Again, I shook my head.

"That's a terrible burden to hold onto. I'm sorry you were alone. I can't even imagine how hard that was." His thumb lightly stroked the top of my hand, and he scooted his chair closer to mine. "I can't say for sure you're better off because it's never easy to lose something so precious, but from what I know of you and what you just shared with me, you truly do sound like you're better off without him."

My shoulders lifted and fell back as if I were shouldering the Earth.

"Do you still love him?" Gabe asked, he locked onto my now-empty glass.

I've since lost count how many I had, but judging from the look in his eyes, it was a few. Amazingly enough, I wasn't slurring my words or even seeing double.

"Do you still love him?"

However, I guess I was losing my thought processes.

Did I love Giovanni still?

I searched my heart and feelings and deep down, very deep down, I did. I shouldn't because at the end, he wasn't very nice. Still, I nodded.

"Guess that's why going to the wedding is so important."

A loud boom shook the building. The storm had advanced quickly during my recollection. So much for it skirting around the city, it was readying to slam into my building.

"Thinking about it now, I'm sure it was a joke to send me an invitation."

It had to be. There was no clear-cut reason for it. We hadn't talked or seen one another since.

"I agree with that. I think he was testing you. To see what your reaction would be."

"And I fell for it, hook line and sinker." Like the idiot I was. Because some things were nearly impossible to let go of. Even bad things.

"Where did you receive the invite?"

"It was sent to me at Westside."

"Ah." He leaned back in his chair and gazed out into the dark sky.

The rain fell in cold, fat drops, bouncing off the lantern tops and railing.

I pulled my heavy feet underneath me and wrapped my arms around me. "We're quite the pair, you and I." My finger waggled between us.

He flipped his face in my direction. "How's that?"

"We've both been on the end of some conniving jerks."

"That much is true."

"Do you still love her, your ex-wife?"

"Hell no. That ship sailed long ago." There was no delay in spitting it out. Which was good. His heart wasn't lingering over her, the way mine was over Giovanni.

"How did you let go?" It was meant as a rhetorical question because I wondered if it was as simple as flipping a switch. Guys didn't seem to have issues letting things go, but women? Well, we could hold onto nothing for a lifetime.

He shrugged and made circles with the base of his wine glass. "I've never forgiven her for what she did, so that helped."

"But is it really letting go? I think it's still hanging on. And if you haven't forgiven her, you can't possibly move on."

"Do you become philosophical when you're drunk?"

"I'm hardly drunk. Tipsy, I'll give you." I gave my wine glass a look. Nah, I was done for now and didn't want any more.

"Just like you and Giovanni. You haven't forgiven him either."

"There's been no reason to."

"So why are you holding onto him? He made it clear it was over. What are you getting out of it by clinging?"

"You tell me, Gabe. What are *you* getting out of your anger at your ex?"

He shook his head in a slow, sad way. "I don't know."

"Me either." I reached for the comfort of his hand and

threaded my fingers through his. "Something's perplexing me. Even though you hold all this rightfully deserved anger at your ex, you still manage to date. How is that?"

The only answer I got was a simple shrug. "Are you saying in all the time since your relationship dissolved, you haven't dated? Not even once?"

Betrayal was a gouge across the heart deeper than the Grand Canyon.

"Because you don't trust guys?"

"No, it's more than that. I don't trust me."

How could I? I fell for someone who broke my heart, and I didn't see his deception along the way. Sadness was inching its way into my consciousness, never a good sign. The alcohol was digging its tentacles in, and I didn't want to start crying in front of Gabe. I was a terrible drunk in that respect.

Thankfully, my bladder ached a reminder of needing the restroom. I pushed against the armrests of the chair and groaned as I tried to stand. My arms gave out, and I fell back into my seat.

"Whoops," I said, laughing.

Once again, I pushed myself to a stand, but my damn feet wouldn't hold me up. Holy shit. When did alcohol affect me so quickly? I only had a couple of glasses. Maybe three. Couldn't have been more than four.

"What's the matter?" Gabe asked.

"I need to pee, but I can't get up." A delirious giggle burst out of me.

Gabe rose with ease. Clearly three glasses of wine did not have the same effect on him. With a grunt and a groan that rivalled the thunder, he pulled me to a stand. "C'mon."

"Thanks, I got this," I said, and grabbed the wet, cold railing and slid my feet one in front of the other. I needed to move slowly since my body was so heavy. Making it to the patio door, the damn thing smashed into my face.

"Whoa," Gabe said, his hands cradling my head. "Easy there." He slid the door open fully.

I fell back against his strong chest as I stepped into my living room, the space around me swimming in violent little circles and the floor tipping from side-to-side.

"Uh-oh. I don't feel so good."

"Okay, let's move." He pushed me down the hall and into the bathroom.

As the room rocked and bobbed, I blinked slowly to figure out where I was when my stomach cried out. Bending over, I just made it. I crouched down in front of the porcelain bowl and prayed for relief. A few minutes later, my stomach was empty, and a cold sweat wrapped around me.

"All done in there?" Gabe's voice came from the hallway, and I didn't blame him for not watching that disgusting revolt.

"I sure hope so," I said, flushing everything, including my pride.

"Let's get you settled down." He led me back to the living room where he'd laid out a throw blanket and the garbage can from under the sink.

I curled up, tossing my arms out to the side to prevent me from rolling off the couch. Overhead the storm cracked, and the building shook. In my drunken state, I was suddenly terrified.

"Don't leave," I begged Gabe and pulled a throw pillow over my ears.

After shifting the can closer to my head, he lifted my feet and propped them up on his lap. "I'll stay for a little while."

It was the peace I needed.

"Thanks, Gabe. I love you."

I drifted off in a senseless and restless sleep.

My mouth was dry as cotton and my head pounded worse than last night's rain when I woke up. I rubbed my eyes and stretched, taking in my surroundings. The stench of dried vomit dribble on my shirt made me nauseous all over again, and I threw the covers off. That's when I noticed Gabe on the end of the couch in the most awkward of positions. How he'd slept with his feet on the table and his head uncomfortably resting on the top of the sofa without a blanket, I'd never understand. Meanwhile, I'd been wrapped in the only available blanket.

I covered him and he hardly moved, only a twitch here and there, and went down the hall to clean myself up. My headache begged for pain relief, something I rarely used, but I popped two into my mouth and chased them down with a palmful of water. A cool washcloth scrubbed over my face felt great, and things were even better when I hopped into clean clothes smelling of fabric softener and not puke. My eyes squeezed shut and blinked a few times, they were as dry as dust.

How much did I have to drink last night? Holy smokes, it had to have been a few glasses and in pretty rapid fashion, especially since I spilled my entire Giovanni story. I clapped a hand to my forehead. How much did I share? I closed my pained eyes as I tried to remember, pretty confident I hadn't shared *everything*. Just the basics. I was sure I excluded the part where Giovanni told me how pathetic and worthless I was, and how he didn't want to be married to anyone like me, but he wasn't sure how to call it off.

That wasn't the most embarrassing and humiliating part. It hit me. I thought I dreamt it, and I prayed that I had, but did I really tell Gabe I loved him? Please let that have been only said in my head. I enjoyed his company and friendship. There were no romantic feelings between us. I could've just said I loved him as a friend. That would make sense. When I get sick, I'm clingy. I probably would've told a stranger I loved them if they'd helped me in any way.

I peeked down the hall, my line of sight zoning in on Gabe who snored softly. Best to let him sleep it off. He'd had a lot to drink last night too. I grabbed my laptop from my office and fired it up as I walked toward him. It was after seven, and I wanted to see how the restaurant faired last night, so I ran a report. While waiting for it to finish, I opened my Mingle More account to see if *Everyday Joe* had replied. My heart sped up a little seeing an unread email from him at the top of a short list of in my inbox, one of which was from Seth.

I quickly skimmed over Joe's letter first.

Well, I'm sorry my suspicions were correct about your former fiancé's invitation. For what it's worth and the little I know of you, I think you are remarkably brave to attend. You haven't yet asked me to accompany you, but I'm sure you have your reasonings. Have you decided to go with one of the others you've met with in person? I won't hold anything against you if you've chosen another.

I know I haven't given you much to go on, but I can promise you, I am a gentleman and will let you lead. If you are wanting physical contact, I can respect that. If you are wanting a little more, I can be persuaded, within reason. My friends would classify me as an old-fashioned guy, who doesn't go beyond a kiss on the first date, and I believe a woman should be courted. By that I mean, holding open doors for you, surprising you with small tokens of admiration, and being the one to drive you around. However, I get that this is a new era, but old-fashioned manners never go out of style.

I respect your need to be in charge and to feel safe.

I'm enjoying our back and forth emails. To answer your questions, I am based in the city but business takes me all over. Currently I am in a land filled with great depression and despair, but the conversation here is chipper and lively. It's a unique place to be.

You haven't provided me many details for the wedding location but I land on Saturday around 11:30, and given security and such, should be out of the airport by noon, baring no delays. I would immediately uber over to you so we can meet and pretend to be a happy couple. Me even showing up at the wedding, and having your genuine reaction to seeing me could be interesting as well. Would lend itself a little authenticity to the circumstances, but I'm just throwing that out there. Like I said, I'm a romantic at heart.

I look forward to future communications with you, so consider me to be one of your hopeful prospects.

Yours in faith,

Everyday Joe.

Oh wow! Electricity poured through my veins as I reread it a second time. Charming wasn't a strong enough word for how I felt about the man who could actually be named Joe, but he caused the butterflies to flutter in my stomach and an ounce of hope to spring. Maybe I wasn't as worthless as I thought.

"Don't you ever stop working?" Gabe's voice, gravelly and raw, broke open the silent air.

"Ah, no," I said earnestly. "I'm running a report from last night."

And when I clicked over to it, it filled my screen with happy little numbers. Things hadn't changed much in my departure, so that was good. No last minute, late-night rush. Robin had shut the place down right on schedule.

Gabe tossed the blanket beside him and put his feet on the carpet. "How are you feeling?" He gave his forehead a rub and gently smacked his cheeks.

"Foolish."

He stood and stretched, the shirt lifting above his belly button. Judging the tautness of his skin, it looked like he still took care of himself. "Why?"

"I shouldn't have drank so much and said what I said." I walked over to the patio and opened the door.

The box of wine sat on the tiny table, the two glasses beside it. Glad it didn't get windy enough to blow them over. Sweeping up shards of glass wasn't high on my to-do list.

I lifted the box of wine and shook, a sloshing sound emitting from it. "There's hardly anything left in here."

"I can get you more."

"It's not that." I set the box on the counter after closing the door. "That's why I feel foolish."

"I think you dumped most of it into the toilet last night."

A flashback to that scene. Great. Nothing like throwing up in front of a guy. "Yeah, about that."

"Don't worry. It's not the first one I've witnessed." Like a cat, he inched his way in my direction.

"Maybe not, but I was out of sorts. I shouldn't have pounded it back, and I apologize that you saw me in that state." The fridge door opened with a yank and cool air circulated around my naked toes. "I shouldn't have shared." Or said those three precious words.

"Shared what?" He turned his body towards me, and I looked away. "Shared what happened between you and Giovanni? I'm glad you did. Maybe now you'll be able to sort

146

through your feelings and figure out how to move on."

"About moving on." Oh, god. How was I going to dance around what I think I said? "Last night, I may have said something I didn't really mean."

He leaned against the counter, head tipped to the side.

"You're not going to make this easy on me, are you?"

"I would if I had the slightest clue what you were talking about it."

I sighed, and my gaze flittered over to my computer. "I'm pretty sure I was sleeping when I said it. And it didn't mean anything."

"Are you talking about those three overused words?"

"Yes!" My shoulders fell with relief. "Yes. I don't want you to think I'm in love with you or anything, because I'm not. I just meant them as an expression of gratitude for being a good friend. I love you as a friend."

Gabe patted me on the arm. "It's okay. I get it."

"You do?"

"C'mon, of course I do. Look at my friend, Charlotte. I love her very much. But I'm not in love with her. She's married. And my other girl friend, Chelsea. I love her too."

I nodded. "Okay. It's just I need to figure out what it is I want from me before I drag anyone else into the mess."

Work. That would consume me and make me forget about the slip of the tongue. I shot a quick gaze to my computer.

"Meghan, you need to stop."

"Stop what?" My head snapped back in his direction.

"Stop beating yourself up."

"I'm not." My eyes scoured his full of life and positive outlook gaze.

"You are."

I couldn't look at him any further and the topic wrapped

uncomfortable tentacles around me. "What are your plans for today?" Maybe I could buy him lunch for making such a drunk ass out of myself.

A quick glance to the clock. "I'm meeting with a client at ten and need to check in with some of the contractors. You?"

There went possible lunch plans. "About the same. Plus, I have a couple of emails to return."

"From Seth?" A lop-sided grin formed on his lips. "I think you have more lovey feelings for him than you do me."

Suddenly though and for reasons I couldn't explain, I wasn't interested in sharing details about Seth. Not to Gabe. Not after last night. Whatever was blooming between Seth and I, it was something I needed to work out on my own.

"Are you taking him to the wedding?"

"He's as good as anyone, and if he still wants to hang out after yesterday…" Which I think he did as the email came in late last night.

Gabe rubbed my arm. "Just don't settle on any one person because of availability. You're better than that."

"And my options are first-date-since-divorce guy, douchebag guy, and Seth. Oh, yeah, and about a dozen or so dick-pic guys. So, it's not really settling, it's making the best of what I was given." Because the first two guys, Gabe and Robin, were already busy.

"What about your mystery guy?"

The thought of Joe brought my insides to life, and a dull roar from the rapid increase in my heartbeat drove past my ears. How was it possible to be attracted to a guy I've never seen and only communicated with a couple of times? It was total desperation and a deep hopeless romantic feeling surfaced.

"He sent me another email late last night. Want to read?" I'd showed him the last one, where was the harm in this one too?

Gabe braced his hands on the table and read out loud Joe's letter. It sounded even more romantic to my ears than it did in my head.

Gabe whistled. "Wow. So, are you taking him?"

Reality slapped me across the face. "No. I can't. I have no idea what he looks like and he's out of town until like an hour before the wedding. What if he turns out to be bald?"

Gabe scrunched up his face. "Is that a bad thing?"

"No, but I picture this amazing guy in my head when I'm reading his emails, and what if the actual is not what I'm expecting?"

"Sounds like real life to me." Gabe pushed the laptop away.

"I'm serious. What if I am expecting to see this young, fit guy and instead I'm face to face with the Comic Book Guy from the Simpson's?"

Gabe laughed, all warm and endearing. "That would be funny. Can you imagine how that would unfold?"

"He knows what I look like, but why's he so afraid to send me a picture? Is it shame on his part? Or does he know how shallow I am? Is he disfigured in some way?"

"Is that a concern for you?"

"No, of course not," I said, feeling tingles of shame.

It wasn't truly a concern, but I wanted the guy I took to Giovanni's wedding to be beautiful, both inside and out. Even if I didn't have a chance with him, I needed to feel I was worthy of being on the arm of someone handsome. Someone everyone thought handsome, not just his mother.

I slumped down in my chair and rested my throbbing head on my arm. "I know it doesn't make sense."

Gabe pulled out the chair beside me and sat down. "It

sort of does. You want to be the high-school dweeb who brings the supermodel to prom."

I looked into his eyes, seeing understanding as if he'd personally been through something similar. "Something like that, but thinking it makes me a terrible person. Someone only interested in superficial qualities."

"I would say for this event, you can pick a guy meeting that criteria. It's one date, not forever, and both Seth and this guy," he pointed to my laptop where Joe's email stared at us, "know that going into this agreement." He rubbed a hand over my arm. "Show Giovanni up. If you take Seth, you'd be doing that. He sounds like a nice enough man and he looks pretty hot... for a guy." He winked.

My dark cloud turned a little less grey. "Perhaps. But this guy has me thinking, and I'm real curious about what he'd be like in person."

Gabe rose. "Here's what I think you should do. Take Seth to the wedding. If you are interested in this faceless and nameless guy, let him know, but tell him you'll meet him after the wedding, where you can meet and see if there's as much a physical attraction to him as you seem to have to his penmanship. That way, it takes the pressure off, secures you an after-wedding date and solves all your problems. Gets you back on that horse again." He waved his hand through the air.

I sat up and straightened out my legs. "Maybe not *all* my problems."

"Got to start somewhere." He walked to the door. "I need to go. Call me later?"

"Sure. Thanks."

"Anytime."

After Gabe closed the door, I opened up my Mingle More account and started typing back to my Everyday Joe.

Chapter Fifteen

Standing at the cash register two days later, I slipped the credit card receipt into the drawer and closed the till. As I looked out across the floor, the supper rush was slowing down, and my front-end staff weren't running about as wickedly fast as they had been just an hour ago. It never failed to impress me how quickly they moved when they needed to, and how they met all their tables demands. My evening crew worked their butts off and it showed; the last customer left a twenty-five percent tip.

Robin—my shift manager—stopped and stood beside me. "What's on your mind, boss lady?"

"Nothing at all. Everything looks great."

A slow smile built on his face. Had I been lax with the compliments to him?

"You're doing a fantastic job and the customers are all happy. Haven't had a customer complaint in ages."

"Well, don't jinx us." Robin rapped his knuckles on the wooden laminate counter.

"I promise I won't." My eyes roved across the floor again.

Seven tables were seated and a group of three walked up to the eating area.

Without hesitation, Robin ambled up to the party of three and escorted them to a table at the back, flagging down Daisy. I enjoyed seeing my crew in motion as they flowed together, helping each other out. It truly was a great group, and I was blessed to have them on my side, working the evening shifts.

I took a walk through the kitchen, seeing what we were running low on, and if anything was amok. Nothing stood out. The restaurant was such a well-oiled machine, I could sit in my office for the evening and there'd unlikely be a problem they couldn't solve on their own. I suppose they were trained well, too well. I felt useless.

As I headed out onto the floor, another couple waltzed in and my heart froze in my chest. I plastered on my best managerial face and walked over. "Good evening, and welcome to Westside. Table for two?"

Gabe gave me a funny little smile but nodded along. "Please. A booth if you have it."

"This way."

Curiosity roared through me. Gabe was not one to frequent my establishment. In all the time I knew him, I was sure he'd been in the restaurant maybe twice. So why was he there? And who was the woman? A work colleague perhaps?

The female slipped onto her side of the booth, and Gabe sat across from her, while I distributed menus to both.

Gabe spoke. "Meghan, this is my new friend, Lorelei. Lorelei, this is my neighbour down the hall."

I shook her limp hand, afraid I'd break it if I squeezed too hard. It was all skin and bones but matched the hallow look of her cheeks and the depressed eyes. "Pleased to meet you."

"Likewise," she said, shaking her hand but keeping her gaze fixed on Gabe.

Seriously, if this was his 'friend' as in a friend with benefits type thing, he should aim higher. I rested my hand on the top edging of the booth on her side.

Gabe looked between the friend and me but said nothing.

"Daisy will be your server tonight, but I'll go and get your drinks. What would you like?"

"What's on tap?"

"What? No wine?" I giggled but kept it to a professional level.

Gabe smiled. "No wine. Not tonight."

"You like wine?" Lorelei said, a sneer colouring her face.

"Gabe's the master at wine-ology," I added for his benefit. Clearly the girl hadn't yet been educated on the finer points of a good wine.

"I don't like anything bloody."

I stepped a little closer to the table, unsure if I heard her correctly. "I'm sorry, what?"

"The grapes. They were killed in a horrible fashion, either stomped on or pressed through a machine, and their blood is what became wine. I can't drink that."

I waited for a smile to crack through, but none came. Surely, she wasn't serious? I glanced at Gabe who shrugged.

For real, buddy? What happened to the likes of women like Jordan?

"I'll just have a warm water with lemon," she said.

A part of me wanted to add that our lemons were hacked into at least twenty-four pieces before they made their death march to a water glass, but I bit my tongue. It was hard.

153

"Okay. Gabe?"

"Just a draught. A big one."

"I'll get them started." With a turn on my heel, I headed over to the server station and zeroed in on Daisy. "Table of two, L4. A twenty-ounce draught and a warm water with lemon. They are VIPs so bring the receipt to me."

Beautiful young Daisy nodded and assembled the drink order. "I'm on it, ma'am."

I cringed. Being called ma'am was almost as bad as being called Megs. Almost.

Secure my team were working hard, I headed back to my office, throwing myself into ad writeups and marketing, and rifling through a stack of art deco samples for the new dining room interior.

An hour later, Daisy knocked at my door. "The VIPs bill." She handed me a white receipt.

Although I didn't care what they ordered, I was curious to see what they'd eaten. A black pepper steak bowl, and that's it? Did the girl not eat?

"Is this everything?"

Daisy grimaced. "She's vegan."

"We have rice bowls suitable for that."

Daisy's voice rose as it sped up. "I know, and I tried. She asked if I knew how the grains were harvested, and when I didn't, she refused to eat."

Fun date. Hope she's better in bed. I mentally smacked myself in the head. *Why would I want to picture Gabe in bed with anyone?*

"Okay, thanks. You did well." I looked at the receipt once again, hoping she was at least a better conversationalist than she was an eater. No wonder she felt like skin and bones. "Have they left?"

"Not yet, I was just about to bring out their bill."

"I'll take it out to them." I stood and dusted my skirt free of wrinkles.

I walked through the emptying restaurant, happy chatter at the few tables I passed and stopped at the edge of Gabe's booth. "How was everything tonight?"

Their table had only a half cup of warm water with a wedge of lemon on its saucer, and Gabe's beer glass with an ounce of fluid remaining.

"It was great," Gabe said with a smile as he ran his fingers through his salt and pepper hair.

"And you, Lorelei, was everything okay?" I said it with as much sweetness as I could pour out, which sadly, wasn't much.

"Fine."

I waited for a complaint that never came. Perhaps she knew it wasn't a lack of food choices on our part preventing her from eating; the choices had been all hers. My gaze flipped between Gabe, who appeared relaxed and full to Lorelei who looked like she would wilt at any moment. She didn't seem to have the stamina to make it outside. How do people find that kind of willowiness sexy? There's nothing wrong with eating in front of a guy.

"Well, your bill's been taken of, but if there's anything else I can get you…"

"Meghan, no. I didn't come here for you to pay the bill."

"I know. That's why I didn't mind." My eyes left the adoration in his and scanned the floor.

Another couple were being seated and the male part of the duo locked eyes with me as he raised his brow. The handsome Seth sat at a table on the opposite side of Gabe's booth.

155

"Well…" I stammered out as my voice dropped. "Enjoy your evening."

A tinge of surprised jealousy flared up in me as I patted Gabe on his shoulder. In saying goodbye, I headed to the front, pushing the surging anticipation at seeing Seth as low as I could.

As a cheap excuse to control myself, I quickly cashed out Gabe's bill and waved them out. Inhaling a deep breath, I strode over to Seth's table.

"I thought that was you," Seth said. His eyes sparkled under the overhead table light.

My fingers tingled with nervous energy. "How are you?"

"I'm great."

I eyed the beauty sitting across from him.

"Oh, where are my manners? Meghan, this is my sister, Violet. She's here from Thunder Bay for the week." He smiled. "Violet, this is Meghan. I'm taking her to her former fiancé's wedding next weekend."

"Hi. I've heard a lot about you." Her gaze fell to her menu.

"So, this is your business?"

"This is my baby." I hoped pride radiated out of me.

"I love eating here."

"Really? You come here often?"

"Not as often as I'd like. It's quite far from my place. I'm in Clareview."

Ah, yes, that was quite a trek to Westside. A good thirty minutes or more.

"Well, there will be a Westside coming to the Ice District in the new year. That could be a closer drive." At least I thought so.

"That's wonderful. Let me know if you need any

marketing assistance. I'd be willing to help you, on the side."

Warmth spread over me as he spoke. Having an extra set of eyes with that would be amazing.

"Thanks, Seth. I'll keep that at the forefront of my brain." I tapped my forehead for good measure. "Has Daisy already taken your drink order?"

"She has."

"What do you recommend?" Violet asked, connecting with me finally.

"Do you like spicy food?"

Seth chuckled. "She does, but it doesn't like her and since she's staying at my place, no to the spicy."

Violet's cheeks flooded with colour. "Something flavourful but low on spice."

"Then I'd recommend the Roadhouse Steak bowl. It's one of my favourites."

She closed her menu. "Perfect."

Daisy appeared, and I stepped off to the side. "Enjoy your meal. You're in great hands with Daisy."

I didn't need to tell her to treat the guests well, Daisy always did. She was my best server, and her tips were reflective of that. In a few months, I hoped to be able to transfer her over to the new store as lead, but I'd also heard she was starting her first semester at university in January as well. Had to figure out if I could keep her very part time or not, although I still had some time to work through that.

The restaurant cleared to just Seth and Violet's table. While they ate, Daisy kept herself busy putting away dishes and restocking supplies, and Robin helped clean up in the back, as we had pared our staff down to the bare bones.

I wandered the floor, ensuring everything was set and stocked and took the opportunity to stop by Seth's table to check

157

on him. "How's your meal going so far?"

"It's great."

"You were right about this steak bowl. I'm loving it," Violet said, taking another bite.

"Do you have a minute to sit down and join us?" Seth asked, a puppy-dog look on his face.

"Sure, for a couple of minutes."

Seth scooted over against the back of the booth wall.

"Tell me, Violet, what brings you out this way?"

Although I'd lived in Edmonton all my life and I loved it, I wasn't sure why someone would purposely visit it, if it weren't for friends and family.

"I'm job hunting for now."

Our province was still reeling from a recession, but we were on the upswing again. I hoped it lasted. At its worst, I had to let go of some of my staff and that was a hard thing to do, considering they were fabulous workers. It was the economy unfortunately.

"What line of work are you in?"

"Engineering."

"That's great." I wished I could offer up a name of a company or business hiring, but I didn't know of anyone off the top of my head.

"She's highly sought after. She just won the Young Engineers Achievement Award in the spring and any company would love to have her."

I turned my focus to Violet. "That's great. Congratulations."

Clearly her brother's glowing accolades got to her, the colour flushed over her cheeks and ears.

"Yeah, she just needs to decide who she wants to work for." He rested his hand on top of mine. "I plan on using my networking skills at the wedding to do some digging."

"Please do."

"But I won't only be networking. I'll be sure you have a really good time."

Violet coughed. "Watch out for him. He can be quite the charmer. He managed to get his last girlfriend–" She stopped with a jolt and shovelled in another bite.

My interest was piqued, and I leaned over the table. From the corner of my eye, Seth glared at his sister. "What did he do?" I asked, my voice dripping in curiosity.

"Nothing." Her eyes remained on the steak bowl, the last of its contents making their way onto her fork.

Seth wasn't much better. Like a lightning bolt hit him, he changed. Squared off shoulders and a serious frown replaced the laughing and relaxed man.

"Well," I said, not wanting to sit around the palpable tension. "I should get back to work. We're closing soon." A quick push, and I stood on my feet.

"It was great seeing you again," Seth said, his mood dramatically different once again. His voice was calm and friendly sounding, but it still managed to make the hairs on the back of my neck stand at attention.

"Yes, you as well. It was lovely meeting you Violet, and I hope you enjoy your stay."

"Thanks." She never met my gaze and for reasons I couldn't figure out, it worried me.

Chapter Sixteen

*a*ll night long I replayed the strange interaction between Seth and his sister. Something was up. What had he managed to charm a girlfriend into doing? And why the death glare between them? I shook my head at the absurdity of it all.

Thirty minutes after Seth and Violet left, the last of the staff went home, and Robin and I locked up and headed out to the parking lot.

"You're doing really well, Robin."

"Thank you."

"I mean it. I should praise you more."

He stopped beside his car, parked next to mine, and rested his arms on the roof. "You're doing fine. I appreciate all that you've given me here. I'm proud to call you my boss and Westside my place of employment."

That lightened the heavy load I carried in my heart. "Thank you."

"So, the wedding is coming up soon. You nervous?"

A nice, summer breeze, ripe with the smell of a distant storm blew around me.

"Nah. I think whatever happens, happens."

"That's a good attitude." He opened the car door. "Because he didn't deserve you."

"Sorry?"

"Whatever happened between you two to cause your fallout, you're better than him, and I think he knows it. Any man worth his salt will treat a woman with dignity and respect. He did neither of those things. No matter what, you won. Don't forget that."

"I appreciate you saying that." I opened my door.

As little as I had shared with anyone, Robin had been the unwitting recipient of a couple of conversations I'd had with myself. Thankfully, as far as I knew, he never gossiped the news to the other staff. A quality to admire.

"Have a great night, Robin."

"See you tomorrow." He slipped behind the wheel and drove out of sight.

As I drove home, a million thoughts lingered in my brain, most of them revolving around Seth and Giovanni. The wedding was ten days away, which didn't give me much time at all to figure out what I was going to do about it. And the whole sudden weirdness with Seth. Although I told him he'd be my date, something strange happened and little flags were going up all around me. Not one to ignore them, they kept me thinking.

I swerved to the side, shaking up my car, as I dodged a parked car on the side road. I gave my cheek a solid smack, knowing better than to be so deep in thought I wasn't even paying attention. That was close.

My adrenaline continued to pulse for the two blocks into my parking stall, and even as I climbed the stairs to my apartment, it pounded. Sitting around my place, it wasn't going to leave, so I changed into my swimsuit and headed to the pool.

I still had an hour before it closed.

Tossing my soft terry bathrobe onto a nearby pool chair, I stood at the edge of the pool, debating if I jump in headfirst or if I wade in slowly and allow myself to get to used to the cool. Although they tried to maintain an even temperature, it was always hit and miss. Some days cooler and other days too warm to swim effectively.

A solid squat, and I dipped my toes in. It was definitely cool, and my heart pounded at the possibility of the first dip.

"To hell with it," I said.

Arms overhead, I launched myself into the cool blue. The first touch of the water slipped over my hands and when it slammed into my head and chest, it nearly knocked the wind out of me. And yet, it was exhilarating. I came up for a quick bite of air and resumed my strokes, focusing on the movement of my arms and the timing of my breaths.

After counting out ten laps, I checked the clock. Thanks to strong kicks, solid strokes, and a channelling of my inner Michael Phelps, I made impressive time. No Olympic time trials speed but still. I'd blame the near accident and the solid whack of adrenaline, but it was hard to send the blame outward. My mind had been focused and not lingering on other thoughts.

Like a knife through butter, my hand sliced through the water, and I reflected on how far my swimming had come. In my life with Giovanni, I'd always been content to sit on the edge of the pools and rarely dip my toes into the lakes and streams. It had been a fear of drowning holding me back. And really, as I look back, it manifested out of nothing. There was no incident that induced the terror; nothing, and yet I allowed fear to control me. It was silly to see it now, but back then it was terrorizing.

A couple of years after Giovanni left me, I joined a gym, one with a pool. It was nerve-wracking and it took five lessons before I could get chest-deep in the water. And here I was now, swimming lengths and besting my personal records. It still amazed me how scared I had been over something so not worth being scared about. I no longer let fear control me.

Another ten more laps, and I was officially worn out. My arms became wet noodles and my legs no longer wanted to propel me through the water. I jumped out and sat on the edge of the pool, looking around as the hairs on the back of my neck prickled. One by one, I spied the video cameras giving a solid stare, but it was the pitch black beyond the slightly fogged up windows that worried me. Anyone on the outside could see clearly into the pool area as it was lit up. They could be watching me, laughing at me, ready to pounce on me the moment I stepped outside.

It was silly, really, to think such things.

I lived in a fairly safe neighbourhood and the crime rates were reasonably low, at least crimes against a person. The pool area was only accessible by key card, which you only received with your signed lease. However, I couldn't shake the feeling of being watched, and I quickly donned my robe and tightened it around my body. My fingers tightened around my phone deep in my pocket, and still wet I inched my way to the door. It was a minute long walk at a brisk pace to the back entrance to my building, so if I ran it, I could cut that in half.

Taking a deeper breath than I would to swim the length of the pool, I stepped out into the brisk air. It chilled my wet skin on contact. One foot in front of the other, I sprinted to the back entrance, my focus directly on the door handle. With ease I reached it and fumbled with my key in the lock until I pulled it closed with a bang.

I sighed, a deep sound of relief. My eyes scanned beyond the reflective glass out into the dark space surrounding the pool house. Nothing out of the ordinary registered. Shaking off my foolishness, I climbed the stairs. Of course, my apartment was at the far end of the hall, and I'd have to walk the length of it still dripping and my shoes squishing with each step.

Just as I passed the elevator, it dinged, and the doors slid open.

"Hey, Meghan," Gabe said as he stepped out, Lorelei on his arm.

"Hey."

Lorelei gave me a solid once over, disgust evident in her hollow, beady eyes. At least I had the strength to walk and not lean against a man. She tugged on him.

"We just saw the new Avengers movie."

"Great." I didn't care what they watched or how they watched it, I needed to get to the safety of my home.

"You okay?" He pulled away from his date and stepped closer to me. Lorelei held tight to his hand.

"Yeah, I'm fine." I didn't want to look at him anymore.

He studied me and cocked his head to the side. "You're still dripping."

My fingers pushed the damp strands off my face and with it, drips of water plummeted to the floor. I looked between Gabe and his date. It wasn't important enough to share anything with her hanging off him like a monkey on his back. "I was just in a rush."

"Gabe," Lorelei whined, drawing out all the letters of his name.

"Just a sec," he said to her and turned back to me. "That's unlike you."

"I got spooked, okay?"

"No, actually it's not okay. I'll let Lorelei into my place, and I'll walk to you yours."

Seriously, it was like fifty feet. I could manage the distance alone.

"Gabe, I'm cold," Lorelei whined.

His gaze flittered between the two of us. "C'mon," Gabe said. "Both of you." He unlocked his door. "Lorelei, you head on in and make yourself comfortable, I'm just going to see Meghan home."

Her lips curled up in a disgusting sneer. "She can't live far, I'm sure she'll be fine."

"Honestly, Gabe, she's right."

"Go," he waved Lorelei into his living room and shut the door. "And you, go." He pushed me down the hall. "What spooked you?"

"I don't know. I just felt like I was being watched."

And just like that, we arrived at my door. I put my key in the lock, but it didn't click when I turned it. It was already unlocked. My heart puddled on the floor.

"Did you leave it unlocked?"

I shook my head and took a step back.

"Back to my place. Now."

He didn't need to say it twice, and I was two steps ahead of him heading back towards his place. With a swift turn of the knob, I was in the safety of Gabe's place. I walked into the living room and gasped.

Lorelei gasped as well. Guess she didn't count on me coming over as she was naked as a newborn sprawled out over the couch. I turned my head.

"Time to go," Gabe said to his date. "The party's over."

"Aw, but we just got started."

"Another day."

She was scrambling into her dress when she waltzed by me. "Don't call me."

Gabe followed her to the door, thumbing through his phone. "I've called an Uber for you." He turned in my direction. "I'm going to lock up and make sure she gets into the car safely, and I'll be back."

I nodded and watched the two of them exit his apartment. The lock clicked and for added safety, I slipped the chain lock on. Leaning against the door, my legs weakened, and I slid down the length of the wall.

Who had tried to get into my place? And why? I didn't own anything of value. Were there other apartments that had been broken into? I really needed to contact the security company, and post on the private Facebook page for our building. The other residents needed to know what happened as well. But what had happened?

I buried my face in my hands.

A key pushed into the lock. Gabe was back.

"Just a second." I slid the chain off and fixed my housecoat, covering myself up once again.

He closed and locked the door. As he turned and ran his fingers through his hair, he glared into the living room. "Well, now I'll need to disinfect the couch." He pulled out a kitchen chair. "Did you make yourself at home?"

I shook my head. "No, I…"

"Have a seat."

I did as I was told, watching him bustle around his kitchen.

The kettle roared to life, and he pulled a mug out of the cupboard and dropped a tea bag in it. "Chamomile work?"

My shoulders lifted and fell, and my lips made an I-don't-care expression. I wasn't thirsty in the least.

Retrieving his phone from his back pocket, Gabe paced through the length of his apartment as he dialled. "Hey, Nico.

Are you on shift?" He disappeared into his bedroom and his voice muted from the distance. A moment later, he was back. "Sorry. My brother's a cop, and I figured he could come and help me check your apartment."

"No, that's okay."

"What are you going to do? Spend the night there? Who knows what cree–"

The air around me turned as frigid as a winter's day.

He knelt before me. "I didn't mean to scare you, that's why I've asked Nico to come. We'll check it out and when it's all clear, you can grab a few things and stay here for the night."

"I can't." It was so sweet for him to offer.

The kettle clicked off and he poured two steaming mugs of tea, however, I think he needed it more than I did.

I tightened the robe around me, suddenly aware I was in nothing more than a swimsuit and my pink, fluffy housecoat and needed to deflect the self-consciousness. "Tell me about your date. Where did you meet her?"

A soft smile sprang up through his lips, and he set down the mug in front of me as he took a seat. "Through a colleague."

"Ah."

"She's a winner, isn't she?" Gabe bobbed the tea bag in his hot water. It was rhythmic and oddly soothing.

I did the same. "She's interesting."

"I knew it wasn't going to last."

"But you brought her back to your place?" I raised my eyebrow, even though it wasn't any of my business. What Gabe did on his own time wasn't my concern. Still, I was curious.

"Yeah."

"I get it. A man has needs." My gaze fell away from him, she had been expecting *something* otherwise she wouldn't have been naked. I hated to think he was so desperate he'd scraped the bottom of a barrel. A barrel that hadn't been harmed in the making of. The thought made me giggle but I suppressed it as much as I could. "I'm sorry."

He narrowed his eyes slightly and relaxed. "It's not like that at all." A wicked grin formed. "You saved me from making what could've been a huge mistake."

"Don't thank me."

My thoughts travelled down the hall to my apartment, wondering who unlocked the door. I shuttered right through to my fingertips. What if I hadn't run into Gabe? What would I have done?

Gabe's phone rang. "Nico's here."

"That's quick."

"He only lives a couple of blocks away." He walked over to the door and cracked it open.

A moment later, a younger, portlier version of Gabe dressed in grey sweats and an ancient U of A sweatshirt knocked.

"Hey," Gabe said.

"Fill me in."

He ushered in his brother. "Nico, this is my friend Meghan. It's her apartment we need to go check."

Nico shook my hand, solid and firm. "Let's go."

"Stay here."

"Hell no, I'm coming." I rose and put on my bravest face. Only a sheer lunatic would attack me with two guys around.

Gabe locked up, and I followed him and Nico down the hall.

Nico bent down and examined the door frame, especially nearest the lock. "No sign of forced entry."

With a quick twist, the door opened and illumination

from the hallway flooded into my kitchen.

I reached past the men and flipped on the switch, the area brightening up like a summer's day. Thankfully, the space was neat and tidy—showroom ready.

Nico headed straight for the patio door.

"Want to grab a few of your things?" Gabe asked, thumbing toward the bedroom.

I nodded and headed down the short hall. My bedroom door was open, not unusual, but my bed was not as nice and tidy as I normally left it. It was almost like someone had been sitting and waiting. The hairs on the back of my neck saluted and a violent shudder rippled through me.

I yanked open my dresser and rummaged through grabbing a few things to get me through the night, and did the same in the bathroom, all under Gabe's watchful eye. Within moments, I was ready to leave. The hairs wouldn't relax and a nagging feeling in my gut refused to dissipate.

Without looking back, I raced into the living room and grabbed my laptop.

"You good?" Nico asked. "Got a few things?"

My mouth resembled cotton, but I managed to squeak out, "Someone has been in here. My bed has an indent."

Nico disappeared down the hall.

"Anything missing?" Gabe asked.

My hands shook like a leaf and a feeling of doom washed over me. The air in the apartment felt wrong, almost like a bad mojo or something, and my desire to get out of there outweighed lingering to see if anything was missing. "Can we just go?"

"Yeah, sure." He wrapped an arm around my shoulders. "Hey, Nico, I'm taking her back to my place."

"Sure thing," he called out.

The pounding of my heartbeat and the racing in my veins propelled me down the hall and breaths later, I curled up on Gabe's couch, draping my housecoat around my knees and my arms around them both.

Gabe handed me my tea from earlier, and it was still warm as it graced my lips. "Guess your intuition was right."

"Yeah." I hated it, but at the same time I'm glad I trusted it. When I think about who could've been waiting for me...

"It's going to be okay. We'll get your locks changed and inform the building management and contact the security company. Maybe they have video footage. In the meantime, you're welcome to stay here as long as you'd like. Me casa es sous casa." A gentle hand rubbed my back and my heart exploded with his kindness and generosity.

My tea was empty and sitting beside Gabe's when Nico came back.

"So?" Gabe asked as I lifted my head off my knees. I was beyond exhausted but in no mood to sleep.

"Nothing. No sign of forced entry can be found on any of the doors or windows. Is it possible someone has a copy of your key?" Nico walked closer to me but kept a respectable distance.

"No. Just the super and myself."

"Did you happen to lose a set of keys at any time?"

"No." My voice cracked.

"It's okay," Gabe said, the soothing motion of his hands across my shoulder blades a welcome distraction.

"Anyone follow you?"

I swallowed. "I don't think so, but after I got out of the pool, I felt like I was being watched and I couldn't get back into my apartment fast enough." My cheek rubbed against the soft terry of my housecoat as it touched my knees again. My body ached with tiredness, but my mind would not shut up. It constantly repeated the evening, scene by scene, in slow-motion.

"Should she file a police report?"

Nico frowned. "We could file a trespassing complaint, but without proof that someone was in there."

"Nico, there's an ass print on her bed."

"I'm sorry, that's not enough to go on. Nothing has been stolen, nothing's out of place, there's no breech of entry. She can file a complaint, but it would go to the bottom of the pile. Now, if you are able to obtain video surveillance of a perp, that changes everything."

I spoke. "I'll contact the building managers in the morning."

Nico pulled a card out of his wallet and gave it to me. "This is my cell. If you see anything out of place, or remember anything weird, call me."

The card fluttered out of my hand as I placed it beside me. "Thanks. For everything."

"Did you want to stay, Nico?"

"Nah. Jen was just on her way home from work."

"That's my sister-in-law. She's a nurse," Gabe added for my benefit.

"Got it." I winked with a bob of my head.

Gabe walked Nico to the door and ushered him out, securing the door afterwards.

"Nice to have a cop in the family."

"Yeah, Nico's good people."

I yawned but tightened my grip around my legs.

"C'mon, I'll set you up in the guest room."

~Chapter Seventeen

J gave myself the night to mope in fear, but by time the sun crested the horizon and filtered in through Gabe's east-facing balcony, I was done.

Sleep wasn't my friend and the couple hours I did get weren't exactly rejuvenating and soul-healing. However, I'd located a locksmith and scheduled a 9 AM appointment, and checked the apartment legislation on whether or not a security system could be installed. It could not. I didn't want to live in fear, but I didn't want to fear for my safety either.

Since I didn't sleep and couldn't shut my mind off, I read my emails, one from Joe and one from Seth.

Seth's email was blunt, and it rubbed me the wrong way, even though there was nothing inherently wrong with it. It wasn't even nasty. But it brought me back to the encounter at Westside.

I still couldn't wrap my mind around what he'd convinced a girlfriend to do. Whatever it was, it wasn't good as he turned wicked all of a sudden.

Down deep in my core, I worried about attending the wedding with him. I didn't want a scene, and I was more than a little nervous about what Dr. Jekyll would do or say. Maybe it was a sign. So far, my gut hadn't steered me wrong.

I was in the process of typing out a long letter, ready to explain to Seth I had changed my mind about attending the wedding *with him* when Gabe padded down the hall into the kitchen.

"Morning," he drawled.

"Morning."

"I didn't expect you up. I took you as more of a night owl."

I closed the lid on my laptop. "Yeah, I didn't sleep much."

"Sorry. You should've woken me." Canisters rattled around as he prepared a pot of coffee.

"No need. I do my best thinking in the wee of the night."

He put his hand down on the counter. "Oh yeah, what were you thinking?"

"I've made a decision. I'm going to the wedding solo." I breathed it out in one breath and hearing it in the air gave it validity, although it sounded better in my head.

"Really. What changed your mind?" He carefully measured out the coffee grounds and dumped them into the filter.

"I don't know, but I suddenly didn't feel comfortable going with Seth." As Gabe finished filling the reservoir, I shared with him about what was said at the restaurant.

He took a seat at the table, fingers pensively tapping his chin. "You don't think it was him, do you?"

I thrust my chin out and crossed my legs as I leaned closer to him. "Him?"

"The one in your apartment."

My back hit the chair. When I left the restaurant, there

was another car in the parking lot, but I never thought much about it. Was it Seth's? I tried to remember what the other car looked like. Under the shadow of the night, it was hard to remember.

But Seth had left some time before we locked up and he wouldn't have waited like a stalker for Westside to close, would he? Had he followed me back to my place and watched me swim? If so, how did he get access to the building?

I raced through a variety of situations. Maybe he gained access via the front entrance as someone was coming out? It was the most logical way to enter the building. I'd witnessed things like that before. But how did he get access to my apartment? And when? And was he waiting for me to return?

"Do you think it could be him?"

"I do now." My hand clapped to my eyes. "But I don't understand why?"

Gabe placed a full mug of fresh coffee in front of me. "No one understands the thinking's of a crazy person. I was married to one for years and I didn't understand her, or see it coming. And you've only just met this guy. If you think he's crazy now, well, maybe it's a good thing you discovered it now."

"I'd never seen a future with him."

"Just a maybe future?" He rose his mug.

"Maybe." I sipped a hot taste. "He emailed me."

"Oh yeah, when?"

That was something I hadn't checked. "Mind if I?" I pointed at my laptop.

"Go ahead."

It didn't take long to get to his email since the reply was still open on the screen. "Last night at 10:36."

"And where were you?"

"With you and whatshername."

"Lorelei." Said as an afterthought, almost as if he too had forgotten.

"Yes, her. At least I assume so. I never really checked the time when I got home."

Gabe stood and disappeared into his bedroom, returning a moment later. He brandished his phone. "I called my brother at ten to eleven."

"Oh."

Well, I guess the wild theory of Seth being the madman was incorrect. Although I hadn't really thought it was him anyway. He had no idea where I lived, and I'd never mentioned it.

"So, what are your plans for the day?"

"The locksmith is coming by in a bit and I'm going to the contact the security company and see if they have any footage. I would imagine there would be surveillance of some sort. Once my apartment's been taken care of, I'll probably get some work done. Not a very exciting day."

My mind drifted over the possibility of being alone today, something I was usually a-okay with, until now. I didn't really want to be on my own.

"Earth to Meghan."

My head snapped up.

"Are you thinking about cancelling your cancellation on Seth?"

"No. I can do this on my own, right?"

With a gentle shrug, he swallowed down some coffee. "You know better than me."

It had been such a wild twelve hours. "Maybe I just don't go." I looked to him for assurance or confirmation, I wasn't sure which.

"You are an incredibly strong woman, and you'll do what's right for you. Go with what you're feeling in there." He pointed at my chest, but I knew he meant my heart.

A chime on his phone, and he focused his attention on whatever piqued his interest. His face went blank and slowly a smile spread across.

"Everything okay?"

"What? Yeah, sorry. Just the company from London I've been dealing with wants to put in an offer. I'll need to fly there next weekend to have them sign the papers."

Noellette Insurance was going international.

Gabe had started his own brokerage and grew it into the national name it was, and now he was expanding. I was thrilled for him.

"That's great. And they agreed to everything?"

"Not everything. But the little points they are heckling over are pretty minor in the scheme of things."

The news completely perked him up and he sported an ear-to-ear grin. "I'll need to head into the office right away and make some calls."

He stood once more and went to the front closet. From a basket nestled on top, he withdrew something shiny. "Here's a key to the apartment. Feel free to come and go."

"Oh, thanks. Once the locks get changed, I'll be fine."

"Keep it, in case you change your mind." He tossed the silver-tone key onto the table. It clattered as it landed. "Please excuse me while I go get ready for work."

"No problem."

He hurried down the hall and once the door was closed, returned my focus to the Mingle More website. The unread email from my Everyday Joe called to me.

Dearest Meghan,

I must say, I am rather enjoying this archaic type of communication with you. It's so much easier to be myself and say what's on my mind from the comfort of my living room. It's freeing. So many hide behind their computers and claim to be the better versions of themselves, and I suppose to a degree that much is true. I've been able to chat freely with you without you seeing the blush that overtakes my cheeks when I think about you. I wonder what you are up to and how your day went. Is that weird?

I've read and read your last email a few times, and to be honest, I'm rather disappointed that you have decided to take another to the wedding, but I understand the reasoning behind it. You're correct it would be difficult to properly act the part without having the chance to meet in person, and I'm sorry I haven't been able to send you a picture. My laptop is used for work and I'm currently breaking the rules by replying on the company's computer as it is. I won't even try to upload a picture. I hope you can understand, and it must be frustrating, and for that, I apologize. If it helps, my friends have told me I bare a small resemblance to Bruce Croxon of Dragon's Den fame. Are you familiar with that show?

I stopped reading and Googled the name to see who he apparently looked like. If he bore any kind of resemblance to the guy, he was an older man, in his forties, with greying dark hair and wisdom on his face. Mind you, that was on the famous name I searched, not on Joe himself. But still, he was a decent enough guy. I continued to read the email.

However, I know you've already made up your mind with whom you are bringing to the wedding, but my plans have changed and I'll now be home the Friday night before. Would you be interested in meeting me for a quick drink?

Even if nothing comes from it, it would be nice to meet you and introduce myself properly, in person. I'll be at the Garden's Edge on Friday for 8pm. If you are curious to meet me, I'll be sitting at the bar in a jean jacket (it's not a fancy place). If you don't show up, I understand.

Yours,
Joe

Oh my god. A possible date. Not to the wedding but just to see who this man was. My heart sped in my chest and the loud drumming drowned out all sounds. All I could imagine was meeting this man and seeing if he was as charming in person as he came across in the emails. It made me giddy just thinking about it.

"You okay?"

I blinked rapidly and focused on Gabe. "Hey."

Dressed in nice beige pants and a short sleeve button up with his hair slicked back, he was ready for work. He even smelled nice; a hint of cologne tickled my nose. "You zoned out there for a minute. Wherever it was though, it put a smile on your face."

Heat crept up my cheeks in a slow-moving crawl. Had I looked that faraway in la-la-land? "Sorry. I was just reading an email."

"From Mr. Dreamy?" He arched an eyebrow as he loaded up a laptop bag.

"Yeah," I said with a sigh. "How is it one man can appear so perfect with his words?" My voice sounded like a giddy schoolgirl's. It was weird.

Gabe patted my shoulder and poured some coffee into a takeaway mug. "Don't believe everything you read on the internet."

"Okay, Abe Lincoln."

He laughed as he understood the joke.

I'd read that meme on social media.

"You know…" Gabe stopped mid-sentence, and as his thoughts hung in the air, he brushed them away with his hand. "Never mind."

"No, what?" Leaning toward him, I waved my hand in a carry on manner.

"I've been thinking about your letter writer." He pointed to my laptop as he set his mug on the table.

"Yeah, and?"

He held his breath for a second. "Do you think he could be your ex?"

"Everyday Joe is Giovanni the Scumbag?" I laughed at the idea. "There's no way. Giovanni was the least eloquent writer I knew. His vocabulary was roughly that of a middle-schooler."

"You're sure? I'm worried he may be leading you on. You've already mentioned you thought it a joke he invited you. Maybe he's messing with you even more."

It would be like Scumbag to mess with someone in a way, but there was no way this letter writer was him. My gaze flicked up to Gabe. "I'm positive this Everyday Joe is not Giovanni. Besides, he said he looks like some dragon guy, and the internet picture is not even in the same ballpark as Giovanni. He was tall and wiry. This guy is older and more filled out."

"You're confident about that?" He wore concern like a badge, and it was endearing how he was looking out for me.

"One hundred percent." That seemed to relax him a bit.

He grabbed his mug and laptop bag. "I'll see you later. Have a good day."

Keys in hand, he headed for the door.

179

"Hey, Gabe. I have tonight off. Why don't you come over for dinner?"

"That would be nice. What can I bring?"

I drummed my fingers on my chin. "Bring a wine that goes well with chicken." I was sure I had some frozen. Now to think about what to create from it.

"Done. See you at six?"

"Six works."

The door clicked shut, and I went back to rereading Joe's letter. I popped the potential date into my calendar, complete with location. Just in case I fully committed to going.

Hours later, my apartment smelled delicious as the four chopped breasts of chicken simmered in the largest pan I could find, combined with rice, tomatoes, enchilada sauce, and a whack of spices. I gave the mix a stir and sampled a taste. For a Mexican dish, it wasn't as spicy as I'd hoped but there was no denying the flavours. This was going to be a tasty meal.

Country music played on the radio and a nice breeze caused the gauzy curtains to float within the living room.

I'd set the table for two with nice linens and a glowing candle jar but decided it bore a highly romantic look and moved the candle off to the edge of the counter. Gabe and I were just friends, and although I kept telling myself that over and over, I was having a hard time truly believing it. My feelings were there, but since Gabe pretty much agreed you could say I love you to someone you considered a friend, I assumed his feelings for me were completely friendship based. Plus, he was clearly on the rebound from Jordan as he dated the food-phobic Lorelei. What an epic disaster she turned out to be.

And even though I told myself it was friends getting

together for dinner, I felt the tiny tingles of excitement grow as I prepared supper. It was a thank you for his kindness; for his help last night and for letting me stay in his apartment and everything else he's done for me. So what if I went a little overboard on the fancy supper? He deserved to be spoiled once in a while, right?

Right at six, Gabe knocked on the door and my heart skipped a beat. Seriously, why was it doing that?

I slid the chain off and opened it.

Gabe stood outside with a bottle of something I likely couldn't pronounce properly and a giant smile on his face. "Wow. What are you cooking? It smells amazing. The whole floor will want to come over."

"Well, I made enough."

Between the chicken breasts and rice and a simple lettuce, tomato, mayo salad my grandma used to make, I thought there'd be enough food for at least us, Mrs. Thompson, and her son two doors down, and the quiet banker at the end of the hall. However, I wasn't sure there would be enough wine.

Gabe made himself at home and dug out the wine glasses right away, removing the cork and filling each about half. "Go easy. It's a sipping wine." He placed the glass in my hand, his fingers brushing against mine.

I raised the glass to my lips and allowed a tiny taste to linger on my tongue. "Mmm. That's nice. What it is?"

"Valpolicella Ripasso."

I knew it was something I couldn't pronounce. The way he said it though was magnificent. "You really are a wine snob, aren't you?"

"Yes, I am." He lifted the glass to his lips. "So, what are you baking?" He took a long lingering gaze at the one dish creation bubbling nicely on the stove.

"It's called One Pan Mexican Chicken and Rice. It's from the internet."

"Very nice." He leaned his back against the counter and propped his hands behind him. "Got your locks changed I take it?"

"Yep. The locksmith was very punctual, and got it handled. Made two additional copies." I tipped my head toward the end of the counter. "By the way, your apartment key is there, beside the candle."

"Keep it. You never know when you might need it."

"Let's hope not ever again." I didn't mean for it so sound bad, but that's how it came out. I raced to cover. "I mean, I hope an incident like that never happens again, and I need to bunk at your place."

He gave me a friendly push to the shoulder. "I know. I'm just messing with you."

"I contacted the security company and they said they'll see about checking the video cameras, but the guy I talked to wasn't overly excited."

"But that's their job."

"Maybe. But he said because there were no filed charges, because there's no one to charge…"

It was stupid, and I had spent nearly thirty minutes on the phone with the company trying to get someone to agree to check.

"I asked the guy what the heck were we paying for security if no one was going to be looking into this, and I'd bring it up with the tenant board meeting to look at other security companies if they weren't going to check things out."

And they were just recently hired as the new security too.

"And?"

182

"I'll have an answer within forty-eight hours he said."

Gabe shrugged. "Well, it's a start. Any word on an alarm?"

"Yeah, that was a hard no. Plus I looked on the condo tenant's act, and it clearly states they are not allowed."

"Damn."

I slipped my hands inside the oven mitts. "Oh well. I don't want to live in fear, but I won't let fear control me either. We'll see if there's anything on the surveillance and go from that."

I gave the rice and chicken another stir, and a blast of rich spices caused my stomach to rumble. I hope it tasted as good as it looked and smelled. I moved the pan to a hot mat to let it sit while I grabbed the salad from the fridge.

"Anything I can do?"

"Just place this on the table, please." I pushed the salad toward him after I tossed in a pair of tongs. A moment later, I set the main course in the middle of the table. "Have a seat."

"Après vous," he said.

"Merci," I responded in the only French I really knew. Apparently nine years of it throughout my school paid off.

He grabbed my wine glass and the bottle. "Top up?"

"No thanks. It's a sipping wine, and I've hardly sipped." I winked at him. "So how was work?"

Such a trivial thing to ask, but it was so nice to be able to ask someone how their day was. Joe had said as much too.

"Great. Things are all lined up for Friday. I spoke to the lawyers and the owners and we'll sign the papers over supper."

I nudged the salad in his direction, knowing it wasn't everyone's favourite and it never looked appetizing, but it was like a comfort food for me. With the wedding hanging in my future, I needed all the comfort I could get.

"When will you be back?"

"Late Sunday night."

I helped myself to the chicken and rice combo. "That doesn't give you much time to visit. You're going to London for crying out loud. You think you'd get more than 48 hours there."

If it were me and that limited amount of time, I'd sleep there and back, and spend all my time soaking in as much as I could.

Gabe put the serving spoon down and gave me a funny look. "It's really nothing exciting to see."

"It's London," I said with a little too much enthusiasm and nearly knocked over my wine glass as my hand sailed through the air.

How could you not get excited about that? The London Eye, Buckingham Palace, St. Paul's Cathedral...

"Yeah, London, *Ontario*." He paused and stared at me. "You didn't think it was London, England, did you?"

"No." I pinched out some salad with the tongs, feeling a tad stupid.

"Don't I wish I could get into London, England?" He laughed and scooped out the rice meal, putting a sizable amount on his plate. "My apologies if you thought otherwise, but it's in Ontario."

Which is still two hours ahead. All the times he needed to be working early, it was because of that? Nine in the morning Ontario time was seven in the morning here. Yeah, I hadn't thought that through at all.

"You're right, it's definitely not as exciting."

"Definitely not. Although London is only a couple hours away from Detroit. That could be fun."

"No, thanks. After watching Michael Moore's film about Detroit, it wasn't a place on my vacation bucket list." I'd much rather visit a beach resort, or the Big Apple, or San Francisco, or any other place.

"Isn't Neil Diamond from Detroit? There must be a museum there or something for him."

I laughed. "Neil Diamond is from Brooklyn. Besides, how do you know I like Neil Diamond?"

Whenever he was over, I rarely played it. Only in my car. At full blast. When I was alone.

"You have way too many CDs to be just a casual fan." He pointed over to the stereo. Beside it were two tall towers, and the Neil Diamond CDs were nearest the top.

Yes, it was old school, but I didn't feel it necessary to rebuy all the songs digitally I already had on disk, so I kept it around. And don't even get me started on iTunes and uploading my music there. Bad idea.

"Guilty," I said, turning back around to the table.

"He's okay, but I prefer good old country music."

My head tipped to the strumming of the guitars and the gentle twang accompanying today's country hits. Not as bad as what my grandfather used to listen to, but it was still country. "That's what I've got on."

"Then you have better taste than I thought." He winked, and I may have melted a little. But only a little.

Inhaling a deep breath to steady myself, I said, "Did I tell you, my Everyday Joe emailed me, and he wants to meet."

"Oh?" His eyebrow popped into his hairline.

"Yeah. Just for drinks. He knows I'm taking someone else to the wedding."

"I'm confused. You're taking Seth? I thought you'd decided to go solo."

I put my fork down and took a *sip* of wine. "I don't know." I hung my head a little as I spoke. "I'm wavering on

185

whether or not to even go."

Gabe lifted a forkful of food into his mouth. "What's the debate?"

"Honestly?" I looked him square in the eyes and relaxed my shoulders. "I have nothing to hide. I'm proud of the direction of my life and sometimes I wonder, if Giovanni *had* shown up and things went as they were planned, my life would be so different now."

Owning my restaurant and having a place to call my own would be a pipe dream as we'd likely still be renting.

"Because you'd be married?"

"Yeah." The wine lingered on my tongue before I swallowed it down. "But also, because we wouldn't be able to have a mortgage, so we'd be renting somewhere in the city. I'd be working full-time while trying to raise the baby, and he'd be out hunting for another job." It didn't sound so pleasant, and yet, had he shown up, it's probably how things would've been.

Gabe's thumb lightly stroked the top of my hand, and he scooted his chair closer. "From what I know of you, you truly do sound like you're better off without him."

I sighed and spoke softly. "There are times I agree with that, and times I don't. I miss his companionship. For all the fighting we did, there was love there. At least on my part. It was really hard to imagine a world where he wasn't in it."

Gabe's lips twisted in a sad smile. "Yeah, I hear that."

"Yes, you, of all people, would understand."

He'd been married to his own version of Giovanni for years before things went sour. I imagine it'd be a harder loss to get over. At least in some small way I got stopped at the gate, my ticket no good for entry into the life-long partner club.

"I'm glad we're friends." He lifted his hand and resumed his meal.

For an unknown reason, my gut tightened with his words. I hoped the coals of longing would spark into more. Instead, they turned into embers. "I'm glad we are too."

Chapter Eighteen

ork was busy, which was great for business. The temperatures soared in the city, breaking heat records, and my restaurant had top notch air-conditioning. It kept the waiting crowds nicely cooled while they waited for a table.

The draught beer flowed like a river out to almost every over-age diner, but no one was getting drunk. I didn't want to have to deal with that. My staff were hopping, and things were going smoothly.

A customer at the till paid their bill leaving a sizeable tip for Celeste, at least twenty-five percent. That was nice to see. High tips meant my staff were doing an extraordinary job. It made me happy for many reasons. A happy customer was a returning customer, and returning customers shared with their friends. It was a wonderful cascade effect.

Because my staff were hard and wonderful workers, I had a little gift for each of them. An end of summer bonus, and to me it felt like Christmas Eve, and I was waiting for the morning before they could tear them open.

After the weekend, things would cool down business

wise. It always did after the long weekend. Students returned to school, and parents were inundated with back-to-school fees of all sorts. It was easy to sort the people who came in right after the long weekend; the upper-class people who aren't burdened with back-to-school costs and the retirees who had no one living at home. It was an interesting shift in dynamic and clientele to watch. Fascinating really.

"Celeste, that was your last table, correct?"

"Yea, ma'am."

"Great. Before you leave, come see me in my office."

She paled a little and stepped backed.

"It's all good. I promise." Seriously, I hoped someday my staff stopped fearing me.

Not every visit to the office was bad. Just once and the guy deserved it. He stole the other servers tips off the table and from the till.

"Okay," she said, but the nerves had already settled on her lips.

I headed to the back and prepared her white envelope with her nightly tips. Digging through the file on the tiny desk, I grabbed the #10 sized envelope that I'd prepared for her specially.

A moment later, Celeste approached the office.

I handed her the first one. "Your tips."

Without looking, she pocketed it into her purse. "Thanks."

"And a special bonus." I handed her the other one, it was thinner than the cash stuffed envelope, but I hope she liked it.

I had a staff of twenty and rather than give them a generic gift, I did a little hunting and listening. As I walked the floor, I wasn't so much checking on how things appeared, but

189

rather hearing what they spoke about it and what interested them, and I started a list.

Not once did anyone mention they'd like tickets to a football game. Dang. However, this was more fun, and I learned something a little personal about my amazing staff. And rather than delay the bonuses as I tried to learn more of each of my staff, in the end, they all basically got the same thing, but tailored to what I thought they needed best.

Celeste held it tightly, unsure of what to do.

I whispered, "It's just a little bonus. You can open it at home. That's okay."

In fact, I preferred it that way. I didn't want a scene. Besides, I knew what was inside. Each got a cheque for ten percent of their pay and a hundred-dollar gift card to a local store. My shift managers faired slightly better with a fifteen percent bonus and a two-hundred-dollar gift card. It had been fun, and I was giddy for the end of each of their shifts.

Celeste looked at the envelope and after a smile broke out over her face, she tucked it into her purse. "Thanks."

She appeared like she was going to give me a hug and since I wasn't a touchy-feely person I stepped back quickly.

"Thank you. I appreciate this." Her hand stayed firmly over her purse.

"And I appreciate all the hard work you do. So, thank *you*." My cheeks pushed up with my smile. Not one to linger unnecessarily, I closed the office door and bid her a good night.

I walked back toward the cash register and stopped in my tracks. Seth stood at the till and his face lit up when he spotted me. Calmly I headed over. "Hey, Seth."

"Hey. You said you wanted to see me, and I couldn't wait until Friday." He had a goofy expression on his face.

Yeah, that had been my now obviously derailed plan.

Thought it was best to meet him someplace public and break the news in person how I was going solo to the wedding. I guess in the dining room of my restaurant would be just as safe as any.

"Sure. Let's go and have a seat." I passed Robin on the way. "I'll be just a few minutes."

"No worries, boss lady." He resumed putting empty glasses on a serving tray. That guy really was a great manager. He had zero issues working the floor like the server he once was and yet, still oversaw everything like an eagle-eyed manager.

"Have a seat." I pointed to the staff table.

Seth slipped into one side, and I sat across from him.

"Two more days."

"Yeah, about that." I put my hands on the table, clasped together tightly. "After some soul-searching, I've decided to go alone."

His face fell with such speed I worried it had been a physical mask he'd worn. "Wow."

"I'm sorry it's short notice."

"Yeah. A little."

"Have you incurred any expenses, like a new suit or anything?"

Would it be weird to pay him if he had? After all I'd stated upfront there would be no additional costs on his part.

"No."

I took a deep breath, keeping it as quiet as I could. One less thing to worry about. "Look, you're a great guy."

"Oh, here it comes." He rolled his eyes. "Let me guess. It's not you, it's me. Am I right?"

"Sort of." I leaned on my forearms and kept my voice low. "When I started looking, I was worried about how to present myself to my former fiancé, and figured I'd need a date who was good looking and secure in his job and well-

191

mannered." Well, the last part was a bit of a stretch, especially after the last encounter we had in the restaurant. "And you are all those things."

"So, what's the problem?"

"It's me. I thought I needed all that, but I don't. I'm secure enough with who I am and how far I've come in my life without him, there's no need to project a false image. I'm okay with me." I pointed at my chest.

"A date wouldn't hurt."

"No, it certainly wouldn't, but it wouldn't be the truth. As nice a guy as you are, it's just not what I need right now."

"Is there someone else?"

My brain immediately plastered up a mental image of the mystery guy's emails. I shook it away. "No."

The hurt on Seth's face was genuine.

"I'm really sorry."

"But the bridge?"

"Yeah, you see. That proved I wasn't ready yet."

"Maybe with more time? I don't have to be your date to the wedding but maybe after?" His voice rose as he pleaded. His hands came up to the height of the table and fell back down to his sides a couple of times, as if he was unsure the best place for them to rest.

However, the air prickled with agitation and my breath picked up a little. I didn't want this to become a scene and suddenly felt like I needed to put out a rapidly igniting fire. "I'm sorry. I'm not ready to be with you."

It was a little white lie, but that's okay. Let the guy down easy, right?

"Fine." He slammed his hands down on the table and from the corner of my eye, Robin straightened himself out and stared towards our table. "Be that way, bitch." He pushed himself out of the booth.

Robin walked closer and spoke in an even tone. "Sir, this is a family restaurant, and I'll ask you to please lower your voice."

"Why? I've done nothing wrong. This bitch here plays on your feelings. She ropes you in and dumps you." He made loud gesturing moves, drawing attention from the patrons still dining.

My cheeks heated the more excited he got.

Robin squared his shoulders and inched closer to Seth. "I'm going to ask you to leave this establishment *right now*." He put a lot of emphasis on the last two words.

I rose from the booth and stepped beside Seth, a united front. "Please leave."

"Good luck with the wedding, bitch. You shouldn't have placed an ad on Mingle More if you weren't ready to actually fucking mingle."

Without warning, his hand flew wildly and connected with my cheek. The sting was painful, but not nearly as painful as the embarrassment rolling out of me. The patrons in my restaurant all stared in my direction with their mouths wide open.

Before I could react, Robin dropped Seth to the ground belly down and straddled him, pinning Seth's biceps with his knees, who groaned and wiggled underneath.

"Are you okay?" Robin asked me quickly while he glared at the side of Seth's face.

I nodded, and my hand instinctively cradled my heated cheek.

"Go call the cops," Robin said to me.

A customer from the table nearest us waved his phone. "They're already on their way."

"Bitch," Seth said, trying to escape from his captor.

I was a little worried he'd overtake Robin, but I shouldn't have.

Robin seemed very in control of the situation. He lowered his face closer to Seth and in a voice that would've raised the hairs on the back of my neck if he were saying them to me, he said, "Is that how you treat a lady? Didn't your momma raise you better than that?"

Seth glared at me, evil and vitriol oozing out of him, so I walked out of his view. I had no desire to see the kind of evil manifesting itself on his face. Again.

"That's it, bitch. You leave."

"I've had just about enough from you." Robin pushed his hands down a little harder on the top of Seth's back. "Not another word."

My two servers stood near the door, my kitchen staff a few feet away poking their heads around the wall separating the server station from the dining room. Two big, bulky guys whispered to each other but kept their focus on the squirming guy on the floor. The tables around us were pin-drop quiet, and the silence of the whole thing was starting to unhinge me.

I dropped my hand from my cheek, the heat remaining but the sting disappeared slowly. My heart beat like I'd swam my fastest time ever in the pool and the sweat building in my pits bore a strong resemblance to having just jumped out of the pool.

Thankfully, the cops arrived within a couple minutes and entered the restaurant, storming straight over to the man pinned underneath the seemingly frail and lanky Robin.

"We've got it from here," the cop said. "But don't go anywhere."

A few more patrons stood from their tables to get a

194

better look, and the scene seemed to grow bigger as Robin jumped up. In that second, the angry Seth rolled over and punched him in the nuts. Robin dropped to the ground, doubled in half.

The cops wasted no time handling the mouthy Seth and hauling his sorry ass outside, presumably into the cruiser.

I knelt beside Robin, who was grimacing but not shedding any tears. That punch nearly made me cry, and I wasn't the target. "You okay?"

It was a dumb thing to ask because obviously he wasn't.

Catching his breath, he said, "Mostly. He caught the inside of my thigh more than anything." Robin glanced toward the door. "But he's no longer in here, is he?"

"You thought he'd do that?" I whispered, wondering how crazy Robin really was.

"The cops were going to stand here and ask questions and take statements and he'd be growling and doing was he was doing. Figured the best way to get him removed quickly was to let him take a swing at me. He missed." He said it with a laugh. "Still, it's going to bruise but I'll have a helluva story to share with my girlfriend later."

"I'm really sorry you felt you had to do that."

"Don't be. I took one for the team." He winked and rolled himself up to a stand. "Are you okay?"

"Yeah." A shiver rolled through me, followed by another.

One cop came back in and sauntered towards us. "You." He pointed at Robin. "Let's talk," with a quick flick of his wrist, "outside."

"Can do, Officer." Robin dusted off his pants. He winced a little as he stepped toward the cop.

I watched him go and motioned for Celeste, who stood

shell-shocked behind the till. "Let's lock the doors now. No more incoming customers for the night." I brushed my skirt down and glanced around, trying desperately to regain my composure. Twelve pairs of eyes stared in my direction. I cleared my throat and addressed the customers. "Sorry you all witnessed that. I promise the situation is under control."

"I'll need to get a couple of witness statements." A cop appeared out of nowhere and left me to walk to the closest table.

Table by table, and customer by customer, the cop made his rounds, but I didn't watch how long he stayed taking statements. I wanted Robin back inside the restaurant. In my mind, he hadn't done anything but defend me. Hopefully, Seth didn't press charges against him, although I highly doubted they'd stick. Robin should be the one to press charges.

As each table finished up with the cop, they made their way over to me.

"Your bill has been taken care of." I wanted each customer to not think poorly of my establishment and hoped they'd return and have a pleasant meal the next time around.

The last set of customers were escorted through the doors, and Robin was let out of the backseat of the cruiser.

I looped my arm through Robin's, more to calm my racing heart, and to steady Robin. "So?" There was a lot of weight in those two words.

"We'll see. I'm free to go."

"And charges?"

"I told Officer Jacobson, I'll press charges if Seth does. Kind of like retaliation."

"You really should. He could've hurt you. Had he missed..." My breath caught in my throat just thinking about how close Seth came to doing a ton of damage to one of my staff. To my friend.

196

"I'm okay, although I wouldn't turn down an ice pack."
I nodded. "I can do that."

"Miss Carter?" The cop stood stoically at the till. "We need to get your statement."

A shiver ran through me. "Sure, no problem."

It was borderline embarrassing giving the cops a rundown of the relationship between Seth and I, and how things ended so abruptly. The officer never cracked a smile while writing down everything I blurted out and showed zero empathy. All I wanted was to finish, make sure Robin was okay, that my staff were fine, and go home. Maybe even stop at Gabe's for a quick visit.

With the statement finished, I usher the cop out and sighed as I leaned against the door.

"All done, Boss Lady?" Robin rose with a bit of a limp and headed to the back of the restaurant.

"All done. Let's shut everything down and call it a night."

Robin walked beside me with a bit of a shuffle.

"I think you should see a doctor."

"Nah, Cara will take good care of me." He flicked off one of the overhead lights and the prep area fell under a shadow. "We'll document it and take pictures of course, but don't worry about me."

"You're my staff. Of course, I'm going to worry." I opened and double checked the walk-in fridge before locking it up and turning off the light. "Where did you learn to pin someone like that?"

"Karate." A huge smirk filled his face. "I've watched my brother earn his black belt."

"Shit! Really?" Who knew? He was a powerhouse

197

under those clothes and my restaurant was a little safer now that I knew.

"He was pretty easy to take down. It's better to disarm a guy than engage."

We walked through the kitchen, turning off 90% of the lights, leaving just enough for the prep cook in the morning to find his way.

A violent wave of shivers ran over me, stopping me in my tracks.

"Are you sure you're okay?" Robin asked.

"Yeah, just didn't expect that, although I'm glad in a way it happened here. I don't know what would've happened had it taken place elsewhere."

"I'm sure someone would've stepped up."

"You have too much faith in humanity." I gave him a sideways eyeing.

Humanity as a whole was decent, but it was the individuals that ruined it.

We walked out to the front. The kitchen staff and front end all huddled together. One thing was good about them all being there, it made handing out their bonuses easier, although not as discreet.

"Are you sure you're both okay?" Celeste asked.

"We're fine," I said, confirming with Robin.

Even if we weren't, we needed to make sure the staff understood they were in no danger, especially if Robin was on shift. However, now wasn't the time for explaining. I needed to be a little more personable. My heart pounded against its holdings.

"That guy—Seth—and I were sort of dating. Sort of." By the surprised looks on their faces, my foray into the dating world seemed as shocking to them as it had been to me.

"Although I was clear from the start about expectations since I just needed a date for a wedding I'm attending, it seemed things became more complicated than that, and Seth didn't take rejection well."

At least Hudson and Cory didn't respond to the emails. The hope of anything was over and it stayed that way. Seth... well, maybe I did lead him on a bit. I really enjoyed our bridge date and the numerous emails between us. Had my words been taken with more meaning than I had intended? Was I doing the same thing with Joe's emails?

"If it wasn't for the quick actions of Robin here, things may have gotten a little more heated."

The small crowd clapped and hollered, and Robin, for the first time I'd ever noticed, went bright red as he tipped his head.

He took a deep breath and looked out at his staff. "Honestly, it was nothing. And I'm sure any of you would've done the same. Westside is family, and we watch out for each other."

I nodded as tears threatened to fill my eyes. What a sweet thing to say. I've always thought of Westside like my family, I just didn't think anyone else did.

"Thank you for staying and helping clean up. I have a little something for each of you. Please open it at home." I handed each their envelopes. My front-end staff had already received their tip outs, so the extra envelope seemed to catch them all by surprise.

A variety as thanks came in my direction as one by one, they walked out the main doors, but not before stopping and giving me a quick hug. It was unnerving and unexpected but kind of sweet.

Robin and I were the last out of the restaurant, out from

the warmth and into the breezy outdoors. The smell of a late-night rain shower hung in the air, a sweet smell of freshness.

I handed Robin his envelope, thinking I made a mistake and should've made his bigger. But it was too late to rectify. Christmas was only four months away, and I could go bigger there. "Thank you for everything you do for the restaurant … and me."

"Always." He held the envelope tightly in his hand. "The wedding will be great."

"You think so?"

"Sure. I don't need to tell you what an amazing person you are. Somewhere in there," he pointed towards my heart, "you know it. You just need to let your confidence shine. Your ex just wants you to fail, and you're so much better than that. Just be yourself, and he'll be the one questioning his sanity."

"Well, that would be nice." A small smile formed as I dreamed to see a surprised look on his face, and that of his family. "Thank you, Robin."

He stepped forward and gave me a big hug. "Have fun. Relax and enjoy yourself. I want all the details on Sunday."

"Oh, you'll get them."

"Good."

Robin hopped in his car, and I waved as I slipped into my own. I wasn't sure what details I'd have to give as I didn't know yet if I was going. I still had tomorrow to talk myself out of it, and tonight to email my Everyday Joe and let him know I wasn't going to show up at the Garden's Edge. One just never knew what hid behind the safety of the internet, and I was concerned about who or what would be waiting for me. I didn't want to deal with another monster, no matter how wonderful he wrote.

Chapter Nineteen

My home stood footsteps away from me, but I found myself hesitating in front of Gabe's door. It was nearly eleven on a Thursday night, surely he wouldn't be up, especially since he was leaving tomorrow? My hand was poised to knock, just once, in case he was in bed. I dropped it before it made contact and walked to my door.

Giggles and goodnights sounded behind me, and I turned to see who it was. A couple were exiting Gabe's apartment. My key was in the lock when he stepped out into the hall to bid his friends goodnight. He glanced in my direction and waved, and the two friends stopped and looked my way as well.

"Hey, Meghan."

"Gabe." I opened my door.

"Come meet my friends." He tipped his head toward the couple.

I wasn't really in the mood, but what the hell, at least I knew Gabe was awake. I locked my door and headed down the hall. "Hi, I'm Meghan."

The male part of the couple extended his hand. "Andrew," he said in a lilting Russian accent.

"So, you must be Charlotte?" I said, turning to the redhead.

Her picture was displayed in the apartment, but she was much tinier in person than the photo accurately showcased. I towered over her, and I wasn't that tall. She couldn't be much taller than five-two, and if she weighed a hundred pounds I'd be surprised.

"I am." She gave me a little wave and placed her hand over the beach ball pushing the fabric of her shirt to its limits.

"Pleased to meet you both. I've heard many good things about you." The former sister-in-law who turned into Gabe's best friend held the hand of her husband, who was somehow connected to Gabe's work.

It was such a tangled web, I had a hard time keeping everyone straight.

"As we've heard about you," Andrew said with a wink. "We'll let you go. Have a good night." He wrapped his arm around his wife's waist. "Come on, Cat."

"Good night," Charlotte called out over her shoulder as Andrew hit the elevator button.

I waved and so did Gabe.

"You have time to come in for a quick drink?" Gabe asked as the elevator chimed, and the couple disappeared from view.

"A quick one. I don't want to keep you up."

"Nonsense." We stepped in and he closed the door.

In a slight flutter, he gathered the used glasses and deposited them into the sink.

"She's very pregnant."

"Very. Her due date is tomorrow." He fumbled with a fresh wine glass and wiggled it in my direction.

I nodded. It was never too late for a glass of red. "Wow,

I don't think I'd be that mobile so close to my due date."

"Baby number two and, bless her, she lets me live vicariously through the pregnancies."

"Really? How so?" I took a seat in the living room as he waltzed in and handed me a glass.

He sat beside me on the sofa and leaned back placing a foot upon his knee. "Since I can't have children, they tell me all about theirs. Charlotte's pretty good at sharing all the details, good and bad."

"That's kind of weird really."

"Nah, I don't mind."

"When you say you can't have children..." I lingered and shook my head.

Was it because he wasn't married? Such an old school thing to expect. I wasn't married when I was pregnant, nor was my one of my staff, but Gabe was an old-fashioned kind of guy.

He took a sip from his glass. "I'm sterile."

The words came out as a matter of fact, there was no remorse or sadness hidden between the words.

Still, the words "I'm sorry," fell out of me.

"It's all good. I accepted it a long time ago. I knew going into my marriage with *her*." Even after all this time, he still never mentioned her by name. He claimed he was over her, but was he really? She truly put him through the ringers.

"Have you thought about–"

"Adoption? Yeah. But I'm a single guy in his forties. I'm sure they are rushing out to find me a child to raise."

That could make it more difficult.

"I have numerous nieces and nephews I dote on, my friend's kids, and of course, Charlotte and Andrew's two-year-old and the new baby. I'm not hurting for baby snuggles."

"That's good."

I wasn't a baby snuggler. Joy had offered, and I turned it down. Mind you I didn't know many pregnant women, so my opportunities were limited.

"Hopefully she doesn't have it while you're gone."

"Until Sunday at least."

"When are you flying out?"

"I meet with the guys at five tomorrow night, and my flight takes off at ten in the morning."

"That'll be exciting." I clinked my glass against his. "And speaking of exciting, do I have something to tell you."

I set my glass on the mahogany coffee table and launched at full speed into what transpired.at my restaurant.

"Jesus Christ," Gabe spit out. "I have half a mind–"

"Don't. Please. It's taken care of." I placed my hand onto his arm, in hopes of settling him down. It was tight with sudden rage.

"And you're okay?"

Inhaling a deep breath, I nodded. "Yeah, it's just a slap. No bruise. I'm more concerned about Robin."

"Just a slap? Let me see?" I turned that side of my face towards him, and he scooted closer on the couch, his thighs rubbing up against mine. "May I?"

I closed my eyes as his hand rose. Tenderly, his fingers touched—and electrified—my cheek as he ran them down from my eye to my chin. Beneath his caress I worried he'd feel the pulsing of my heated blood, so I took a slow breath to quell the roar of my heart. His fingers on my cheek and the slow deliberate way he stroked them was the most intimate moment I've experienced in a long time.

"Any man worth his salt would never ever strike a defenceless woman."

I opened my eyes and stared into his, mere inches from

204

mine. "You think I'm defenceless?"

A smile cracked on my façade and his fingers moved as my cheeks inadvertently pushed them away.

"That's not what I meant."

Gabe was right, I did know what he meant, but still.

His voice was low and deep, and the distance between us spanned only a heartbeat and a breath. "I think you're beautiful and kind and brilliant."

Butterflies I didn't know I had, suddenly swarmed around my insides. And until he dropped his hand, I didn't know how badly I wanted a kiss from him.

"Sorry," he mumbled and pushed away from me. "I was way out of line."

What? NO!

I tried to keep the disappointment off my face. I wanted to beg him to come closer and start something with me, and on the flip side of that coin, I wanted to be bold enough to make the move toward him, but he backed away. He was so close and yet, *he pulled away*. A nasty feeling of not being good enough flared up. Sudden anger replaced my warm and fuzzy feelings.

Gabe scooted over to the edge of the couch and his hand covered his face. It came across as looking regretful. No point to me being here. Seeing his disappointment was too much.

"I need to go." I stood and unceremoniously set my still full glass on the counter.

There was a large amount of self doubt still lingering in me, and it was screaming at me to leave because I wasn't worth it. Gabe had said as much loud and clear when he pulled away and allowed the silence to build a wall between us.

I didn't wait for a goodbye or a friendly wave, and marched into my own apartment, deadbolting and chaining the door. How did I not know my feelings for him were so strong until that moment? I wanted him to kiss me and feel those lips upon mine. I wanted to be wrapped in his protective arms and melt.

He'd made a move and, in a heartbeat, realised I wasn't worth it. He claimed I was smart and all that, and yet he pulled back. What was so wrong with me that guys weren't really interested? Just a quick poke, like Hudson had hoped, or something fun to get away from kids, like Cory. Maybe I was better off with the likes of a Seth, since a guy like Gabe wasn't interested in me.

Tonight, I needed to drown my sorrows. With a bottle of Butterscotch Ripple, the only hard liquor I had, I poured myself a full eight-ounce glass and downed most of it, feeling the burn as it made its way into the pit of my stomach. Instead of drowning anything, it fired up everything as it wasn't as good as the wines Gabe had made me try. And I hated how I wanted another man who wanted nothing to do with me. Once again, I was all alone in my apartment ... and there was an emptiness in my heart.

Chapter Twenty

The alarm on my phone buzzed the most awful sound one should ever wake up to. Especially one with a nasty friggin' headache. With more force than necessary, I smacked my phone, cancelled the alarm, and sent it flying onto the carpet. I hardly ever woke up with a headache, but I sure did this time. A headache and eyes so puffy, I could hardly see through them. An empty bottle of hard liquor and a glass stared down on me as I looked up from the couch towards the coffee table. That bottle was half full last night. Damn.

Slowly, I pushed myself up into a sitting position and covered my head with the movement. Inhaling a few breaths, I walked to the bathroom and poured a couple of pain relievers into the palm of my hand and chased them with a glass of warm tap water. Yuck. I wiped the back of my hand over my parched, scratchy lips.

"Good thing he didn't kiss me," I said to the mirror as I analyzed the condition of my un-kissable lips.

A good smear of balm should help to soften them, not that anyone would touch them anyway. The rest of me looked like hammered shit too; hair all askew and enough bags under my eyes to take me to London.

Sigh. London. Gabe. Another sigh.

Shaking my head, I gave my face a rub.

He's not interested. Made it perfectly clear last night.

I popped into the shower and checked my schedule once I'd located my phone. I ignored the text messages from Gabe, sent a few minutes before my alarm went off.

Whatever.

I cleared them off my screen and focused on the running list of meetings I'd booked with the builders and contractors. Thankfully today was a busy enough day I wouldn't have time to think about Gabe. I could worry about tiles and wall colourings and décor items for the new dining room and all the latest appliances for the kitchen. It would be nice to have more modern equipment. The current store ran off of very dated ones, yet they still functioned... somehow. Today I'd get to pick out some top-notch equipment, and that was worth getting excited about.

Hours later, I stumbled back into my apartment, my feet sore, my bank account much, much thinner, but delighted all the same. The new restaurant was going to be amazing. With the help of a trusted consultant, I'd picked out higher grade equipment, not quite as high as I'd hoped for, but still great quality. Whoever I hired for the kitchen should be impressed. It all needed to be ordered in ahead of time, so with a little luck, it would be here by early December, and baring no set backs, the framing would all be completed by late October, and the electrical by November. But I knew better. These things never went according to plan. It was the story of my life.

I dialled my mom and put it on speaker as I logged into

work to see how things were going.

"Hey, darling." Based on the excitement in her voice when she answered, you'd swear I only called her once in a blue moon. Fact was I called her every single week.

"Hey," I said, letting my voice sag.

"What's up?"

"You got a minute?"

"For you? Always." The chair in the kitchen echoed through the phone as I imagined she pulled it out to sit on it. "What's on your mind, honey?"

"Everything."

"Well, I can't help with that kind of ambiguity. Break it down for me."

Where to begin?

"I'm wavering on going to Giovanni's wedding."

"Why am I not surprised?" Her eye rolling was loud and clear. "Because?"

I felt like a child who had been caught with a hand in the cookie jar and had to explain why she was grabbing the cookie. It was easier to say you weren't doing anything wrong.

"I'm worried about what he'll say, or what his family will say to me."

"I'm glad you're not worried about the obvious, like having to answer questions about the state of your life."

"There's nothing wrong with my life." God, I was tired of having this discussion with her and everyone else it seemed.

"I know and that's my point. I'm glad you're not worried about it. I'm very proud of how far you've come. Four years ago, you were shut down and lived like a zombie. Everything was routine and monotonous, and you lived paycheck to paycheck. Then a small spark happened, and you went to secure a business loan for your restaurant and got a mortgage somehow on top of that. You own your own home, and not one, but two businesses. How could I not be proud of all that?"

It was rare to hear such pride leak out of my mother, and it never failed to produce a tear. "Thanks, Mom."

"Giovanni has not faired as well, and you and I both know if he had shown that fateful day, your life would not be what it is right now. I don't need to remind you of his lack of work ethic. That bike repair business he dreamed up, well, it's not putting food on the table. She's the one making the money, and in many ways, I'm glad you're not in her shoes. That's not a life I'd dreamed for you. What you are doing now, that's what I wanted. You are a bright, successful woman. Go to the wedding and own it."

"Even if I'm single?" As much as I tried, I couldn't shake the possible images of people laughing at me because I showed up to the wedding solo.

"Damn straight. Look at me. I haven't taken a lover since your father passed away, does that make me less successful?"

"Of course not." But she's mom; powerful and strong. I could never live up to her. She raised me on an art gallery curator's salary, which wasn't a lot of money, and she made sure to set money aside for my college years.

"And at any point since your father passed, has not having had a man made any effect on my life?"

"I don't know, aren't you lonely?"

"Who has time to be lonely?" She laughed, but it was true. For a woman in her sixties, she kept the busiest social calendar, filled with all kinds of activities her sorority hosted, or the university put on. "Honey, what I have always told you growing up?"

"To put on clean underwear?"

"Yes, of course, but what else?"

And here it was. The thing she always made me repeat. "A successful woman is one who can build a firm foundation with the bricks thrown at her."

"Do you believe it?"

"Yes."

"I don't hear it in your voice."

"I believe it," I said, the enthusiasm for it bubbling up and out of me.

And I did. I could go to the wedding a strong person, who succeeded in the goals most didn't think I would. Giovanni included.

"That's my girl." Pride radiated through the phone. I could hear her smile.

"Thanks, Mom."

"Anytime." Before I could hang up, she added, "Having a man on your arm doesn't define who you are, Meghan. A man who is truly worthy of your love will help raise you up. And when you find him, you'll know it in your heart."

I hung my head. "What if that's passed me by?"

"It hasn't happened for you. I know you'll hate to hear this, but it wasn't Giovanni. You never got excited by his presence. To me, it seemed like you figured it was time to settle with someone and it may as well be him."

"I was in love with him, Mom."

She huffed. "I doubt it. You were in love with the idea of being in love, but you really weren't. For two people who claimed to be so in love, there was a lot of arguing and distancing and breaking up and getting back together. If you look objectively into your heart, you'll know it's true."

I hated how she even put a spark of doubt into my head,

but even as I glazed over our time together, it had been less than exciting. Even the way he proposed was ho-hum, like an after thought between periods of hockey. He gave me a ring he'd purchased at a pawn shop, and it was tarnished and in rough shape.

"Is that what it was like for you and dad?" She never talked much about him, and I didn't really know him since he died when I was nine.

"Oh, your father had a way of sweeping me off my feet. It wasn't so much with words, but actions. He could take asking me about my day and make it the best part of his. We didn't need to do anything special, we just needed to be together. And some day, that guy will show himself in your life."

"Some day."

"Who knows? Maybe you'll meet him at the wedding. Wouldn't that be something?"

It was a crazy enough idea to make me smile. Imagine that scenario.

I walked to the bedroom and eyed the dress hanging in the closet. "Okay, I'll go. I'll go to the wedding and face Giovanni's family and the man himself. I'll hold my head high."

"But be yourself. Don't pretend to be anything else. You are special, and if they can't see that, then screw them."

"MOM!" Always so eloquent, it shocked me to hear my mother speak like that.

"Call me on Sunday, or tomorrow night if you're finished up early."

"I'll text you some pictures."

"I'd like that."

I sat on my bed and placed the phone on the table. "Thanks, Mom, for everything."

"I love you, Meghan."

212

"And I you."

In that moment, I was strong and powerful, and wanted to share it with the world. Towards the end of last night, I had felt weak and unworthy, but a surprisingly upbeat chat with my mom had flipped it on its head.

Everyday Joe was at the Garden's Edge, maybe waiting for me. Maybe not. I hadn't confirmed nor denied my coming. Until a moment ago, I wasn't even sure if I should. Now that I knew I possessed the courage and confidence to attend the wedding solo, meeting my mystery man would be the icing on the cake. Maybe he was the one I was meant to be with.

What would be the harm in checking him out? It would be neat to see the man behind the words, unless it was a woman pretending to be a man, or a serial killer out for his new victim. Truth was I knew nothing about this guy. Nothing. Maybe I could stealthily sneak up on him and see how he was with the wait staff. You get a strong feeling about people based on how they treat others. Especially wait staff. If people treated servers like shit, they were usually shitty people themselves.

Oh, what the hell, I was going to go meet him. I owed it to myself.

After a quick bite to eat, I freshened up, and slipped into a sundress with little sunflowers on it. Since he said he was going to be wearing a jean jacket, I dug an old one out of the closet. Cut nicely, it actually paired very well with my dress.

Unsure of where exactly the Garden's Edge was, I Googled it. It took me to a hotel on the southern edge of town, near the airport. Ironically, according to the aerial view, there was no garden on any edge of the property.

Grabbing my keys, my phone pinged.

Gabe texted. *The deal is done. Paper's were signed an hour ago.*

Still feeling the sting of rejection from last night's advance and retreat, I replied with a happy face emoji and left it at that. Truly, I was happy for him, and it would be great for his business, but I couldn't deal with him right now. Maybe on Sunday, after the wedding. After some distance.

Thirty minutes later, I pulled open a glass door and walked in the main entrance of the hotel. It transported me back to a time and place before I was born. Heavy, room darkening drapes like I'd seen in Grandma's house hung beside the window, and between each was a huge velvet painting completely out of place. The images of wolves howling at the moon in no way tied to the deco with its bright colours of navy blues and greys. The carpet was the industrial variety direct from the 1970's. Dark coloured wood panelling throughout, and macramé plant holders hung on the wall wherever a free space was found. Either it was a blast from the past, or this was the in thing in hotel decorating. I hoped it just meant the hotel hadn't been updated in forever. It was scary to think this was planned.

A long hallway with a single elevator at the end divided the wood check-in desk from the restaurant. I peeked in to check it out. Red carpeting, and not of the fancy Hollywood variety, was laid wall to wall. Amazingly enough, it was in great condition. The dining room was spacious but dated. Everything from the lamps to the tables to the golden velvet drapes screamed from decades gone by. Still, with a little investment…

But that's not why I was here.

A bellhop pushing a rickety old cart stepped off the elevator.

"Excuse me, where could I find the Garden's Edge?" I pulled on one of the buttons of my jean jacket and twisted it.

"Top floor. Follow the signs." For good measure, he pointed up.

Simple enough. Did this place contain one of those hidden gems people talked about? I stepped into the elevator and hit the button beside *Garden's Edge*. The higher I rose, the drier my mouth got. Here I was, about to meet the man of my inbox, because I wasn't yet sure he was the man of my dreams. All I had to go on was a Dragon's Den lookalike.

My pulse raced and my leg twitched a little, and when the elevator chimed and the light flashed on the five, my heart stopped.

Breathing sharply, I stepped out of the claustrophobic box and into an open-air space, complete with twinkle lights strung between light poles and off to the sides. This I wasn't expecting, and it was enchanting in how completely different it was from the interior. In its simplicity, it gave off a very romantic vibe. Jazz melodies played at a level you could talk in and didn't need to shout over, a pleasant level indeed. The music spewed out from speakers anchored on the edge of concrete half-walls.

Still standing beside the closed metal doors, a security guard gave me a once over and waved me in, but he didn't keep my focus for long.

If there was a lack of a dance floor, there was no lack of available seating as bar height tables littered the area, some with huge umbrellas. I imagined during the heat of the day, the space would be bathed in shade, but it would lose the feeling the twinkle lights provided. With the sun setting now, the lights were beautiful.

Toward the back of the place, past many full tables of customers sitting on high-backed wooden chairs, a long mirror lined the wall. It gave the space a much larger feel than it needed. Along the wooden bar with its brass railing, which was the only piece that captured the 70s look from the main floor, patrons sat on stools, pounding back drinks, and laughing with friends. I spied them all, hoping to catch a glimpse of a man in a jean jacket. It shouldn't have been hard considering most of the men were in t-shirts or sport coats.

Foot by foot, I slowly weaved my way through the small crowds of people lingering around the tables, excusing myself as I squeezed between. Sheesh the place was crowded.

A lightness descended upon my chest, and I greeted the excitement with a giant welcome mat. I nodded at a couple of guests who were enjoying a breezy cocktail and retrained my eyes to the length of the bar. I tried to blend in and tugged my jean jacket back into place as I pushed my confidence level up. This guy wanted to meet me, so this was a giant start, and I could do this.

I danced around a couple of tables to avoid being spotted. I was the one wanting to do the spotting first.

Finally, three tables away from the bar, I saw the only person in a jean jacket. His back to me, he had broad shoulders, but not so much so, and a decent looking ass, at least what I could make out from the stool. A full head of darker hair. Perhaps it was the weight of stare because he slowly turned around, a huge smile on his face, and I gasped as my jaw fell off my face and crashed into my heart on the way to the floor.

I turned right around and stormed back to the elevator.

Chapter Twenty-One

My finger cramped from stabbing the elevator button, but it wasn't opening.

"Ma'am, it doesn't come any faster the more you push it," the security guard informed me.

"Meghan, wait!"

His voice called out from behind me, but I didn't dare turn around. How could he deceive me like that?

"Meghan, please."

The doors finally opened and a couple moving the speed of snails shuffled out, laughing and touching.

Breathless, he caught up to me and grabbed my hand before I stepped in. "Stop. Let me explain."

Torn between being thrilled and feeling betrayed, my vision blurred as it rolled up from where we were joined at the wrist up into his blue-grey eyes. "What, Gabe? What do you need to explain? You're supposed to be out of town. Did you hack my email? Because I never showed you the last letter Joe sent me."

"I'm Everyday Joe." He pointed at his chest with his free hand.

I raised my eyebrow. I've known Gabe for a few years and he never spoke with such eloquence and romance.

"I'm no one special. Just an ordinary, boring guy who happened to fall for the sweetest neighbour ever."

My legs weakened underneath me, and I needed to sit down. Instead, I leaned on the security guard's joke of a desk. "All this time? All. This. Time?"

"Yes." His voice was warm and soft, a complete contradiction to mine which spiked in both volume and pitch.

"Why?"

"Let me explain, but first, let's sit." He led me over to the first free table, beneath an umbrella tipped to shade us from the setting sun. It also provided a small sense of privacy in the otherwise crowded area.

I hopped up onto the tall chair and leaned my forearms on the table as my stomach rolled with both sourness and butterflies. Under a careful eye, he shrugged out of his jean jacket and draped it around his chair as he slid into it. His eyes sparkled but his face was sorrowful, the lines around his eyes pulled down.

"Why did you lie to me?"

He narrowed his eyes slightly. "That's what you wanted to ask me first?" A smile followed the question.

"Fine. Why did you set up an account on Mingle More and lie to me about it?"

All those times I showed him the emails, and he acted like it was something brand new I showed him. How deceptive. He even made me question for a microsecond that Giovanni had sent them.

A perky little voice interrupted the stilted conversation. "Hi, welcome to Garden's Edge. My name's Mindy and I'll be serving you tonight."

She wore booty shorts and a tank top knotted between her breasts which bared her midriff. For a place like this, it seemed to me to be a lack of proper attire. Something a little classier would've been a smarter look in my opinion. Always err on the side of classy rather than smutty. However, considering the clientele in the place, her tips were probably higher than what my staff would make. Shame, really.

"I'll take an iced tea."

"Long Island, Garden's Edge or Standard." Standard was said as if it were a dirty word. It must've been the non-alcoholic version.

"Standard."

"Fine, and you?" She focused on Gabe.

And why wouldn't she? He was quietly handsome; the kind of guy whose sweetness came through and made him even more attractive. If he hadn't lied first. That put a dark smudge on him.

"A 20 oz draught."

"Dark or light?"

"Dark."

"Any particular brand? We have Guinness, Hockley, Rickards–"

"Hockley please."

"Fair enough." She sauntered away, giving a little shake of her rear as she went.

I cleared my throat and looked at Gabe.

He wasn't watching her. At all. He reached for my hands and wrapped his over them.

My heart strummed loudly in my chest, threatening to break through with the vibrations. "Are you going to answer why you set up an account on Mingle More?"

"Because I like you."

My chest tightened with his admission, but it didn't calm me down any. "Then why not just come out and tell me?"

"You weren't ready to hear it."

"Sure I was. I had asked you to come with me to the wedding. If memory serves me correctly, I think I even asked you the night I got the invite."

He shook his head. "You didn't ask me because you were interested in me. You asked because you didn't want to go alone. There's a difference." Those grey-blue eyes of his searched mine. "So, I didn't turn *you* down, I turned down the invite. Does that make sense?"

In some sort of weird way, yeah it did. Had I expressed any interest in Gabe, his answer would've been reflective of that.

"And then, despite my insistence you should go alone, you joined a dating site. And suddenly, all these others were interested in you, and you were planning dates. There was an excitement in you I hadn't seen before. You were finally ready to get back onto the proverbial horse, if you will."

"So, you lied to me instead?" My words were laced with more venom than I meant. "If it's one thing I can't stand, it's being lied to because it makes me feel as if I'm not worthy of the truth."

His hands squeezed mine, and his voice lowered. "Oh, believe me, you're worthy. I told you as much last night."

"So why did you pull back?" A little fire sparked inside me. Whatever reason came flying out of his mouth, it needed to be the truth. I deserved that much.

He hung his head. "I didn't want to seem like I was taking advantage of you. You had just been hurt, and I wanted nothing more than to comfort you, but I felt I'd overstepped."

"Overstepped? I disagree. Wholeheartedly." I

swallowed and inhaled a breath of air.

The fight within me was dying as fast as the sun was setting. Gabe was being a gentleman, not wanting to act until he knew I was in the same place as him.

"When I got home last night, you were the one I desperately wanted to talk to about it. I almost knocked on your door."

"What stopped you?"

"I didn't want to wake you up."

He gave me a half smile. "You can wake me anytime at all."

"And when you touched me, it ignited feelings and sensations I haven't felt for a really long time." Feelings I knew I'd act on, and I'd do so without any hesitation or regrets.

With perfect timing, the waitress came back and dropped off a coaster, followed by our drinks. She patted Gabe's shoulder. "Can I get you anything else?"

"Just some privacy, please," Gabe said without looking away. His blue-grey eyes stayed locked on mine.

A small huff steamed out of her, but none the less, she wiggled herself over to another table, her high-pitched sing-songy voice irritating another couple.

My hands tingled with each graze of his thumb across my knuckles. It was enough to ignite the lustful yet hopelessly dusty coals. "You still haven't answered why you set up an account and emailed me."

"Because it's easier to hide behind the anonymity of the internet." A sweet rise of his eyebrow. "If I had come and out and said anything before you were ready to hear it, you would've run, and I'd miss out on the best thing to have happened to me since my ex-wife."

"You hated her."

"Only at the end. Before that, she was the love of my life."

My tongue turned to lead and failed to move. Obviously, he had loved her, he married her. They'd been together for years, despite her deception to him about her lover; his estranged brother.

Gabe took a long sip of his dark beer and set it down, a ring of condensation formed on the table as he made circles with his mug.

I wrapped my free hand around the base of the cool glass.

He stopped the movement. A crack in his exterior formed as he said, "You seemed pretty relaxed around me, like a friend would. But the excitement you held for this mystery man was intoxicating, kind of like an addiction. I wanted you to feel that for me, but I couldn't do it face to face. I was just Gabe; this guy was Joe." His shoulders fell. "I'm a coward."

Definitely not a coward, a little insecure, sure. But who isn't?

"In all that time I was writing you, you knew it was me. You had an unfair advantage."

"Maybe," he said, a small smile reforming on the edges of his lips. "But it worked. Every time you spoke of him, you'd get this dreamy look, like anything was possible, and I couldn't wait to see it again. Like I said, it was intoxicating."

The butterflies he thought I only got reading Joe's letter were nothing compared to the ones taking flight in my stomach. The mystery guy was an enigma, Gabe was the real deal.

"Was it an act?"

"Not at all. He said everything in writing, I would've liked to say in person." Truth coloured his eyes and deepened the stretching smile.

I stroked his fingers, from base to tip. They had cooled slightly in the dusk, but it was soft, and I liked touching him. A thought from one of his more recent emails surfaced, and a tiny grin spread from ear to ear.

"You think you look like Bruce Croxon?" A shy giggle escaped me.

"That's who Charlotte said I resembled. Personally, I don't see it."

"Did she know?"

Would that be why she was so sweet the first time she met me? Or was it just her nature? I tried to remember if she gave me any kind of look, and my mind was blank. Mind you, it was on other things.

"Yes. She suggested it, and I went with it."

"I'll have to thank her next time I see her."

"You're not mad at me?" The innocence in his tone melted all hostility, not that I had much. I was surprised it was Gabe, but truthfully, I was thrilled.

I shook my head. "Not anymore. How could I be? You're the one I want to share everything with. I feel so completely safe and secure around you, and I know you would never do anything to hurt me."

"Never. I'd rather protect you."

"I sensed that last night. Had you continued to touch me like this..." I took the bold initiative and trailed my fingers along his whiskered cheek. "You would've found I was more than willing to accept it and take you in."

I slipped off my chair and positioned myself between his legs. My face mere inches from his strong jaw, and salt and peppery whiskers. Close enough to hear the quickened pace of his breath and to see the beating of his pulse near his temples as my finger caressed it. The pupils in his eyes widened just a fraction, but they took me all in. That was a level of intoxication I'd never felt... the desire burning in him for me. Me, of all people. My free hand wrapped around his other cheek and I cupped it, tipping my head to the side.

"It's you I want, and I'd love it..." I placed a sweet, tender kiss upon his lips and lifted off again. "If you'd be my date to the wedding tomorrow, because I want you, and I need you."

With the featherest of touches, our lips met again. I teased him, barely skirting over his soft pink skin before I pulled back.

"Only if there will be more dates following." Breathless, he reached out to kiss me again as my hands locked behind his neck.

A genuine smile bubbled to the surface. "There'll be many others." I brushed his pucker again, eliciting a promise of more. Later.

He wrapped his hands around my waist and pulled me in tight. "You're pretty damn awesome, Meghan."

"As are you, Gabe."

Under the twinkle lights as the sun set on more than just the day, I gave my heart to him.

Chapter Twenty-Two

"Are you nervous?" I asked Gabe, sitting beside me and holding my hand.

He dressed in a nice suit with a silver button-up nearly matching the shade of my hi-lo dress. "Are you?"

I laughed longer than was necessary. "Nope."

"Liar." He brushed a wayward piece of hair off my cheek and trailed his finger down my neck and over my collar bone.

Last night I learned the little divot in the center was highly erogenous and his finger rested there now, surely feeling the race of my pounding heart beneath.

I reached for his hand and pulled it into mine. As much as I liked the distraction, this wasn't the place. My head rested against his shoulder and my hand squeezed his. "I'm not nervous at seeing him, just the rest of his family."

"That's why we're seated at the back." He gently moved his hand to my thigh and gave it a rub as he glanced around.

My body was at war. Every little touch poised to send me back into the stratosphere, but for the moment, I needed to stay grounded. Deflecting his touch, my vision hunted through the seated guests ahead of us, and those who lingered on the sidelines. No one present was familiar to Gabe, but a few faces closer to the archway were familiar to me.

Giovanni's younger sister, Trinity, kept staring at me and nudged the person beside her. He too looked at me like a bug to be squashed. Thankfully, I hadn't laid eyes on Mr. and Mrs. De Luca. All the preparation in the world couldn't prepare me for the stare-down I was sure I'd receive. Even though I had done nothing wrong.

Not wanting to draw attention to myself by stretching my neck out and checking out the seated guests any further, I huddled into Gabe, even though the temperature in the full sun pushed the mercury over thirty degrees. I was sweating, but more from the sun soaking. At least that's what I told myself.

Music started playing, soft and romantic and immediately my stomach did a triple flip.

"You okay?" Gabe whispered into my ear.

I shuddered against his arm. "Do you hear that? Pachelbel's Canon? That was *our* wedding song."

How freaking odd. Of all the songs in all the world, they chose that one?

Gabe patted my thigh, his body twisting as if he was searching for someone. However, I doubt he knew what Giovanni looked like. I never showed him and kept all the pictures tucked in a box, buried in the back of the bottom part of my closet. Time to burn the box of bad memories.

While the music played, the mingling guests took their seats on the appropriate sides of the main aisle. There weren't many in attendance, perhaps a hundred at most, and the sides were definitely uneven. Giovanni's out-numbered hers two to one. With all guests in their seats, Pachelbel's Canon ended.

The loud, staccato beats of Wagner's March blared out of the speaker beneath me, its volume high enough to make me jump out of my seat rather than a polite rise. Fingers interlocked with Gabe's, we stood connected as the bride began her walk down the cobblestone path from the hall to the garden where the guests awaited with bated breath.

One thing was for certain, Carla, a former friend and college buddy, was gorgeous. The white dress contrasted nicely with the golden, fake 'n bake tan she sported, and the corset had been tightened enough around her to give her a very Jessica Rabbit look. But whatever, it was her wedding day. Her bare arm looped through her father's, they walked to the garden's entrance before pausing. Even through the shoulder-length veil, Carla locked her gaze on mine and her mouth dropped open a smidgen – confirmation the invitation was a joke. She hadn't really expected me to attend, even though I'd RSVP'd.

Well, the joke was on her, because here I was, connected to this beautiful man whose hand I squeezed again for strength, and for the first time in a really long time, I couldn't have been happier. To prove it, I gave her a genuine smile as I leaned into my boyfriend.

She cast her gaze around as she inhaled deeply, her chest pushing against the tight constraints of her bodice.

My slick palms needed a wipe, but I didn't want to let go of Gabe, so I squeezed tighter still, hoping to keep him close. Despite the heat, he cozied up beside me.

Carla sashayed up to the front, as a couple of Giovanni's family gave me a questionable glare. I wanted to wave back, just a little smirk of a wave, but I refrained. I had a feeling a head-to-head moment was brewing.

As Carla got to the archway, the guests had yet to sit, but the microphone on the justice of the peace was on.

And broadcasting.

"Where is he?" she said through gritted teeth, the mic picking up her hushed tone amazingly well.

With the arrival of the bride, I hadn't looked to see where Giovanni was, or who the groomsmen were. Was the person she growled at Colton? Had they remained friends?

The crowd's mumbles mingled their way through and settled before me. Giovanni was not at the front. Did the guy have serious commitment issues? Surely, he wouldn't stand another bride up? I twisted and looked into Gabe's curious face.

"No show?"

I shrugged. Deep down, I truly hoped he didn't ditch her. I wouldn't wish that on anyone, not even Carla.

"Just kidding," a loud voice carried over the guests, and the unmistakable face bounced into view.

I knew that voice anywhere, however, instead of it making me giddy like it used to, it ruffled my feathers. Coming to the wedding was starting to make me see *I* hadn't lost out, he had.

The guests sat glued to the benches while I got a good look at Carla's face. Horrified anger wouldn't describe it; her eyes were thin little slits, her jaw tight and locked, and her shoulders were ramrod straight. She was the polar opposite of a blushing bride.

"What do you think you're doing?" Carla leaned closer to Giovanni.

The people in the front row may not have heard her, even though her voice was low and guttural, but everything she said was clear as a bell thanks to the speakers placed at the back. A wave of empathy rolled through me.

Giovanni wore his smugness like his bow-tie, a little misplaced and off kilter.

"I thought it would be funny. Sort of like a repeat of last time. Except this time, I actually showed up." In a ta-da motion, he threw his hands out to the side and broke into a smile, one that used to be so easy to forgive him his errors when he gave it to me. Now, it curdled my stomach.

And it appeared like it was doing the same to Carla. Daggers shot from her eyes. "She's here, you half-wit."

Trying my best to swallow down my trepidation when eyes searched out and then found the *she* Carla referred to as they turned in my direction, I sat there nearly breaking the bones in Gabe's hand while meeting each of their expressions. They ranged between amusement, like Giovanni's, to down right anger, like Carla's.

I wanted to throw up and thought for a brief moment I might as my stomach swirled and soured.

I curled my toes inside my shoes and forced myself to be as professional as possible, as if this were an interview. In many ways, it was similar. Silently, I nodded at each expression and hoped the forced smile wasn't as uncomfortable looking as it felt.

"Oh," he said, turning his look back to fiancée number two. "I'm here, baby. I want to spend the rest of my life with you. I love you. I would never ditch *you.*"

The bile rose higher in my throat, burning it as it advanced.

The Justice of the Peace cleared his throat.

Carla twisted away from Giovanni, who continued to stare in her direction.

"Shall we begin?" the JP asked, his gaze flipping between the bride and groom, although his body remained relaxed as if he'd seen this type of shenanigan many times before and how this too will pass.

"I need a minute," Carla said.

Giovanni's face fell, and his expression morphed into concern. "It was a bad joke, and I'm sorry. Please don't be angry with me."

"You're an idiot."

I was glad she said what I was thinking, and probably that of many others. Who in their right mind makes a joke like that? Talk about wrong place at the wrong time.

The gathered guests all leaned in a little closer and through the masses Mr. and Mrs. De Luca in the front row pulled back, huddling into each other. How I'd missed her tight ballerina bun and puckered up face was beyond me.

"Carla, I'm sorry. Do you want to start over? You go back to the hall, and I'll stand up here like we planned, and we can redo it." His voice pleaded and begged at an embarrassing level.

With an angry finger, she pointed in the direction of where she started. "If I walk into that hall before we say 'I do' I'm not coming back out."

Whoas moaned out from the guests.

"So, let's get those underway." He nudged the Justice of the Peace. "You can start now."

"No." She turned around, tears falling down her cheeks. With a flick, she tossed her bouquet to the bridesmaid. "I can't marry you, Giovanni. This was the final straw."

"Baby," his voice broke with plea.

"You are the biggest god-damned jerk." She looked at her parents sitting in the front row. "I'm sorry for all the expense, and I'll find a way to pay you back, but I can't marry him. I just can't." Head shaking, she lifted her gown and stepped onto the grass.

"Carla!" Giovanni's cry echoed through the crowd and

actually stung my heart a little. Just a little.

"Stay away from me, you two-timing thug."

Thug? Two-timer? Those were new. Giovanni was many things, but not a thug. At least he wasn't. And two-timer? Wow. Suddenly, I was very glad I got dumped. Marriage would not have been a happy road.

"I should report you to the security company you work for." She slipped a gold bangle off her wrist and threw it at him. "This is probably stolen too. Asshole." She stormed down the aisle and screeched to a halt in front of me. "He's a security guard in your building. I'd watch your back and your belongings."

Wait, what? My heart skipped a beat as I connected the impossibly distant dots. Our building had just hired a new security company, was Giovanni one of the guards? Oh, dear god. Was Giovanni the one who broke into my apartment?

That night replayed in my head, over and over. How I felt I was being followed. How he got into the building, and into my home without forced entry. How the security team said they'd review surveillance and get back to me.

Oh my god.

It was a good thing I was already sitting as I melted with the realisation. The only question I had was why? Why would he pursue me like that? He'd left me. I was going to have a long talk with Nico when I got home and see if there was a way to get the police involved. There had to be.

The bridesmaids blew by in a sea of green, interrupting my thoughts and plans, and the bride's side of the crowd dispersed into the parking lot behind us, their voices quiet yet the murmur remained constant. The De Luca's walked by, noses in the air, shoulders back, almost as if they were proud of the joke of a son they had.

And to think, I almost married into that family.

Shaking my head and gathering up my dignity, I rose, and Gabe followed, never letting go. "I'm done. I came, I saw, and I'm so happy for the way things turned out." I smiled up at him, content that life had a way of working things out.

"This is your fault."

I inhaled and spun around, looking into Giovanni's pissed-off face.

No hi, surprised to see you here?

"Why? Why is this my fault or my problem? You made your bed, lay in it."

"Because you came."

I laughed. I couldn't help myself. "You are deluded, De Luca."

"Get bent."

Gabe stepped in front of me and placed a protective arm across my chest.

Lovingly, I pushed it down but wrapped my hand around the fist he created. "I've got this. I've had a lot of time to think this through and there's a lot I want to say." I pulled all the courage I had and pushed it to the surface.

The words spit from Giovanni's mouth. "So, say it."

How was I ever attracted to this man? The surfacing ugliness was mind-blowing. A face some would call handsome was contorted with tight anger and a thin-lipped scowl. A definite product of his mother. I shook my head, debating which words to use. They needed to be small.

In the end, with my dignity intact, I said, "Nah, you're not worth it."

He chuckled an uncomfortable laugh. Many parts of me were feeling pretty content how this time he was the one in the awkward position. He turned away from me.

"Wait, there is one thing I want to say." It was my chance to say everything I'd bottled up in me over the last four years. All the hurt and anger and mixed feelings floated on the surface. It was now or never to put it all out there.

"What?" A smug looked crossed his face.

"Thank you," I said, in my most sincere voice.

He stepped closer and Gabe, who also sported a look of surprise, pulled me back.

"Thank you? And you say I'm deluded." His hands flew out to the sides in a you've-got-to-be-kidding manner.

"No really. Your wedding invitation put a lot of things into perspective for me, and it made me realise I truly am better off without you, and today's performance nailed it on the head."

"You work for a restaurant, I'd hardly say you're better off." He scoffed and for the first time in my life, I wanted to smack someone across the face as hard as possible.

Restraining myself, I inhaled sharply.

"You can think what you like, but I'm here to tell you thanks. And I truly mean that."

Man, it felt good to say it, because really, if he hadn't sent the invitation, I never would've started down the journey to learning about myself and letting go. Along the way, I found happiness within myself and love, an honest, pure love. Gabe didn't knock me down the way Giovanni always had, and still tried. The love Gabe gave me was the kind my mom said was the best. I smiled at Gabe, happiness radiating out of me. I hoped Giovanni saw how truly happy I was with Gabe.

"Oh," I said, as I gathered up my clutch from the bench. "If there's one piece of advice I can give you, it's love yourself. Love yourself so much to the point that your energy and aura rejects anyone who doesn't value your worth."

I loved that clip by Billy Chapata I discovered while

researching something work related on the 'net. Last week I'd printed it out and hung it in my bathroom and it became my daily mantra. Because it was the truth.

"It worked for me." With a broad smile on my face, I pulled Gabe away from Giovanni's slack jaw expression.

My shoulders back, I left my past behind—literally and figuratively. I was no longer worried about what Giovanni thought about me, although I was going to speak to the powers that be about his job. I was through with him and completely over him, and every cell in my body echoed that sentiment.

I was glad for the invitation, as it really was an invitation to explore me and my life. As I looked into Gabe's eyes, I couldn't be happier. And mom was right, I didn't need a man to make me happy. He complimented all the happiness I had inside. It was just waiting for him.

Six months later...

The new opening for my second restaurant had been pushed back a couple months and instead of the January opening like I'd hoped, I was now readying for a late-March celebration. All things being ready, the doors would open to the public on March 31st, and with it I was launching a menu with new tastes. In consultation with my cooks, we came up with ten new varieties of steak bowls.

In order to narrow it down to the top five that would make the new menu, I invited all my staff—past and present—to a celebratory night at the flagship restaurant. Invitations had gone out over a hundred people to come and sample free-of-charge the new dishes and rate them. So far, and quite surprisingly, sixty-seven staff responded in favour.

Celeste dropped the printed list of confirmed guests on the hostess podium, beside the invited guest list, just in case someone changed their minds at the last minute. She'd planned on acting like the bouncer and letting the guests into the dining room, past the lengthy buffet station where the new steak bowls sat.

The spicy aroma was comforting on my nerves. I wanted this evening to be a success. If my staff all visited and hung out enjoying the space like family, even better. Afterall, Westside was my family and the smile I wore hadn't left my face all day in preparation.

Robin, the General Manager of the new store, walked beside me. Like captains on a ship, the expanse of the dining room stretched out before us, readying for the evening.

"I think this is great idea, for the record."

"Stated. I knew I could count on your support." I rested my hand on his shoulder. It had taken some time, but I was trying to be softer in my approach with the staff even though Robin and I had an easy rapport with each other. "Doors are unlocked?"

He gave me a quick nod and surveyed the lay of the land. "It'll be a nice to see who comes through the door."

Let's see who the eager beavers are.

I had a list in my head with my suspicions.

We both looked over as the first sound of chatter came through the doors.

Joy, a shift manager on maternity leave, came in with her boyfriend on her arm.

I totally forgot his name, having only met him a couple of times.

She walked straight over to Robin, who had moved out from behind the counter, and embraced him. "Hey," she said, beaming like usual. She glanced in my direction. "Hi, Meghan."

"Hey," Robin said. "Hi, James. Where's Destiny?"

James, right. I could always count on Robin to remember these things. Mind you, he and Joy had become great friends outside of work.

Joy leaned her head against her boyfriend and patted him on the chest. "Am I a bad mother if I needed a night away? Ana's home for a couple of weeks and offered to watch her."

"She still enjoying life in Australia or is she ready to move home?" Robin stepped back from the couple and smiled.

"Oh, she's enjoying it. Did I tell you? Her and Ollie

finally set a date. New Years Eve. Just nine short months to get it all planned."

"Is the wedding going to be there or here?"

"Oh, there for sure. And Destiny will be the flower girl." Joy waved her hands around. "Oh yeah, Destiny just cut her first tooth."

"There goes any more breastfeeding," James piped up.

Joy turned back to face him. "I haven't decided that yet. She understands the phrase no biting."

James raised an eyebrow. "Does she?"

Pink tinged her cheeks and her arm crossed over her chest.

"Excuse me," I said to the three of them and stepped away to give them some privacy.

I wasn't sure where exactly the direction the conversation was going to end in, but I wasn't going to be there for anything more personal than what I'd just heard.

A few more guests had come in, kitchen staff mostly as well as a former server. But one blond former manager whom I hadn't seen in roughly eighteen months just entered. He was chatting with Celeste, who in heels, towered over the shorter man.

"Niall." I walked closer. "How's it going?"

His face split in half. "Meghan. So good to see you." He closed the distance between us and held back. "Don't worry, I remember. You're not a hugger."

"It's okay." Instead of waiting for him to make the first move, I did, surprising us both. His eyes were wide as I pulled back. "How's the hotel business?"

He looked good, a little worn down like I remembered, but there was a light in his eyes I'd never noticed before. "Things are great."

"That's really good. What's new?"

"Well, I'm getting married."

"Really?" I hope it sounded sincere, but judging from the confused expression on his face, I failed.

"Really," he said, the smile pushing the corners of his eyes up. "I know it surprised me. Always figured I wasn't the marrying kind, the too-devoted-to-my-work kind of guy."

Something I could totally relate to. Although... things within my own life over the past few months had changed my outlook substantially. "Tell me more." I led him over to a booth. "Did you bring a guest?"

"Nah, figured I'd come solo. Wanted to check this out." He slipped into one side and motioned for me to sit across from him.

"For a minute," I said, tucking my skirt under me as I sat down.

Robin could most certainly handle everything, but I also wanted to walk around and chat. Plus, I was sure Niall wanted to chat with the others too since he had managed the people I could see from where I sat.

"I must say, this is a different side of you, Meghan." He rose his eyebrow.

"I'm trying to leave the bitch behind and be a better person."

"You were always a good person."

"Just hard to deal with, right?" He didn't need to answer, I knew. But it was okay. Gabe had shown me and told me repeatedly as long as my staff respected me, liking me was secondary. "Anyways... tell me about you."

He shifted in his seat, but a broad smile cut across his features. "She's a sous-chef within the chain but not at my hotel. She works on the southside."

"And does *she* have a name?"

"Justina." As the name rolled off his tongue, a dreamy look settled on his face.

It was nice to see him so happy. Was he still addicted to working?

"And work? Are you still dedicating your life to the hotel?" He always had to Westside and was always eager to fill in when another manager couldn't. Even before as a server, he worked too many hours.

"Nah, not as much. It's still good and I'm paid quite handsomely, but it's not my life's work. Justina got me involved with The Mustard Seed over Christmas and to be honest, it's changed me. I love working with the homeless and poverty-stricken people, trying to help meet their basic needs. Who knew there were so many homeless within our own city?" He shook his head.

It was just like Niall to want to help others, it had always been part of his personality.

"You sound very happy."

"I am. What about you?"

I sat a little higher and folded my hands together. "I'm doing very well. Business is going great. New store opens next week, and I've put Robin in charge as the GM."

Not long after I said his name, Robin walked by talking to another former server I recognised but couldn't immediately put a name to. Someone from a while back.

"That's great." His gaze followed Robin. "If he hasn't changed, I'd imagine he'd be quite perfect in his role."

"A born leader."

Niall returned his attention to our table. "And personally? How have things been?"

Niall had known a little about Giovanni, back when I

239

was dating the jerk. And Niall was around when I'd done the one thing I knew I could control after it all collapsed – throw myself into work.

"Things are going well. I have the most wonderful man in my life."

"And his name is?" He chuckled.

"Gabe. He owns his own business, so he's been a great collaborator."

"Wow. Look at you, you're positively glowing."

I glanced back around the dining room again and sunk a little into my seat. "He's really amazing. Someone who sees me as an equal."

"And do you have a wedding set?"

I scoffed. "No, no, no. We're not even living together yet."

"Still pretty fresh then?"

"Six months. But we've both been in hard relationships so we're taking things slowly."

"Sounds fair enough."

I certainly thought it was. We'd discussed joining apartments, but it never evolved into more. Something always popped up and we changed the topic, but it was usually me who was responsible for the switch.

"How's Audrina doing?"

She'd been a fantastic manager after Niall left. Had been through the ringer a while back, but she made a comeback. I was really worried we'd lost her after her brother died as I didn't get the sense she had any kind of support, but she hung in there for a little bit. Until she left Westside after obtaining her accounting degree and started helping out her boyfriend's business.

Niall nodded toward the door. "Ask her yourself. She

just arrived." Niall pushed himself out of his seat and walked over to his friend, wrapping her in a hug. "Audrina. Chad."

I joined them and when they pulled away, I couldn't help but notice the bump pushing out against the fabric of her shirt.

"Congratulations," I said without any kind of restraint.

She smiled and melted against Chad. "Thank you." Her hand protectively covered her belly.

"When are you due?"

Niall placed his hand on the swell of her belly and looked at Audrina.

She smiled weakly in Chad's direction before turning to me. "Two days before the second anniversary of Michael's passing." Tears welled in her eyes and she brushed them away.

Chad squeezed her shoulders tight and placed a kiss on her cheek. "It's perfect." He ran a finger down in her cheek in a seemingly very intimate way.

It felt hugely personal, and I turned away, unable to stop myself from doing so.

"The heavens have healed Michael and given him new life. And who better to be his guardian angel."

That's a different theory. But whatever, it was his belief and it put a smile on her face. Its not like I had any experience with religion and spirituality.

"And all the tests came back negative for any defects, not that we cared either way." Chad linked his fingers through hers.

Yes, I remembered her mentioning her brother had cerebral palsy and muscular dystrophy, something I was sure she'd want to prepare herself for.

"And we know what we're having." Audrina looked over at Niall.

"And..." Niall said with bated breath, as he rocked on his heels.

"It's a boy."

Chad gave Audrina's belly a rub. "A healthy baby boy."

Audrina beamed like she'd won the lottery. I was so happy for her, and she deserved it.

"Congrats," I said. "Well, I hope you're hungry enough for two because there's plenty of new flavours to sample. There are survey cards at the table, please try them all and mark your choices."

I pointed to the buffet table behind me and the small yet manageable line of patrons eager to taste the new creations.

"I'm always hungry."

"Yes, she is." Chad laughed.

Lily, one of newest evening servers walked by. She was shaking her head and muttering to herself, obviously distressed.

"Excuse me," I said, and followed after Lily.

She stepped into the server station and braced her hands on the counter.

"Are you okay?"

She reacted like she'd been shocked and bolted upright. "Yes." A pause. "No."

I stared down at her having dealt with a fair share of drama before, but this was no teenager. She was older than me but looked like she was about to have a child-like meltdown.

"There's someone out there from my past I was hoping to see, but now that she's actually here, I'm chickening out and don't want to see her."

I nodded. Slowly. Which direction to take this, I wasn't sure. It wasn't my place to get involved in their personal lives. However, I was trying to be a better person. I'd said as much to Niall.

"Yeah, that can be tough. It's hard to rise above and be the better person."

"She took care of my girls when I left my husband twenty months ago."

Ah. Well, that would make seeing them tricky.

"And I'd cut off any contact with her. Or my husband. Or my kids."

As much as I wanted to ask if this person was in the dining room with Lily's husband, I refrained. It was none of my business, even if the curiosity was a tad overwhelming.

"The best advice I can give you is to just rise above. You can't hang out here all evening until she leaves."

Lily sighed a huge, breathy sound and pushed herself off the counter, straightening up and steeling herself. "You're right. I can do this."

"Yes, you can. Believe in yourself."

She passed by me and turned into the dining room.

"Lily?" A voice I imagined only belonging to the woman in question punctuated the air.

"Shayne." Lily sounded deflated.

Shayne? I searched my memory. I once had a Shayne who worked for me for a few months; a prim and proper young lady who had quit to follow one of my more charming servers when he moved south. Sure enough, as I rounded the corner, there she was. A little more mature looking, for sure, but huge questioning looks hung on her face.

"What are you doing working here?" Shayne asked Lily.

"Making my way in the world."

"But your family? Does Jason know you're here? Do the girls?"

Lily leaned forward in a nearly aggressive stance. "Do

you still keep in touch with him?"

Shayne hung her head. "No, not so much anymore."

The older of the pair backed away. "Well, then I'll have you know, that yes, he does know where I work, and we are … working on things."

Shayne's face broke into a huge smile. "That's great!" She lunged forward and wrapped her arms around Lily. "I'm so happy for you."

A surprised expression crossed Lily's face, and she stepped back to put some distance between them. "What about you? Are you still in Lethbridge? And how did you get an invite here?"

Actually, it was a question I wanted to hear the answer to since I didn't remember sending out anything with her or Korey's name on it. There had been no forwarding address.

"Yes, we're still living in Lethbridge, but we came up for a week to see Sean and Randy's new baby boy. And since Korey and Niall are still friends, he mentioned it when they were chatting last week." Shayne turned in my direction. "Oh, hi Meghan. Sorry I didn't say hi earlier. I'm just so surprised to see my… best friend here."

"It's all good. And I'll let you catch up for a minute. Excuse me."

Shayne stepped off to the side.

Head held high, I walked past the two ladies and joined the crowd in the dining room. Lots of happy chatter and metal spoons clanging against the dishes. Scanning, I spotted Niall talking to a handsome young man. I needed to squint a bit while taking in the man. Long gone were his dread locks and fuzz on his face. Instead, he appeared taller, if that were possible.

"Hi, Korey. So nice of you to come." I shook his hand upon approach.

"The timing was quite perfect really."

"Don't ask until I'm there."

I stopped in my spot and turned in the direction of the voice.

Shayne walked over and looped her arm through Korey's. "We were wondering…"

Niall and Korey both looked at Shayne. Korey nudged her on.

"Well, since we met while working here, we were wondering if we could rent out Westside and have our wedding reception here. We'd pick a Sunday or a Thursday evening so as not to take away from a busy night. We've looked at all other locations, but nothing seems to be as perfect as Westside."

It was certainly the most unique request I've had from a staff member. "When would the wedding be?"

"We were thinking in early May? It's not going to be anything formal since neither of us is traditional in that respect, and we'd have less than fifty people in attendance. Of course, we'd order from the menu and make sure to pay the staff for their time." Shayne's words were practically tripping over themselves.

"Let's discuss it in more detail. How about we sit down and go over the plan? You said you're in town for a bit, so can I squeeze you in tomorrow afternoon?"

I've never noticed someone light up quite so much. It was interesting to watch the expression take over her face and move down her body.

"Yes." She squeezed Korey's arm. "Yes." Surprising me completely, she gave me a huge hug.

A variety of issues sprang to mind as I started to work out the possibilities of hosting a wedding reception. All things I'd need to look into for sure. It could be neat to do. Weddings could be fun, they didn't always have to be traditional. I broke out of the embrace and looked at Niall. He appeared as if he were holding back a laugh.

After setting up a tentative discussion for tomorrow afternoon, I backed away from the trio and circulated around the dining room, chatting with everyone, and getting more updates in people's lives than feedback. However, the comment cards were visible on the tables and some had pen marks on it. Perfect.

The work end of the evening had wound down and it was time to go home. The cooks had kept the buffet station filled with the ten delicious steak bowl creations and the serving staff had kept everyone perfectly hydrated. The stack of comment cards grew, and early indications were that the Polynesian-inspired dish with the coconut milk, ginger and tamarind was in the lead and the Serrano Spice a close second. One was flavourful, and the latter was quite a hot little spicy dish.

Once home, I kicked off my shoes into the corner of the closet and dropped my keys into the bowl by the door. A loud sigh blew out of me while I walked over to the refrigerator. Inside I spied the bottle of red, complete with a bow and a note that read *happy birthday*.

Gabe had placed it in there before he left but I was given strict instructions to not touch it until today.

"Oh, Gabe. I wish you were home," I said, pulling out the chilled bottle and resting it against my body.

Suddenly, an ache spread across my chest. I wanted him here, always, and didn't want to go back and forth between apartments anymore. It didn't matter how we had exchanged keys with the other a few months back and had access to the other's place, the decision to merge had rested on my shoulders.

I wasn't ready. Then.

But I was now. Coming home to an empty apartment, my escape from the hustle and bustle of a busy work environment was no longer high on my wish list. I wanted—I needed—to come home to the sanctity that was Gabe, his quiet nature and how just being with him was the most perfect version of coming home, even if all we did was hang out in pajamas and watch tv together. Too bad Gabe was in London, and I had to wait until he came home tomorrow to tell him I was ready to become his roommate.

The chorus from *Sweet Caroline* started playing on my phone – Gabe's ringtone.

"Hey, Gabe." I put back the special birthday wine with its fancy Italian writing and pulled out another brand, a knock off brand, that was perfect for me and drinking alone. I'd save the good red for when my honey was home.

"Happy birthday, my sweet." His voice was loud and clear through the speakerphone.

"Thanks." I picked off the shrink wrap on the cheap bottle of wine.

"How did the sampling go?"

The cork made a popping sound as it wiggled itself free of its confines. "It was good. Ended up with lots of feedback."

"Is that the wine I left for you?"

"No, no, no. I'll save it for when you get home."

A huge grin broke my face in half as I imagined our meet up. My place or his, it wouldn't matter. We'd be together again, arm in arm, hand in hand, just enjoying the other's presence. I couldn't wait. Less than twenty-four hours to go. I grabbed a clean wine glass from the dishwasher and set it on the counter.

"So, my flight got changed again."

"Damn, really?" Every time he flew out to London, his flight home got changed. "Time to switch airlines."

"Maybe. But it's cheaper."

"Sometimes the fifty-dollar difference is worth it." \

A knock sounded on my door. Who'd be knocking on the door at this hour? It was almost ten.

"Hold on a sec, Gabe." I opened the door, keeping the chain on.

A lovely bouquet of flowers smiled at me between the door and the frame.

"My flight got changed. You're right, the fifty dollars was so worth it." From behind the flowers and out of sight behind the wall, Gabe's voice was music to my ears.

I closed the door and yanked off the chain, pushing the flowers off to the side.

"Yes, best upgrade ever." I wrapped my arms around my man.

He'd been gone for a week, seven days too long in my opinion. Tender kisses covered his lips and his whiskery cheeks.

"May I come in?"

"It's your home too."

He gave me a quizzical look but proceeded to step inside my apartment anyway, setting the flowers on the counter top. I closed the door with a little too much enthusiasm and snuggled my arms under the heavy weight of Gabe's jean jacket. The embrace I'd needed to be engulfed in surrounded me in a heartbeat, my hands wrapping around his waist and pulling him closer. The safety of his arms greeted me like a warm blanket.

"I missed you." I gazed up into his eyes, noticing a fresh sparkle in them.

"I missed you as well."

My lips found his and crushed against him, many lonely

nights passionately coming out of me. Tonight was going to be magical in more ways than one.

He lifted me onto the counter, and I wrapped my legs around him. So what if it pushed my skirt up a little? I was hoping to get my party started right away.

"I have a birthday present for you." His hand slipped into his coat pocket.

"And I have one for you." I threaded my fingers through his salt-and-pepper hair and brushed his cheek. Slowly, I brought my hands over his arms and threaded my fingers through his. "Tonight was an interesting night at work."

"Oh yeah?" His gaze never left mine.

"Indeed. Inviting all the staff, former and present, was a great idea. I got caught up on some of the staff's latest going ons, but one thing struck me hard."

"What's that?"

"They're all moving on with their lives. Some are having babies, others are getting married. Some have changed interests in their lives and are focusing more on matters of the heart verses the size of their wallet."

"Sounds like an inspiring night."

"It so was." I gave his hand a squeeze. "And when I came home, I was all alone."

Tenderly, he brushed back my hair.

"And I don't want that anymore. I want us to have one home so when you're gone, I can still smell you on the bedsheets and I can spray your cologne all over my washcloth."

"You could've slept in my bed and showered in my bathroom."

"I did… three times already this week." Heat tinged my cheeks. "My point is..." I sighed.

This was so hard to ask even if I did want it. I wasn't

afraid of his answer, in fact I was quite confident of what it would be but still, it was a question with so much weight behind it.

"Will you, Gabriel Noellette, move in with me?"

His lips brushed against mine, the promise of more lingering when he pulled back. "Absolutely. Are you sure?"

"Completely. One hundred percent sure. There's nothing I want more."

And it was true.

Gabe wore the biggest, sweetest smile. A smile I could look at for the rest of my life.

"I guess the only question I have to that would be which apartment? Did you want to move into mine, or shall I move into yours?"

"It doesn't matter. Yours, mine, someplace new. I don't care. You've given me a new sense of hope that all my dreams will come true. I love you, Gabe."

"And I love you too, Meghan."

Dear Reader

Oh my – that Meghan – who knew her true love was right under her nose? If you've read any of my other books, notably the *Courting of Charlotte Cooper* duology, you would've recognized a few characters as they made their appearances in *Serving Up Hope*. It was exciting as an author to bring back a few beloved characters and have them interact (and fall in love) with the new characters. If you haven't read them, may I recommend hunting around for a copy of *Ask Me Again*? That's where three of the characters came from, and the book where Gabe was introduced. In my opinion, it was a great way to draw this series – The Ladies of Westside – to a close. I may drop hints about some of the other supporting characters (namely Robin and Celeste) in upcoming books. All my stories are set in the same city, so you never know who you will run into. Maybe Aurora? Or Lucas? Who knows? Maybe they've all dined at Westside and have crossed paths without actually meeting.

As an author, it makes my day when someone shares their thoughts and gives me feedback on the characters you've invested your time with, so I'm asking you a favour. If you are so inclined, I'd love a review or a rating of *Serving Up Hope*. It doesn't have to be long, even something as simple as "Loved it, great series" works. Reviews and ratings help me gain visibility and as I'm sure you can tell from my books, reviews are tough to come by. As a reader, you have the power to make or break a book.

Thank you so much for spending time with me.

Yours,

H.M. Shander

Other Books by H.M. Shander

Visit www.hmshander.com for up-to-date listings

Acknowledgements

Gosh, it's hard to believe I am writing my ninth public thank you. Ninth! I'm in a perpetual state of shock. A million thanks to my family – Hubs, The Teen and Little Dude – and to my parents and sister-in-law. Where would I be without your support and endless cheerleading? I may get a raised eyebrow or two when you've read what I've written, but I know you'll love it regardless, and I've come a long way since that very first story written at fourteen. Thank you for giving me time to sit and write while you played your games so I could make my daily word count. Thanks for all your help with signings (especially you my little PA – you are always out there smiling beside me and helping people pick out their swag.) Love you all always.

To my wonderfully dedicated critique partner – Julie – you always know the best way to pull the better version out of me. And I love how you adored Meghan and her quirkiness, and how thrilled you were that Gabe was back. Your thoughts and comments mean so much to me, and as I write, I often ask myself, WWJS (what would Julie say).

To my tribe of alpha readers and beta readers. Nathalie, Emma, Josephine, Lacey, Mandy, Miranda and Moreno. Thank you from the bottom of my heart for all your comments and advice and wisdom, for pointing out what didn't make sense and what needed to be expanded on. Thank you for falling in love with Meghan and rooting with her as she dated the three potentials and wanting to know more about her Everyday Joe.

To my cover designer – Megan – Thank you for your talents on redoing this cover. In my heart I wanted the identity of the mystery writer to stay a mystery, but after conducting research on trends in my genre, and with the tropes, in the end we went with the couple who conveyed the best representation of the couple, as Meghan finds her happiness. I appreciate all

SERVING UP HOPE

your work on this, and for incorporating my brand of colours and fonts. I'd be thrilled to work with you again on any projects. Thank you for your excellency.

To my editor Irina – Whew – I made it to you in time, and you made it back before Christmas, giving me the time I needed to correct the red and polish my baby up even more. Thank you.

If I missed you, it certainly wasn't intentional. I know I couldn't be where I am without the help of so many others. Thank you! And thank you for reading and making it all the way to the end. You all rock.

About the Author

H.M. Shander knows four languages—English, French, Sarcasm and ASL—and speaks two of them exceptionally well. Any guesses which two? She lives in the most beautiful city in Canada–Edmonton, AB, a big city with a small-town feel, where all her family live within a twenty-minute drive, although her parents are contemplating moving away. As much as she'd love the beach under a blanket of stars, this is her home.

A big-time coffee addict, she prefers to start her day with a mug before attending to anything pressing, like driving the #momtaxi as she shuttles her kids off to school and various extracurricular activities. Secretly she loves it as when the vehicle is empty, it gives her time to think about what crazy things those characters will do next. She is a self-proclaimed nerd (and friends/family will back this up), reveling in all things science, however likes to be creative when there's time. Right brain, left brain? Both.

Did you know she once wanted to be a "Happy Clown" as she enjoys making people smile, but she's beyond terrified of scary clowns? How ever many different jobs she's worked, her favourite has been working as a birth doula and librarian, in addition to being a romance author. Because, let's be honest, who doesn't love falling in love?

Five things she loves, in no particular order; The Colour Blue, The Smell of Coconut & Shea Butter, Star Wars (the original three), The Ocean, and Chocolate.

You can follow her on Facebook, Twitter and Goodreads.

Thanks for reading– all the way to the very end.